# The Phantom Child

AJ WILLS

Cherry Tree
Publishing

Cherry Tree Publishing

The Phantom Child

Copyright ©   A J Wills 2024

# Content warning

There are many reasons we love to read stories. For entertainment and escapism, for example. But we also read stories and particularly thrillers, consciously or not, to help us deal with trauma in a safe setting.

That's why many psychological and domestic thrillers deal with themes of abuse, controlling behaviour and violence.

It helps us to understand these issues and, in many cases, to experience troubling emotions without the real threat of harm.

That's why I don't usually include trigger warnings in my books, and also because recent research published in the journal of Clinical Psychological Science has shown they actually can have the opposite effect.

Merely the mention of trigger warnings can lead to anxiety in anticipation of what's to come.

It's a bit like going for a walk in the woods and telling your friend that at some point a monster is going to jump out from behind the trees and chase them. Admittedly, the friend could choose not to go on the walk, but if they did, they'd probably be in a state of heightened terror throughout.

That said, I wanted to mention there are a number of themes covered in the book you should be aware of before you begin.

Notably, these are: domestic abuse, including controlling behaviour and psychological abuse, child abduction and abortion.

# MISSING

In precisely three minutes, my life as I know it will end.

My phone says it's past nine, but that can't be right. Jacob never sleeps this late. He's always in our bed before the first light of dawn, wriggling and chatting, his cold feet on my bare legs jolting me rudely from sleep.

I bolt upright like a jack springing out of its box, the duvet crumpling in my lap as a spike of fear needles through my veins. Ronan's still comatose beside me, his breathing deep and slow, his hair matted to his head.

My feet skid across the tiled floor as I scramble out of bed and yank back the curtains. The heat of the Turkish sun is already radiating through the glass doors. Outside, there's not a ripple on the surface of the pool. A beach ball floats past lazily, but there's no little body bobbing around face down in the water, thank god.

So why do I still have this suffocating sense that something is horribly wrong? A heavy throb of doom that beats in my chest?

I race through the villa, a stranger's home that smells of polish and citrus, and head for Jacob's room.

Oddly, the door is shut, although I always leave his door ajar and the landing light on at home in case he gets up in the night.

'Jacob?' I whisper.

The door creaks as I ease it open. The room's in darkness. It takes a moment for my eyes to adjust and to make out the shape of the bed pushed up against the wall under the window.

There's no lump curled up under the duvet. No head lolling on the pillow. No bare leg hanging out over the side. I flick on a switch, flooding the room with light, but the bed's empty.

'Jacob!' I scream, spinning on my heel and running back into the lounge, frantic.

In less than a minute, I've searched the entire villa. I've looked everywhere he could be hiding. He's not anywhere inside.

Ronan catches me by the arms as I hurtle past our bedroom. He's bleary-eyed and scratching his crotch. He holds me firmly, not letting me squirm free.

'Karina? What the hell's going on? What are you doing?'

My panic is so intense, so crushing, I can hardly think straight. I stop and stare into his eyes.

'It's Jacob,' I yell. 'He's gone.'

# Chapter 1

'Mummy, who's going to be driving the plane?'

I force a smile as I swivel to face Jacob, who's strapped into his seat in the back of the car, for what feels like the millionth time since we left home half an hour ago.

'The pilot drives the plane, remember?'

'What's he called?'

'I don't know, sweetheart. Anyway, it might not be a man pilot.'

'Do ladies fly planes?'

I suppress a laugh. *Ladies?* 'Of course they do. Ladies can do anything men can do, and usually better.'

I glance at Ronan, who raises his eyebrows, but has the sense not to contradict me.

'Will we be able to see him?'

'Or her. We might see them when we get onto the plane but then they have to go into the cockpit and close the door,' I explain.

'Why?'

Jacob's not stopped talking about the holiday from the moment he woke up this morning. It's the first time he'll have been on a plane, and although he's been looking forward to it, he's obviously anxious. His incessant stream of questions is giving me a headache. I wish he'd give it a rest for five minutes, but I don't want to get the trip off to a bad start by losing my patience. I want it to be a holiday he'll always remember, for all the right reasons.

Until a couple of weeks ago, I wasn't sure we'd be going at all. Originally, we'd planned a week in Crete but at the last minute we discovered the villa where we were supposed to be staying had been double-booked. I was furious. We'd been excited about the holiday for months, not only because it was going to be Jacob's first time abroad but because I hadn't been to Crete in years, and couldn't wait for a break from the monotonous routine of life.

I love being a stay-at-home mum, but four-year-olds are so demanding, especially when they're always up so early. I've been feeling the strain lately. It's probably why Ronan and I have been so grumpy with each other. That's another reason for the holiday, to spend some quality time together and hopefully seal up the cracks that have begun to fracture our marriage.

Fortunately, Ronan and his silver tongue managed to talk the travel firm into paying out some compensation which allowed us to upgrade to a more luxurious villa than we'd normally be able to afford. It's why I left it to Ronan. He's better at dealing with people than me. It's his superpower. An uncanny ability to charm almost everyone he meets.

The villa he found in Turkey, high in the hills surrounded by olive groves and orchards, looked amazing in the pictures online, although I'd never have chosen Turkey as a destination. It's just somewhere I've never fancied. I can't put my finger on why. Some inbuilt, irrational prejudice about it being too politically unstable. Too arid. Too dangerous. I never used to be like this. I've visited all kinds of inhospitable places for my job, but having children changes you. It makes you view everything through a different prism.

While Greece remained my first choice, going to Turkey was better than not going anywhere at all. It's going to be a week relaxing in the sun, eating good food and spending precious time together as a family. It's exactly what we need, especially as Ronan's been working so hard we've hardly seen him in the last few months.

Predictably, I've done all the packing and organising, while all Ronan's had to do is throw a few T-shirts and a couple of pairs of shorts into a case. He didn't have to worry about getting the laundry done. Or popping to the bank to change some money. Shopping for holiday toiletries. Or remembering to pack the factor fifty and make sure we had the right travel plugs. He didn't have to pack for Jacob and stress whether he had enough clothes, which of his toys to bring or what we needed to keep him entertained on the flight.

That was all down to me. I'm sure we've left something behind, but what the hell, we're halfway to the airport now. If we've forgotten something, we'll just have to buy new. It's not as though they don't have shops in Turkey.

The car's buffeted by a speeding white van that shoots past in the outside lane.

'Did you download your boarding pass?' Ronan asks, glancing in the rear-view mirror.

'Yes!' I hiss.

*Did* I remember? I was tackling a large pile of holiday ironing when he was nagging me about it last night.

'And you picked up the passports?'

'Yes.'

'You're sure?' He glances at me, like he doesn't trust me. As if I didn't have enough to worry about.

I put them in my bag, didn't I? They were on the dining room table, left in plain view so I didn't forget them. But now he's said it, he's put doubt in my mind. A worm of uncertainty that burrows deep into my brain.

In fact, now I think about it, I don't actually remember picking them up, but then I forget all sorts of things these days. Mummy brain, Ronan calls it.

'Mummy, are there toilets on the plane?'

A flush of anxiety sweeps hot and then cold over my body.

'Yes, darling. There are toilets on the plane. Don't worry.'

I remember grabbing my handbag and a packet of tissues, but did I actually pick up the passports?

Casually, I dip into my handbag at my feet. It's only a small quilted bag I picked up from John Lewis for the holiday. Something lightweight I can sling over my shoulder. Not my usual tote bag I cart around weighed down with a ton of

Jacob's things. Books. Toys. Emergency snacks. This holiday, I was determined to travel light.

No passports.

Shit!

I bang my skull against the headrest, squeezing my eyes shut, feeling sick. I can't believe I've forgotten them, but is it any wonder? I was so flustered when we left. If Ronan hadn't been hassling me to hurry up, standing outside the door, swinging his car keys around his fingers, glancing at his watch, I'd have had the chance to check we had everything we needed.

'I don't have them,' I mumble.

'What?'

'I've forgotten the passports.'

'You're kidding?' Ronan sighs, casting a reproachful glance my way. 'Bloody hell, Karina. You only had one job.'

One job? Is he serious? All he had to do this morning was get himself ready and out of the door. The only helpful thing he's done is load the cases into the boot.

'*You* could have looked after the passports, you know,' I snap. 'I don't know why it's always down to me.'

'Mummy, can you open the window on the plane if you're feeling sick?'

'No, you can't!' I instantly regret raising my voice.

'Why not?'

'There's not enough oxygen.'

'What's oxygen?'

Oh, for pity's sake.

'Right, we'll have to go back.' Ronan's face has turned an angry shade of puce. 'We're not going to get far without our passports, are we?' I hate it when he takes that patronising tone with me.

I glance at the clock on the dashboard. We were already cutting it fine. If we go back to the house, it's going to add at least another hour onto our journey. But he's right. We're not getting to Turkey without our passports.

'*You* could have checked before we left the house, you know,' I say. 'You had little else to do this morning.'

Ronan shoots me a withering look. 'There's a junction up ahead where I can turn around. If we hurry, we might still make it,' he says through gritted teeth. 'But it'll be touch and go.'

# Chapter 2

Ronan races back to the house like a man possessed, his foot heavy on the accelerator. I grip onto the edge of my seat with my feet firmly planted on the floor, pressing an imaginary brake pedal, feeling slightly sick. At least Jacob's questions have finally stopped. Until we reach the house.

'Why are we back home, Mummy?' he asks as we pull up violently, my seatbelt locking against my collar bone and catching me as I'm jerked forwards.

'Silly Mummy forgot the passports,' Ronan tells him with more than a hint of a dig at me.

I glare at my husband, but button my mouth. I'm not going to have a row in front of our son. He deserves better than to hear his parents tearing strips off each other. It can wait. And besides, we don't have the time to bicker. We need to get to the airport or we can kiss goodbye to the holiday.

I already have the keys to the house in my hand as I stumble out of the car and race up the path to the front door, but in my hurry drop them in the dirt.

'Come on, come on,' I mutter under my breath as I jiggle the key in the deadlock. The lock springs back with a satisfying clunk. I slot another key into the latch and the door falls open.

I dive inside, not even bothering to kick off my shoes or stopping to worry whether I'm trailing mud over the carpets. The passports are exactly where I left them, on the table in the dining room. Three burgundy booklets, stacked in a neat pile. I must have walked right past them on my way out without seeing them. How could I have been so stupid? I snatch them up and hurry back to the car. In and out in record time. Now we just have to pray there are no hold-ups on the way to the airport.

'Did you get them?' Ronan asks, as I throw myself into the car.

'Yes, drive!' I yell, waving the passports under his nose.

We wheelspin away as I'm still pulling on my seatbelt.

'Yay, Mummy got the pathports,' Jacob declares joyfully from the back.

Ronan's driving is no safer as we hurtle back to the airport, along winding country lanes towards the dual carriageway. He wilfully ignores all the speed limits, jumps countless red lights and narrowly misses a reversing delivery van as it manoeuvres out of a side road. All the while, he keeps shooting worried glances at the clock on the dashboard, his knuckles white on the steering wheel.

I can tell he's angry with me, but maybe if he'd taken responsibility for the passports and not left it all to me as usual, we wouldn't be risking life and limb to make our flight. But I keep my mouth shut. It's been stressful enough as it is without us arguing, especially with young ears listening.

So instead of picking a fight, I engage with Jacob, encouraging him to name the colours of the cars we pass, making up stories about the sheep and the cows in the fields and getting him to count the number of lorries we overtake. Just because we're in the car, and my stomach's cramping with anxiety, it's no excuse to pass up an opportunity to broaden his education.

By some miracle, we swing into the airport car park with forty-five minutes to spare before our flight is due to take off. Although we still need to make it to departures and through security.

'Grab Jacob and I'll bring the cases,' Ronan yells as he piles out of the car and pops open the boot.

I unstrap Jacob from his seat and hitch him onto my hip before half-walking, half-jogging to keep up with Ronan, who's striding purposefully towards one of the transfer buses.

'Why are we going on a bus, Mummy?'

'It's taking us to the airport, darling.'

I check the time on my phone. There's no way we'll be able to get our cases checked in, pass through security and reach the boarding gate in time. Jacob's going to be devastated.

The bus trundles along painfully slowly, jerking every time the driver shifts gear. I silently will him to hurry, but we're entirely in his hands.

Ronan's jaw is clenched tightly shut. He can't even bring himself to look at me, staring intently at the road ahead instead as we perch on the edge of our seats, Jacob on my knee.

It takes an achingly slow ten minutes before we eventually make it to the terminal. Ronan drags the cases off the bus as I struggle with Jacob and our cabin bags, and I'm left trailing in his wake as he rushes into the building.

We dump our luggage at a self-service baggage check-in without any issues but just when my hopes are rising that maybe we'll make the flight after all, they're dashed by the sight of long queues snaking through security. Hundreds of people segregated by a lattice of retractable barriers, shuffling along like sheep in a pen.

'Terrific,' Ronan sighs, bowing his head in defeat.

We should have paid extra to go through the express security checks. It wasn't even that expensive. If I'd have known we were going to be this late, I wouldn't have thought twice.

Fortunately, the queue moves reasonably quickly and despite my initial concern, we make it to the front in a matter of minutes. I peel off my jewellery, belt and shoes and dump them into a plastic tray with our cabin bags. They all fly off along a conveyor belt to be X-rayed while I guide Jacob through a body scanner, a bemused look of wonder on his face.

I follow him through, gritting my teeth. I've passed through airport body scanners in countries all over the world, but I still get nervous, convinced the alarms are going to go off and teams of burly security guards with dogs are going to come running to arrest me. I guess I have a natural guilty conscience even when I haven't done anything wrong.

But nothing happens, and Jacob and I are waved through.

Before I know it, we're pulling on our shoes and belts again and running through duty-free, barging past hordes of people all ambling along as if they have all the time in the world. Don't they know we have a plane to catch?

We skid to a halt beneath a departures board. Our flight to Ankara is listed at the top. The next plane due to depart.

'Gate thirty-six. Hurry,' Ronan shouts.

As he charges off, I notice they've already made the final call, but at least the gate's not closed. Not yet. We might still make it.

I grab Jacob's hand and tug him along, but he's too slow, oblivious to the urgency, wide-eyed with curiosity as he gawps at everything in the unfamiliar environment.

'Jump up, I'll carry you.' My back's already aching but I swing him onto my hip and follow Ronan who's disappearing among the crowds.

Sweat breaks out on my brow and dampens my shirt. I almost lose my sunglasses as they topple off the back of my head, but Jacob catches them and hands them back to me with a smile.

I really hope we make the flight, for his sake.

Gate thirty-six is miles away. Or at least it feels like it, carrying a wriggling four-year-old whose avalanche of questions continue unabated.

'Why's that man got no hair, Mummy?'

'How do planes fly?'

'Will I be able to drive the plane?'

Ronan's disappeared from view but hopefully he'll be able to persuade the airport staff to keep the gate open for us.

With my arm aching under Jacob's weight, I'm relieved to see a travelator up ahead. I drop Jacob onto his feet and stretch my back. He stares up at me in disbelief. He's never seen anything like it.

'It's like an escalator but it's flat,' I explain.

He stands with his feet wide apart, arms out to catch his balance, worry etched across his face.

Over a loudspeaker, a disinterested woman's voice informs passengers that gate thirty-six is now closing.

Shit.

'Run!' I yell, pulling Jacob's arm.

We sprint, whizzing past people who've opted not to take the moving walkway.

Finally, I catch sight of Ronan, who's at the gate, remonstrating with a member of staff from the airline.

'Sorry, we're here now,' I pant, fishing in my bag for the passports.

I present them to her with a friendly smile, my chest heaving and sweat dripping down my back.

She glowers at me. 'As I was explaining to your husband,' she says, her voice devoid of emotion, 'the gate is now closed. I'm sorry. You're too late.'

'But the plane is literally right there.' I point through a plateglass window overlooking the runway and a waiting Airbus A320.

'I'm sorry,' she repeats. 'There's nothing I can do. The plane's ready to leave.'

# Chapter 3

Doesn't this jobsworth realise we've raced almost a hundred miles to make the flight, more if you include the detour home to pick up the passports? Is she seriously going to turn us away for being less than thirty seconds late?

'I want to speak to your supervisor,' I demand, waving our passports in her face, anger coursing through my veins. 'We've paid good money to be on that flight.'

'Madam, the gate closed three minutes ago. There's nothing I can do. But if you'd like to speak to someone on the sales desk, I'm sure they'll be able to find you seats on a later flight.'

'There are no later flights to Turkey,' I grumble. She knows that as well as I do. We'd have to wait until tomorrow. Book into a hotel overnight or, god forbid, drive home again. If only I'd remembered the passports. Or better still, Ronan had taken responsibility for them.

He steps between me and the gate attendant, his hands on my shoulders, gently edging me away.

'Why don't you let me handle this?' he says with a smile that could defuse a bomb from fifty paces.

My blood's steaming but he's probably right. Ranting won't get us onto that flight.

'Fine,' I huff, and with one last poisonous glance at the obnoxious woman behind the barrier, I turn and walk away.

Jacob reaches for my hand.

'Why did that lady say we couldn't go on the plane?' he asks, confused.

I guide him to a bench in the corridor over-looking the deserted waiting area.

'Because we were late,' I say, cross with myself as much as anyone.

'Was it because you forgot the pathports?'

I take a deep breath and let it out slowly. I should have put them in my bag last night. Now I'm going to have to break it to Jacob that the holiday we've been promising him for months isn't going to happen. There will be no plane. No beach. No swimming pool. We're not going to Turkey, at least not today.

I drop my head into my hands and rake my fingers through my hair.

This is so unfair.

'It's okay, Mummy. Daddy's talking to the lady.'

Jacob sits next to me swinging his legs, seem-ingly oblivious to the seriousness of the situa-tion. I pass him his rucksack, which is filled with toys and books I packed for the trip. He pulls out a pair of plastic dinosaurs.

Ronan's trying his best, but even with all his charm, changing that stupid woman's mind is going to be an uphill struggle. We might as well admit defeat and see if there are any other flights. Although if anyone can talk their way onto the plane, it's him.

I wasn't looking for a relationship when I met Ronan. I was happily single, my heart broken, and adamant I didn't want or need a man in my life. But there's something about him that is undeniably attractive and when we met in a chance encounter in the park, he bowled me over. He made me feel like the only woman in the world. Those eyes. That smile. The unwavering confidence.

He spotted me with my head buried in my phone, enjoying the warmth of the early spring sunshine on my skin. He asked for directions to the library, and when I looked up, he told me I had beautiful eyes, then blushed, apologising. I'm used to men hitting on me. They've been doing it since I was old enough to notice, but it was the way he said it. Not in a creepy way, like a cheesy chat-up line, but like it had caught him by surprise and the words had tumbled accidentally from his mouth.

When he asked if he could sit with me for a minute, I found myself nodding. I was intrigued and he seemed good company. He wasn't one of those men who just wanted to talk about himself. He wanted to know about *me*. What I did for a living. What I did for fun. Why I'd come to the park. Whether I'd ever truly been in love.

Looking back, it was all a bit forward for a conversation with a complete stranger, but I fell for it. For him. He was respectful and attentive. He had a great sense of humour and wouldn't stop complimenting me on my looks. I didn't know it then, but it was exactly the ego boost I needed.

I've never been one to swoon over a man in a uniform, but when he dropped into conversation that he used to be a firefighter and was now running his own health and safety consultancy, I was impressed, because there's no denying the attractiveness of a man who's willing to put his life on the line to save others. And I suppose all little girls dream of the day they'll be rescued by a real-life hero.

So when he asked for my number, I didn't hesitate to type it into his phone. He called later that evening to ask me out for a drink, but, still not sure I was ready to date again, I had a pang of uncertainty and turned him down. I didn't know anything about him and life was complicated enough after the acrimonious end to my marriage. But he was so persistent, I eventually gave in with no expectation it would be anything other than a bit of fun.

We went to a quiet Vietnamese restaurant he knew. He ordered goi cuon and pho for us both without looking at the menu, and he talked about poetry and philosophy, his love for nature and his sadness at all the poverty in the world, wishing he could do more to help others. I was hooked, and the feeling was mutual.

I never looked back. I never had the chance. After that first date, he would send flowers or chocolates or some token or gift every day, and he'd leave me these adorable voice messages on my phone telling me how much he was missing me and that he was counting down the hours until he saw me again.

'Karina? Come on, let's go.' Ronan's voice snaps me out of my trance.

When I glance up, he's standing on the other side of the boarding gate next to the female attendant who's now smiling sweetly. He's waving at me to come over.

I've always said he could charm a river to change course, but this is nothing short of a miracle. For all his faults, the man's a bloody genius.

Jacob's on his stomach under the bench, lost in an imaginary Jurassic world.

'Jacob, we've got to go. Time to get on the plane.'

He pokes his head out and beams at me. 'Yay!'

The attendant hurriedly checks our passports and scans our boarding passes on our phones before urging us to run.

I've no idea what Ronan said to make her change her mind but he's saved the holiday and averted a potential meltdown from Jacob. Who knows, he might just have saved our marriage as well. I'm not sure it would have survived the strain of the holiday being cancelled for a second time.

'How?' I whisper in Ronan's ear as we reach the end of a boarding bridge where a flight attendant with a wide lipstick smile welcomes us on board the waiting plane.

'I told her we were on our honeymoon and that Jacob was recovering from a rare illness,' he says, grinning.

'Ronan,' I gasp, not sure whether he's joking. But who cares? We're on our flight and that's all that matters.

Most of the passengers are already seated and I'm conscious of a hundred pairs of eyes staring as we shuffle down the aisle looking for our seats, everyone watching the latecomers on their walk of shame.

Jacob leads the way as I struggle with our bags behind him, trying not to bang people's arms and heads. Ronan's behind, unusually quiet. I guess he's embarrassed we're the last on board.

I check my boarding pass. Row twenty-six, right behind the wing. Jacob has the window seat and I'm in the middle, but as we amble closer, it's clear the aisle seat, Ronan's seat, has been taken by a large man with curly grey hair and who's wearing a crumpled tweed jacket.

'Excuse me, I think we're in there,' I say, nodding to the seats on his left.

He unbuckles his seatbelt and wheezes as he stands, shooting me a filthy look. Some people are so grumpy. I might as well have asked him to drink curdled milk.

Jacob squeezes past the man's legs and flops into his seat, squealing with joy as he peers out of the window.

'Look, Mummy. I can see more planes.' He jabs his finger at the glass, a million tiny scratches caught in the glare of the morning sunshine, and points to a whole fleet of aircraft lined up on their stands.

After all the stress and hassle of getting here, and the crushing disappointment that we might have missed the flight, my heart balloons with happiness at Jacob's excitement.

I slump into my seat and fish out the belt from under my thighs.

Ronan's further back down the aircraft, studying the seat numbers under the overhead lockers.

'I think you might be in the wrong row,' I say to the man in the tweed jacket as he's about to sit down again. He probably spotted the empty row and took his chances that we would be a no-show.

He shakes his head and points to the number above the seat. 'Twenty-six C. It's my seat,' he mutters.

That can't be right.

'Ronan,' I call. 'We're down here.'

A team of flight attendants are marching officiously up and down the cabin, checking the lockers and instructing passengers to push their bags under the seats in front of them.

Ronan glances my way and mouths, 'Sorry.'

Sorry? What's he sorry about? He's putting his bag in the locker above a row of seats a short distance in front of us, but he should be back here with us.

And then he slides into an aisle seat, disappearing from view. Why's he sitting there and not with me and Jacob?

Surely he's not booked us seats apart? I can't believe it. Why didn't he say something earlier?

The man next to me puts his head back and closes his eyes.

'Sorry, I guess there must have been a mix-up. I don't suppose you'd mind switching seats so my husband can sit with us?'

His eyes crack open, he rolls his head towards me and raises an eyebrow, making it clear he does mind. Quite a lot.

'No? Right, fine,' I mumble to myself. What's wrong with people?

As I pull out a pack of baby wipes from Jacob's rucksack and clean the armrests and his foldaway table, disturbed by the black film of dirt that comes off the filthy surfaces, an insidious thought creeps into my head. Did Ronan deliberately book a seat in a different part of the plane so he didn't have to sit with us? So *he* didn't have to entertain Jacob for the duration of the flight?

No, he wouldn't do that. Maybe there was a limited choice of seats because we had to book late after our holiday to Crete was cancelled. I wish he'd mentioned it though. It means I'm in sole charge of keeping Jacob amused for the next four hours while Ronan gets to read, sleep and relax. I shouldn't be ungrateful, but sometimes our parenting responsibilities feel a little one-sided.

Just wait until we land, then I'll give him a piece of my mind. Really, Ronan can be so infuriating at times. And this is unforgivable.

# Chapter 4

At first, the novelty of being on a plane, taking off and watching the fields and houses below us grow smaller as we climb through the clouds, holds Jacob's attention. Until the pressure builds in his ears and I have to show him how to swallow to equalise them. After that, he's just restless.

It's going to be a long flight.

He still has so many questions and I know I shouldn't be cross with him because it demonstrates an inquiring mind, but really, half an hour's peace and quiet would be a godsend.

'How does the pilot know where to go?' he asks.

'I expect he has a map.'

'Are there parachutes on the plane?'

'Probably. I should think so.'

'What happens if the wings fall off, Mummy?'

'Why don't we read a book together?' I suggest, pulling out one of his favourite picture books from his bag, conscious there may be some nervous flyers within earshot who don't want to contemplate what would happen if the wings fell off the aircraft.

'Mummy, I'm bored. Can I get up?'

We're only forty minutes into the flight, but he's not used to being strapped into a seat and told he can't run around. He's always been an exuberant, energetic little boy.

Behind me, a child, not much older than Jacob, starts kicking the back of my seat. A slow, steady, rhythmic drumbeat that raises my hackles. Why aren't his parents keeping an eye on him? I'd never allow Jacob to get away with disturbing other people like that. It's rude.

I begin reading the book out loud, but Jacob's attention keeps wandering. There are too many distractions, including a little girl in the row opposite. She's maybe a year or two older than him. She has her hair tied in bunches and her eyes laser-focused on the iPad in her hands, playing a game. Her parents aren't paying her the slightest attention. They're too busy chatting, flicking through magazines and drinking gin and tonics. It's lazy parenting.

'What's this animal?' I ask, pointing to a tiger in the book as I desperately try to regain Jacob's interest.

'Lion,' he says without even looking.

'No, come on, you know this one. Look properly.'

'Don't want to read a book,' he cries, throwing himself stroppily back into his seat.

The man in the tweed jacket, who was trying to sleep, turns his head and glares.

'What about doing some drawing?' I produce a pad of paper and some crayons, lining them up on the pull-down table. 'You could draw the aeroplane and all the people on it. How many people do you think are on the plane?'

He puzzles the answer for a moment before announcing, 'Seven?'

I laugh. 'I think there are more than seven. Shall we try to count them?'

Jacob struggles with his seatbelt, trying to take it off so he can stand on the seat.

'No, honey. You need to sit down.'

Behind me, the kicking becomes faster. Stronger. Jarring my body until I start imagining the unspeakable horrors I'd inflict on the irritating child if I had my way.

'Don't want to sit down. Wanna see Daddy.'

I glance at the time on my phone. We have another three hours of this. Maybe bringing Jacob on a plane at his age wasn't such a good idea.

'Wanna see Daddy. Wanna see Daddy,' he chants over and over, rocking back and forth, banging his head against the seat. Another glare from the grumpy tweed jacket man.

'We'll see Daddy in a minute. What about a game?'

Jacob momentarily stops his rocking. 'What game?' His eyes flicker towards the girl with the iPad. I'm not against technology but Jacob's too young to be playing on a phone or a tablet. I'm not having his brain rotted by some mindless computer game, as tempting as it is right now to simply hand over my phone and let him get on with it.

'How about I Spy?'

He pulls a face.

'Alright then, what about a rhyming game? I'll think of a word and you have to say a word that rhymes with it.' It's good for his linguistic skills.

'I know,' he says, holding a finger in the air like he's been struck by an idea of great importance. 'What about chase?'

My heart sinks. 'We can't play chase on the plane, sweetheart.'

He sticks out his bottom lip, his shoulders slumping. 'Why not?'

'Because you'll annoy all the other people.'

'I won't.' He looks imploringly at me with angelic eyes.

'I know. Why don't I pretend to be an animal and you have to guess what it is by asking me lots of questions?'

Jacob stares at me like I've lost my mind. Another glance at the girl in the row opposite. She's so absorbed in her game, she seems completely oblivious to everything going on around her. Would it really hurt to give in and let Jacob play on my phone for the rest of the flight? As a special treat?

No, it's a slippery slope. If I let him play on my phone now, it'll be the parenting equivalent of letting the genie out of the bottle. He'll forever be pestering me about it.

It's only a few hours. Surely I can keep my own son distracted for that long without resorting to video games.

The kicking against my seat ratchets up a notch. It's both feet now. One after another. Ta-Dum. Ta-Dum. Ta-Dum. A never-ending barrage of thumps. It's worse than water torture.

'Wanna get off the plane now, Mummy,' Jacob whinges in my ear.

'You can't get off the plane until we land.'

'Wanna get off!' he screams.

'You can't. It's not like a car.'

'I don't like it. Wanna get off. Wanna get off.'

'Jacob, stop it,' I soothe, resisting the temptation to raise my voice, conscious of what all the other passengers must be thinking.

Ta-Dum. Ta-Dum. Ta-Dum.

I swear to god, if that child doesn't stop kicking me I'm seriously going to lose it.

Jacob pretends to cry, screwing up his face, rubbing his eyes and wailing pitifully.

Ta-Dum. Ta-Dum. Ta-Dum.

That's it.

I unbuckle my belt, jump out of my seat and turn to the mother of the child behind me.

'Will you please control your son and stop him kicking my fucking seat, for pity's sake,' I scream.

All around us, people fall silent. The boy in the seat behind and his shocked mother stare at me in disbelief.

Next to me, Jacob stops his pretend crying and looks up with his mouth wide open. And then he grins.

'Mummy said a rude word.'

# Chapter 5

I've flown on plenty of aircraft in my time.
Before I had Jacob, my job took me to some
wonderful, exotic locations all over the world.
Back then, I used to enjoy flying. All that time
to myself with nothing else to do but listen to
music, watch a film or read a book. It was fun.
Exciting. The flight to Turkey has been none of
those things, and when we eventually land, I've
never been so pleased to get off an aircraft in
my life.

The cabin crew plaster smiles on their faces
and wish us a pleasant stay as we slowly file
off, but I know they're judging me. Making a
mental note of my face. The crazy woman who
completely lost her shit with a child and had
to be taken to one side by the senior flight attendant, who warned me that if I didn't calm
down, they'd have no choice but to alert the
Turkish authorities and have me arrested when
we landed.

The shame of it.

At least Jacob finally settled down after my
outburst. He happily read his books, drew
colourful pictures of the plane and how he
imagined our holiday villa would be, complete

with swimming pool, nearby beach, and, oddly, what looked like a five-legged zebra.

Jacob holds my hand tightly as we tramp down a set of wobbly steps from the rear of the aircraft and onto cracked concrete. The heat hits our faces like we've opened the door to a blast furnace. Ronan finally catches up with us as we march in line behind the other passengers towards the arrivals hall, an amused grin on his face.

'Enjoy your flight, did you?' I can't resist sniping.

'Very relaxing,' he says. 'Hey, Jacob. What did you think about the plane?'

'It was awesome.' Jacob grabs Ronan's hand and swings between us, squealing with delight.

The intense, suffocating heat from the midday Turkish sun is a fleeting taste of the week to come. As we step inside the terminal to run the gauntlet of border control and baggage reclaim, we're greeted by an arctic blast from the air conditioning which brings goosebumps to my arms.

We show our passports to surly-looking officials, none of whom appear remotely pleased to be welcoming yet another planeload of British tourists into the country, and follow the signs to the baggage reclaim area, where our cases are among the last to emerge, predictably.

Ronan's hired a car and while he goes through a mountain of paperwork and waivers, Jacob and I sit on our cases and wait.

'Can I go in the pool when we get to the house?' Jacob asks.

I brush his hair with my fingers. I can't believe I swore in front of him. What kind of example is that to be setting to a four-year-old? Note to self - must do better.

'Of course you can. Just remember to put your armbands on before you get into the water, okay?'

'Will it be cold?'

'It might be.'

He screws up his face in disappointment.

The pool is something I've been worried about. What if Jacob accidentally falls in and drowns while neither of us is watching? It's been preying on my mind ever since Ronan showed me the pictures of the property online.

I've always been nervous around water, ever since my mother threw me into a pool when I was five in a misguided attempt to teach me to swim. It was one of the most terrifying things that's ever happened to me and still brings me out in a cold sweat just thinking about it. I'm sure I would have drowned if it hadn't been for my father who fished me out by my arm, coughing and spluttering. I can still remember the debilitating panic as I floundered around wildly in the water and then sunk to the bottom, not able to breathe, thinking I was going to die.

We should have taught Jacob to swim, but I've not been able to bring myself to take him to a pool for lessons. At least he's not inherited my fear of the water. He's too young to understand the danger.

'We'll keep an eye on him,' Ronan said with a shrug when I raised it. 'It's not as if he's going to be wandering around by the pool on his own, is it?'

He thought I was overreacting. But it only takes a second. A moment of distraction. You read about it in the news all the time. Kids who've fallen into rivers and lakes and even shallow ponds barely an inch deep, and drowned, even if they could swim.

Ronan strides back to where he's left us with the luggage, clutching a folder of documents in one hand and swinging a car key around one finger.

The hire car is a basic white Hyundai with few frills, although at least it has air con. We're going to need it. It's so much hotter here than I thought it was going to be. The heat drier. The sun more intense. Not great when you have a complexion like mine. Pale freckly skin that sooner burns than tans. Jacob's the same. With his blonde hair, he's as liable to burn as I am, and you can't take any risks with young kids. He won't stay in the shade, so I'll have to make sure he's smothered in factor fifty when he's outside.

While Ronan loads the cases in the boot, I strap Jacob into a grubby car seat in the back.

'Want my dinosaurs,' he says, reaching out his hand for his rucksack.

'What do you say?'

'Pleeeeeaaaaase.'

'Good boy.'

It takes almost an hour to drive to the villa and although I try desperately to stay awake to take in the scenery, I find my eyes growing heavy. Sleep soon envelops me in her comforting blanket. I'm vaguely aware of Ronan changing gear. The drone of the tyres. The hum of the air con. And Jacob chuntering happily in the back. Occasionally my head rolls onto my chest, ripping the muscles in my neck, and I jolt awake, only to fall back into sleep moments later.

I finally wake when the car comes to a halt and Ronan kills the engine. Although I've seen pictures of the villa online, it's even better in real life. It's a modern, modular design, clad in ochre timber and set high in the hills, overlooking the sea. I have to hand it to my husband, it's a brilliant find. There are three more villas on the complex, all the same size and design, but it doesn't feel crowded. Far from it. It's such a remote spot, it's going to make for a perfect week away to relax and chill. Plus, it's noticeably cooler than the stuffy heat we encountered at the airport. It's certainly nothing like some of the places we looked at where the properties were crammed in on top of each other like the developer was trying to squeeze every last penny of profit out of the land.

Ronan puts a hand on my thigh. 'So, what do you think?'

'It's stunning.'

'Can I go in the pool now?' Jacob asks, struggling to unbuckle himself.

I laugh. His enthusiasm is infectious. The journey might have been a trial but now we're finally here, I have a feeling we're going to have an amazing week. Just the three of us.

There's hardly a cloud in the sky and the heat burns through the windscreen. There's nothing to worry about other than being a family. Being together, making memories and sharing an amazing time.

The keys are in a miniature safe by the door. We're both beaten inside by Jacob, who pushes us out of the way and charges in. Ronan's face momentarily clouds with irritation, but it's gone as quickly as it gathered.

'He's just excited,' I say.

We follow him in, cooing our appreciation for the sophisticated decor, cool white walls and clean, modern furniture. It's as impressive inside as it is from outside, although I can't imagine we'll be spending much time inside the villa, other than when we're sleeping. It's been designed for outdoor living with a beautiful decked area shaded by a trendy triangular canopy, the same colour as the ochre cladding, and laid out with comfortable chairs and a dining table, plus a paved sun deck surrounding a kidney-shaped pool.

Jacob runs from room to room, taking it all in in a matter of seconds. It's not huge. It only has two bedrooms, but it's plenty big enough for us, especially with the outdoor space and the incredible views stretching out over the Black Sea in the distance.

'Where am I going to sleep?' Jacob asks.

'In this room.' I show him the room with the single bed and a picture window that looks out over rolling pine-clad hills, glad to see it has no direct access outside, unlike the master bedroom with its sliding patio doors which lead straight out to the pool.

Jacob looks puzzled for a moment before launching himself onto a springy bed.

It's lovely to see him so happy.

'Can we go in the pool now?' he asks.

'Sure.'

'I'll grab the cases,' Ronan says.

Jacob and I head out through another set of sliding doors in the living room which open effortlessly on well-oiled runners. Jacob darts away from me, making a beeline for the pool.

'Jacob!' I scream. 'Be careful. You don't have your armbands on.'

'It's okay, Mummy. I'm just looking,' he replies sulkily.

My heart's in my mouth as he approaches the edge of the water. I race after him and grab his arm, my pulse hammering, and pull him away from the edge. I can't blame him for being excited. The water, so clear you can make out a seashell pattern on the bottom, glistens in the bright sunshine. Even I can see the appeal, although the bikini I brought is purely for sun-bathing purposes only.

'Can I put my swimmers on and go in?' Jacob looks at me with doe-eyed innocence.

I have a distinct feeling of being watched and when I glance up, there's a woman in a long, floaty summer dress staring at us from the villa opposite. When I catch her eye, she vanishes back inside, as if she's embarrassed I've caught her spying on us.

'As long as you put your floats on first. And you'll need to put on some sun cream or you'll burn.'

'Yay!' Jacob pulls away and sprints back inside, bumping into Ronan, who's dragging in our cases.

'Steady on, young man,' Ronan warns.

'I want to go for a swim.'

'Come on, then. Let's find your trunks.'

I can already feel the stress and strain my body's been holding onto for the last few weeks evaporating. It really is the most idyllic spot. An absolute jewel. And so peaceful. Apart from the cicadas, whose constant buzzing is so loud, it makes my ears purr.

I pull up a chair on the decking under the shade of the canopy, all the tension in my neck and shoulders softening. The holiday wasn't cheap but I have a feeling it's going to be worth every penny. The perfect place for Ronan and me to reconnect and rediscover some of the lost intimacy that's become a casualty of our busy lives, working and raising a young child.

We don't talk like we used to. When our relationship was in its infancy, we chatted about everything and anything. It was so easy with Ronan. He completely understood me, like he knew what I was thinking and feeling, sometimes even before I knew myself.

I'm not so naive to think it was always going to be chocolates and roses, but I miss the couple we were in the first few months. Our wedding wasn't a big affair. Just a small gathering of friends and family at the local register office. It was one of the happiest days of my life, but it wasn't long after we tied the knot that we started to drift apart. We moved to Norfolk for a new start and to give Jacob the kind of childhood I dreamt of as a kid, and we stopped talking. I'm sure I'm as much to blame as Ronan, but neither of us put in the effort our marriage needed. The wedding was almost a year ago, and things haven't been getting any better between us. If anything, they're worse. We never do much together as a family and Ronan's away so much for his job, we've become like ships passing in the night.

Jacob comes barrelling out of the villa wearing nothing but a pair of navy trunks, chubby white arms and legs pumping.

'Have you put on any cream?' I yell after him as he shoots past, attention laser-focused on the pool.

Typically, he ignores me, plagued by a sudden deafness.

His bare feet slap across the paved sun deck, his hips waggling and his shoulders rolling.

But he's not wearing his armbands.

I jump up and open my mouth to scream. But nothing comes out other than a strangulated screech of terror.

I stare helplessly at my little boy, watching him in slow motion as he races towards the pool.

My body's frozen, my muscles locked in inaction. All I can do is watch helplessly. Terror swallowing me whole.

He jumps.

Launches himself into the air.

Arms wheeling. Legs kicking.

And then he's falling, plummeting into the water.

And with a loud splash, his body disappears below the surface.

# Chapter 6

I know I should do something. Anything. My son is drowning. But I can't move. It's as if my brain, like an unresponsive computer, circuitry locked and commands frozen, urgently needs a reboot.

I don't even know what to do. I can't dive in and save Jacob. I can't swim.

But then a miracle materialises in the shape of my husband who sprints out of the villa, head down, like a desperate animal acting on instinct.

He launches himself off the sun deck and into the pool with his back arched and arms reaching forwards, his elbows tucked into his ears and his hands clamped together in a classic diver's pose. He enters the water with barely a splash and disappears below the surface.

I can vaguely see shapes, indistinct patterns and colours, distorted by the water. Seconds tick past as slowly as hours while the non-stop grind of cicada legs vibrates noisily through the air.

Ronan's head bursts through the surface and a moment later, he hauls Jacob's tiny body out, manhandling him towards the side.

'For god's sake, Karina, help me,' Ronan splutters.

I rush to the pool, grab my son by his arms and yank him out, water soaking the paving stones. Jacob flops lifelessly onto his back, limbs as loose as seaweed on a rolling tide. His eyes are closed and he's not breathing.

Oh god.

Ronan hauls himself out with what seems like half of the water in the pool. He shoves me out of the way and turns Jacob onto his side, tilting his head back. Ronan's face is ashen, his shirt and jeans clinging to his body like a second skin, his hair plastered to his skull.

This can't be happening.

My baby. My darling boy.

My throat tightens painfully as tears cascade from my eyes.

And then another miracle happens.

Jacob coughs. And chokes. Water and spittle pouring from his mouth. And he stirs.

'Jacob!' I gasp, holding his head, stroking his hair.

He retches, pulling his knees up to his chest. He moans and begins to cry, but he's alive!

I pull him to my chest and hold him tight. Tighter than I've held him since the first day he came into my life. A bundle of joy and happiness.

'I'll get a towel.' Ronan stands. He puts a hand on my shoulder.

In the villa opposite, the woman in the floaty summer dress I saw earlier is half-hidden in the shade of the canvas canopy over her own deck, watching. God only knows what she must think of us, letting our little boy nearly drown. We've not been here an hour.

'Thank you,' I whisper to Ronan through my tears as he squelches back to the villa leaving a damp trail in his wake. 'Thank you for saving him.'

We don't talk about what happened. What *could* have happened if Ronan hadn't acted so quickly when he saw Jacob run off without his armbands. Instead, we focus all our attention on our little boy, smothering him with love and reassuring him that nothing bad is ever going to happen to him again. Because what's the point of shouting at him? He's learnt his lesson the hard way. I'm confident he won't be going near water without his floats again.

I spend the rest of the afternoon with Jacob close by my side, reading stories to him on the deck, under the shade, while Ronan heads out to find a supermarket to buy food. I don't think any of us could face a meal out tonight.

He returns with pizza and wine. Comfort food. The perfect choice. Pizza for Jacob. Wine for me. After the shock, I really need a drink.

We put Jacob down early. After all the excitement and trauma of the day, he's exhausted. A good night's sleep is what he needs and we can start afresh tomorrow. Put today behind us.

When I return from settling Jacob, tucking him up under the duvet when his eyes fluttered closed halfway through one of his favourite stories, the one about the park keeper taking in all his animal friends during a snowstorm, Ronan hands me a second glass of wine. We drink together in silence on the deck watching a shimmering amber sun set slowly over the horizon. But by nine, I'm struggling to keep my eyes open. Tiredness consumes my body. I feel like I could sleep for a week.

'It's all the adrenaline.' Ronan watches me over the rim of his glass. 'It's been a stressful day.'

He's not kidding. Even so, the exhaustion is debilitating. I can't ever remember being quite so tired, my limbs quite so heavy with fatigue. At least not since Jacob was a baby and teething, when I hardly slept a wink at night.

'I think I'll take myself off to bed.' I yawn. 'Sorry to be a party pooper on our first night.'

'It's fine. It's been a long day. I'll clear up.'

'Leave it. We'll do it in the morning.' It's only a few plates and the wine glasses but I can't face it tonight. All I want to do is sleep.

'It won't take long.' Ronan gives me a reassuring smile.

'Thanks, love.' I attempt to stand, but my legs give way under my body.

'Careful.' Ronan grabs my arm and steadies me. 'Want me to help you to bed?'

I shake my head. I'm not a two-year-old. 'I can manage, but will you make sure all the doors and windows are locked before you come to bed?' I ask. 'I don't want Jacob getting up in the middle of the night and getting out to the pool again.'

'Of course,' Ronan says, but I can see he thinks I'm being over protective. He's always thought

I'm a neurotic mother, but after today, surely he'll understand it's with good reason.

It's not that I don't trust him, but I make a quick circuit around the villa to check the doors and windows myself, ensuring they're all secured and the keys have been removed from the locks. And then, with a final check on Jacob, who's sleeping soundly with his thumb jammed in his mouth, I shuffle off to bed. It takes all my energy to clean my teeth, remove my make-up and pull on my pyjamas.

And when my head hits the pillow, I instantly plunge into the depths of a big, black hole of thick, dark sleep.

I don't even wake up to use the toilet in the middle of the night. It's as if my mind and body have shut down to recuperate and recover. It can't just be the stress of today. It's probably the culmination of weeks' worth of disturbed sleep and the anxiety that constantly seems to wrack my body when I'm at home. I worry about everything. Whether I'm doing enough for Jacob. Whether I'm being a good mother. I fret about Ronan. Our marriage. And what the future holds, my mind constantly taking me to sinister places. Fear holding me in its grip.

Like an air bubble rising to the surface of a jar of oil, I float back to consciousness through a delicious cloud of dreams, feeling happy and unusually calm. Until I check the time on my phone.

It's gone nine which means I've slept for twelve hours. I haven't slept that long since I was a teenager.

But if it's really that late, where's Jacob? He's always up early, wriggling into our bed at the first sign of light, oblivious to everyone else's needs. Ronan's still comatose, with one leg hanging out from under the crumpled sheets, but we have the bed to ourselves. There's no Jacob, and beyond the drone of the air con, the villa is silent.

Something's wrong. I feel it in my gut. A cold prickle of fear dancing across my skin.

What if he's woken up disorientated and managed to let himself out of the villa on his own and in his semi-awake state has wandered out to the pool?

I fly out of bed, skid across the floor and tug open the curtains. A beach ball floats past on the surface of the pool, but there's no sign of Jacob. He's not face down in the water, his pyjamas ballooning with air like I'd imagined. But it's only a small relief.

I hurry to his room. The door's been pulled shut which instantly makes me suspicious as Jacob hates sleeping with the door closed. It's why I always leave it ajar with a light on.

Jacob's bed is empty. And he's not sprawled out on the floor reading or playing with his dinosaurs either.

I scream his name, frantic.

The villa's so small, it only takes a minute to check all the rooms and cupboards, but he's nowhere to be found.

Ronan catches me as he emerges from the bedroom, curious about all the fuss I'm making.

'What the hell's going on?' He has dark bags under his eyes and his face is shadowed with dark stubble.

'It's Jacob. He's gone.'

'What?'

'I can't find him anywhere. He's not in his room and he didn't come into our bed this morning. I've looked all over. He's not here!'

My chest tightens, panic blooming in a flush of heat across my body.

'What are you talking about?' He narrows his eyes, confused.

'Jacob! He's vanished!'

'Why don't you sit down for a minute,' Ronan implores.

I don't understand why he can't grasp the seriousness of the situation. Our son is missing and he wants me to sit down?

'I don't have time to sit. We need to find him,' I yell, shrugging Ronan's hands off my arms.

'Why don't I make some coffee and you can tell me what's really going on,' he says.

'But he could be in danger,' I gasp.

Ronan scrapes his fingers through his tangled bed hair and sighs. 'What's going on with you, Karina?'

'Maybe he managed to get outside. Did you lock the door in the lounge like I asked?' I was so tired, I don't even remember hearing Ronan come to bed. Maybe it was so late, he forgot.

'Karina, stop it,' he says with a weary sigh.

'We should call the police. Where's my phone?'

'Stop!' he yells, making me jump.

'Please,' I beg.

'Karina, no more. I don't know if this is your idea of a joke or whether the strain of the last few weeks is finally catching up with you, but you're making no sense. We don't have a son. We don't have any children.'

I hear the words but I don't understand why he's saying them.

'This isn't a joke. I'm serious. Jacob is missing. Didn't you hear me? We have to find him.'

He shakes his head sadly. 'You're scaring me, Karina. This isn't funny.'

'You have to help me.'

'I can't help you if I don't know what you're talking about. I don't know what's got into you but we don't have any children. No one's missing. It's just you and me. We came to Turkey on our own.'

# Chapter 7

I stare at Ronan like he's a stranger, unable to believe what I'm hearing.

'Maybe you had a bad dream,' he says.

A bad dream?

'I'm talking about Jacob, our son.' It's as if I've woken up in a scene from *Alice in Wonderland*. What's next? A parade of playing cards waltzing through the villa on their way to a tea party?

Ronan shakes his head again, pouting out his bottom lip like he's trying to remember a vague acquaintance he once met.

This is insane.

'It's probably the heat. You're not used to it,' he says. 'Maybe you should have a lie down?'

He attempts to take my arm but I pull away.

'This isn't funny, Ronan.'

'Karina, I seriously don't know what you're talking about. You're worrying me. Do you think I should call a doctor?'

'I don't need a doctor. I need to find our son.'

'We. Don't. Have. A. Son,' he repeats, emphasising each word like I'm a simpleton who can't understand plain English.

'Don't say that!'

He throws his arms out in exasperation. 'So this son of ours, where is he?'

'That's the point. I don't know!' I scream. 'He's vanished!'

'That's convenient.'

This can't be happening. It's madness. Why would Ronan say these things?

Oh god, unless he's ill. I've heard about people who start acting strangely or who suddenly lose their memory when they've had a bang to the head or a clot on the brain. Is that what's happening? Has Ronan had some kind of stroke in his sleep and now can't even remember our own son?

'Do you remember yesterday we had to turn back on the way to the airport because we'd forgotten the passports?' I ask.

'Because *you* forgot the passports,' he says, pointedly.

'Yes, yes, whatever. And then we were late, and the gate was closed and they wouldn't let us on the plane?'

'What does that have to do with anything?'

'But you remember, yes? And you sweet-talked that irritating woman into letting us on board but you hadn't told me you couldn't book seats together?'

He hangs his head.

'Do you remember? Jacob and I had to sit with this grumpy old guy. You must remember that?'

Ronan draws in a deep breath and lets it out with a long, slow sigh. 'I remember you kicking off and yelling at a woman and her kid in the seat behind us,' he says. 'And anyway, the guy wasn't grumpy. He just wanted some peace and quiet. But it was just you and me. There was no one else. And there definitely wasn't anyone called Jacob, okay?'

I squeeze my eyes shut and hold up my hand to silence him. I can't bear it. 'Stop saying these things. I don't know what's wrong with you and why you're being like this, but you're really scaring me.'

His body softens. He comes towards me, arms out wide as if he's planning to hug me. I take a step back. I don't want him near me when he's being like this.

'We're wasting time. We have to find him.'

Ronan groans and throws his head back. 'Karina, just listen to yourself. I don't know what's going on inside your head right now, but this isn't funny.'

'No, it's not! You've just told me we don't have a son.'

'We don't! There is no Jacob! We don't have any children!'

'Fine. Be like that, but I'm going to find him. He needs me.'

I storm off towards Jacob's room with tears of anger and confusion pricking my eyes. Whatever's going on with Ronan, it'll have to wait. One crisis at a time is all I can manage and right now, Jacob has to be my priority. He's only four.

The light's still on in his room, but there's something odd I hadn't noticed before. The bed doesn't look as if it's been slept in. The duvet cover is pulled up over the pillows and smoothed out, even though I distinctly remember putting Jacob to bed last night and tucking him in. We snuggled up together, his little body tucked into mine as I read him stories until his eyes grew heavy. I brushed his hair behind his ear and kissed him on the forehead. He was already fast asleep and curled up in a foetal position under the duvet when I left the room. There's no way Jacob has risen and made his own bed. He doesn't even know how.

Ronan appears in the doorway and leans on the frame, watching me with his arms crossed and eyebrows raised.

'Did you make his bed?' I demand.

'I've not even been in this room.'

Hang on a minute. I see what's going on here.

I smile, my shoulders relaxing. Any minute now, Jacob's going to spring out from a cupboard or from under the bed to surprise me. This is something they've cooked up together. A hilarious practical joke at my expense.

'Come on then, where is he?' I whisper.

Ronan's eyes grow wider. 'Where's who?'

'It's okay, I'll act all surprised.'

'About what?'

'Look, a joke's a joke but this has gone too far. I was worried for a minute.'

He stares at me blankly and gives a slight shake of his head.

So, he's going to keep this whole charade going until Jacob pops out and scares the living daylights out of me. Fine. I'll play along.

'Oh, no, where can Jacob be?' I put my hands to my mouth in mock horror. 'He's not anywhere I can see. He's not in his bed and he's not in this cupboard...'

I creep across the room on tiptoes and throw open the wardrobe doors, fully expecting Jacob to throw himself out with a monster-like growl, hoping to make me jump, before collapsing in hysterics at the prank.

But the wardrobe's empty.

And, strangely, his clothes have gone too. I spent some time hanging all his T-shirts and shorts in the wardrobe yesterday afternoon and now they've disappeared.

'Where are his clothes?'

'Whose clothes?' Ronan creeps up behind me and stares over my shoulder into the wardrobe. 'This is really creepy, you know.'

I yank open the top drawer of a chest that's built into the wardrobe where I put all of Jacob's pants and socks. It's also empty.

'What have you done with them?'

I spin around, shoving my husband out of the way, and dive under the bed where I left Jacob's empty case so it would be out of the way. But it's not there anymore. I can't even find Jacob's Thomas the Tank Engine rucksack with all his books and toys he had on the plane.

In fact, when I look around the room, there's not a shred of evidence that Jacob's been here at all.

If this is a joke, they've gone to some trouble. God knows when they concocted their plan. I guess they must have set up the room like this while I was sleeping this morning.

'Please, I don't like it. Just tell me where he is, okay?'

'It's all in your head,' Ronan says, tapping my temple with his finger. I swat his hand away angrily. 'There is no Jacob. There's just you and me. Now come on, why don't you let me make you breakfast.'

'I don't want any breakfast,' I yell.

'Suit yourself.' Ronan holds up his palms in submission. 'But I need a coffee.'

I bunch my hands into tight fists at my sides, my nails digging into my palms. The sharp stab of pain gives me focus.

Jacob has to be here in the villa somewhere, but he's clearly not inside. If this is a joke, I hope Ronan's had the sense not to leave him hiding alone near the pool.

I race for the sliding doors in the lounge, thumbing open the lock and spilling out onto the decking. The heat is already building, the sun high in the azure sky. It's going to be another scorching day.

'Jacob!' I scream. 'Jacob!'

I look left and right, scanning for any sign of my son, squinting in the bright sunlight bouncing off the tiles around the pool.

A short distance away, the woman in the villa opposite is watching again, cradling a coffee cup in one hand, sitting at a table on the decking under the shade. Does she have nothing better to do? Although I'm sure it's all quite entertaining for her. She must be wondering what kind of bad mother I am.

What if it's not a joke? What if Jacob's been abducted? Could someone have come to the villa in the middle of the night and taken him? We're so remote up here in the hills, it's entirely possible someone could have driven here without being seen. Although it doesn't explain why all Jacob's clothes have gone. Anyone intent on abducting a child wouldn't waste time packing their belongings and making the bed, would they? It just doesn't make sense.

My mind is a tumult of confusion and worry. If Jacob's disappearance is a prank conceived with his father, it's gone way too far. And there's no way Jacob would be able to contain himself hidden away for this length of time.

But it's the only plausible explanation that fits the facts, although they've never played a prank on me like this before. I don't like it. It's not remotely funny.

When I rush back into the house, Ronan's in the kitchen pouring hot water into a cafetiere, still only wearing his boxer shorts.

'If you don't tell me where he is, I'm going to call the police,' I announce.

He turns, folding his arms over his bare chest.

'I don't think that's a good idea,' he says. 'If you rant on to them about a missing fictitious son, they'll probably section you. At best, they'll arrest you for wasting their time.'

'Don't talk rubbish.'

'Why, what do you think's going to happen when they realise you're delusional?'

'I'm not delusional.' I stagger backwards in shock. Why is he saying these hurtful things?

'But you keep talking about this Jacob boy like he's real, when it's all in your head. I'm sorry, Karina, I don't know what's going on, but it's freaking me out.'

'Jacob's our son!'

'No, he's not! How many times do I have to say it?'

If only I could prove to him he's wrong. I glance around the villa looking for something, anything, to confirm Jacob's existence and my sanity.

We've been here less than twenty-four hours and we haven't really spread out yet. Most of what I can see was already in the villa when we arrived. There's nothing of Jacob's, not even a carelessly discarded T-shirt or a pair of shoes.

'I'm sorry, love,' Ronan says. 'I didn't mean to shout, but I'm worried.'

And then I see it on the table in the corner. The pile of our passports. Jacob's only four but he needed his own documentation to travel abroad. If ever there was incontrovertible proof we have a son and his name is Jacob, this is it.

I catch Ronan's eye and he follows my gaze to the table as I throw myself across the room like a woman possessed. There should be three passports. But to my surprise, there are only two in the pile. With a sense of dread, I flick open the first. It's mine. That awful picture of me with dead eyes and lank hair glaring out from under a protective laminate film.

The second belongs to Ronan, his picture making him look ten years younger, with darker hair and a thinner face.

'What have you done with it?' I cry.

Ronan looks at me with the kind of expression you'd give an old dog whose days are numbered.

'What have I done with what?'

I open my mouth and let out an ear-bursting, anguished scream of anger and frustration.

# Chapter 8

As my legs give way, the floor races up to meet me at a dizzying speed. I slump to the ground as weak as a newborn lamb, my mind a blizzard of confusion and fear. Is this what insanity looks like?

My own husband is trying to convince me our missing son doesn't exist. That he's never existed beyond the realms of my imagination, which is patently untrue. I'm not in a dream. I can't pinch myself on the arm and wake myself up. This is all really happening and I have no idea why. It's utterly bewildering.

I let my head fall into my hands. Thick, wet tears roll down my cheeks onto my bare knees. My throat is tight, my mind a maelstrom. It's as though I've fallen asleep in one world and awoken in a parallel universe where my life looks the same but everything is different.

And to top it all, Ronan's staring at me as if *I'm* the one having a breakdown. That I'm the one who's lost their mind. But I haven't. I know the difference between illusion and reality. If anything, there's something wrong with him. He's the one being weird, pretending he can't remember Jacob. Denying him. All his memories lost.

Did something happen to him after I went to bed last night? Maybe he banged his head after drinking too much and tripped over. If he slipped and cracked his skull on a wall or the floor, it's possible he could have a clot pressing on his brain without knowing it. Should I be trying to get him to a hospital?

Possibly. Probably.

But not until I've found Jacob.

Even if there is something wrong with Ronan, it still doesn't explain what's happened to Jacob and why all his clothes and toys, even his passport, have vanished. It's too weird for words. I can't explain any of it and that's the most terrifying part of it all.

'Karina, are you okay?' Ronan crouches on his haunches with one hand lightly resting on my shoulder.

'I just need a minute.'

I wipe away the tears. Crying won't fix this. I need to think straight and work this through logically. There has to be a rational explanation.

My mind might be a little woolly this morning from too much sleep, but I'm not going mad. I've not made up memories of my son. That would be utterly ridiculous. The biggest insanity of all. No, there's something else going on here that I'm not seeing. I just need to work out what it is.

I close my eyes and focus on the shape of Jacob's head, the slant of his eyes and the smell of his hair. The softness of his hand tightly gripping mine. His little snub nose. The freckles on his cheeks that are only really noticeable in the summer.

I have other strong memories too, bottled up and sealed so I'll always remember, even when I'm old and he's grown up with a family of his own. The day he sat up on his own for the first time. When he first crawled, snaking unsteadily across the floor towards me. When he pulled himself up onto his feet using the dining room chair for support. Taking his first steps. Speaking his first words, 'Mumma', not 'Dadda', which gave me a thrill of delight.

There are other memories that stick with me. Not necessarily happy memories, but recollections that have a resolute toehold in my mind. The hours I spent pacing up and down with him in my arms when he was a baby with colic and wouldn't sleep. The darkness that crept into my brain in the weeks after his birth and left me wondering if I'd made a terrible mistake deciding to become a parent. The helplessness that enveloped me as it occurred to me I didn't have a clue how to look after a newborn baby.

And raw, intense emotions that I couldn't possibly have imagined and that still evoke a physical response, spiking my heart rate, dampening my palms, whenever I think about them. The panic that gripped me when Jacob tripped in the park when he was two, grazing his head so badly on a bench I thought he'd need stitches. His plaintive cries in the night when he woke up hungry and I needed to haul myself out of bed to feed him when it was the last thing I felt like doing. The anxiety of bathing him when he was tiny and wriggly and

I was constantly worried about him slipping from my grip and drowning.

You can't make up those kinds of memories. They're not the imaginings of a crazy woman.

And what about all the photos? I have thousands of them charting every stage of Jacob's short life. Many taken on my phone. Quick pictures or video clips capturing a brief moment in time to be treasured forever.

I snap open my eyes. Ronan's still crouched in front of me, looking concerned.

'I need my phone,' I say.

There must be hundreds of photos of Jacob on it. I even took some on the plane and at the airport when we arrived. There was one I particularly liked of Jacob sitting on one of our cases with his head propped in his hands looking sulky and bored while Ronan dealt with the hire car paperwork.

Even my lockscreen is a picture of the three of us I took on the beach near our house when the sun was setting and casting a stunning glow across the sand. When I show Ronan, he'll have to accept the problem's with him and not me and we can get on with looking for Jacob.

'Just try to take it easy.' Ronan puts a hand to my forehead, checking my temperature, as if I'm sick. 'Stay here, I'll bring you some water.'

'I don't want any water. I want my phone.'

I drag myself to my feet, my legs still shaky.

'You look a little pale,' Ronan says. 'Are you sure you're not sickening for something?'

I brush past him. My phone's still in the bedroom, by the bed, the charging cable lying limply on the floor. I should be out looking for

Jacob, but this is important. If I can prove to Ronan that there's nothing wrong with me, we can get on with the search.

The phone's screen lights up as I collapse onto the unmade bed.

But immediately I can see something's not right. I should be looking at a picture of me, Ronan and Jacob, standing on the beach with long shadows cast from our feet across the rippled sand. The lockscreen image I installed months ago. A reminder of a happy time and place that always brings a smile to my face.

Instead, I stare at an image of the Milky Way, a colourful spiral of stars against a black sky. It's a familiar picture, but it's not one of mine. It's one of those standard images that comes pre-loaded with the phone. I'm sure I've not changed it, but I suppose it's possible the phone's defaulted to its factory settings because we're in a different country. I can't think of any other reason.

It doesn't matter. I have plenty of other photos of Jacob. I type in my passcode and navigate into the photo app.

The last image I took comes up first. It's a selfie of me and Ronan on the sun deck last night after I'd put Jacob down and we were sharing a bottle of wine. We actually look happy. At least I do. Ronan's face is drawn and he looks a little anxious, although he's never taken a decent picture. He can't relax in front of the camera.

I scroll back. The next shot is of my feet with my bright red toenails freshly painted for the holiday, the swimming pool in the background, slightly out of focus. It's a clichéd Instagram shot but I quite like it. And then there are a few of the villa. Some close-up pictures of the olive trees dotted around the complex. And a panorama of the view with the hills giving way to the sea.

Still nothing of Jacob. I hunt further back and find a few shots I took on the plane. Some images I snapped through the scratched window as we flew over Germany and Austria, the Alps on the horizon, but none of Jacob, which is odd. I distinctly remember taking several of him looking out at the view, framed artistically in the window with a shaft of sunlight falling across his amazed face.

But they're all gone.

# Chapter 9

With a rising panic, I scroll further and further back through the album. There are plenty of selfies, of me, and me with Ronan, but nothing at all of Jacob. This can't be right. I had loads of him on my phone. Ever since he was born, he's been my favourite subject.

'What are you doing?' Ronan appears at the door, looking weary.

'Have you been on my phone?' I snap.

'Of course not. Why?'

'All my photos. They've gone.'

He shakes his head, eyes narrowing. 'What are you talking about?'

'Look!' I thrust my phone towards him. 'They're all gone.'

'Maybe you accidentally deleted them.' He takes the phone and uses his index finger to scroll.

I watch him closely, studying his reaction.

He shrugs. 'I don't know what you're talking about. There are loads of photos.'

'Not the ones of Jacob! I took pictures of him on the plane and at the airport while you were sorting out the car,' I yell, the heat of panic and confusion flushing my body. 'But they're all gone. Every single one. It's like he doesn't exist.'

'Karina,' Ronan says in such a pitiful, patronising voice I could cry.

'No! Don't say it.'

'I think you might need to see someone. A professional,' he says. 'I'm sure we can find someone in the area who'll take a look at you.'

'I don't need someone to take a look at me. I need my son back.'

I snatch my phone angrily, fear pricking at my insides. But I'm not going crazy. The recent photos I took of Jacob might have gone, but I have plenty of others all backed up to the cloud. I'm fastidious about it.

I open another app where I keep all my old photos and log in. I meticulously catalogue all my images, storing them in hundreds of folders corresponding to dates and locations. It's a good habit formed when I was a young professional photographer because I learned early on that you need to have a system or you might as well give up.

There must be thousands of photos of Jacob and in any given folder there's bound to be at least one of him, but I choose one labelled November last year. That's when Jacob had his birthday and I know there are tons of pictures of him from his party when I surprised him with a rocket-shaped cake and the three of us spent the day on the beach, wrapped up in our coats and hats.

A second or two passes after I click on the folder.

But when it opens, there's nothing inside it. It's completely empty. It doesn't contain a single image. Not one frame of Jacob's party, or from any other day in that month.

Frantically, I click into another folder at random. One from July last year. It was a hot summer. We ordered a paddling pool online for Jacob and set it up on the front lawn, filling it with water from the hose. It was Ronan's idea. I thought Jacob was too young and spent most of the summer worried he might slip and drown in it. But he loved it. I took dozens of pictures of him splashing around in the water with his plastic boats from the bath.

But all those photos have also vanished. The only images left are a few of a particularly spectacular sunset I captured one evening, some shots of a hedgehog that paid a visit to the garden one night and some of Ronan goofing around with a pair of underpants on his head. There's nothing of Jacob at all.

I glance at Ronan with horror. 'It was you, wasn't it?'

'It was me what?' There's a catch of irritation in his voice, but I couldn't care any less about his feelings right now. If he's deleted my photos of Jacob, I'll never forgive him.

'You've deleted everything. Every photograph I've ever taken of Jacob.'

'For the last time, there is no Jacob,' he shouts.

'What have you done with him? Where is he?'

'There is no Jacob, Karina. How many times do I have to repeat myself? We don't have any children. What the hell is wrong with you?'

'With *me*? This is all you, isn't it?'

He shakes his head sadly. 'I knew we should have spoken to a therapist, but you were adamant you didn't need help, weren't you? Of course, you always know best. But this is exactly the sort of thing I was worried about.'

His words take the sting out of my anger. I genuinely have no idea what he's talking about.

'Why would I need a therapist?'

'You assured me you were dealing with it,' he says, one hand on his hip, the other raking anxiously through his hair.

'Dealing with what?' He's talking in riddles.

'I thought this holiday would help, not make things worse. You know, I really thought it would help us reconnect after everything.'

He's trying to confuse me. I have to stay focused. Jacob is missing and he needs me.

*Think, woman, think.*

'Maybe we should just pack up and go home.'

'I'm not going anywhere until I've found Jacob.' I'm not abandoning him. I'll stay for as long as it takes, with or without Ronan's help.

We should never have come. This whole holiday has been a disaster from the moment we left the house. Forgetting the passports was an omen, a warning that we shouldn't have come, and I ignored it. First there was Jacob almost drowning in the pool and now he's vanished, probably abducted from his bed.

'The pool,' I shout, making Ronan jump. 'Yesterday when we arrived, it's all Jacob was interested in. Do you remember, you helped him find his trunks but he jumped in without his floats.'

Ronan wets his lips as he watches me, listening.

'Come on, you must remember that. You dived in fully clothed and pulled him out. You saved his life. I didn't make that up.'

'It didn't happen,' he says so softly it's barely a whisper.

'It *did* happen. You hung your jeans up outside to dry.' I race out of the room, through the lounge and out onto the sundeck.

There, hanging on a railing, right where I remember he left them, are Ronan's jeans, still damp around the lower legs.

I offer them to him with a raised eyebrow as he follows me outside.

'I spilled some wine, remember? I rinsed them out in the sink so they wouldn't stain. I never went anywhere near the pool.'

I stare at my husband, trying to work out what's going on inside his head. Whether he's lying to me or if there's something else going on. Something in his brain that's made him forget.

Or something worse.

It's almost unthinkable but what if Ronan arranged for Jacob to be abducted and now he's covering his tracks by denying his existence? It would certainly explain everything that's happened, why Jacob's clothes and passport are missing. What if Ronan has sold Jacob to a child trafficking gang for a family who wanted a beautiful, blonde, blue-eyed little boy like Jacob?

No, that's even crazier than any other explanation. There's no way Ronan would sell his own son. What am I thinking?

But what, then? What other possible explanation can there be? Because there *has* to be an explanation. The alternative is that I *am* losing my mind. That everything I believed was true was all a fiction in my brain.

'Jacob!' I scream at the top of my lungs. 'Jacob!'

With a quick glance at Ronan, I race around the front of the villa in my bare feet. He's out here somewhere. I just need to find him.

I don't see the van until it's too late.

It's roaring along the track outside the villa, kicking up a cloud of dust in its wake, but I only see it when the driver blasts his horn. It's bearing down on me fast, tyres skidding on the loose gravel.

I scream and squeeze my eyes closed.

And the last thought that goes through my mind is not that I'm going to die, but that I've let my son down.

# Chapter 10

Every muscle in my body solidifies as I brace for the inevitable collision with the van, but instead of being tossed into the air and sent sprawling across its windscreen, I'm bundled sideways as Ronan rugby tackles me to the ground and out of harm's way.

We land in a heap in the warm dirt, Ronan on top of me, my shoulder bearing the brunt of the impact with the ground. I blink open my eyes with my heart thumping and a part of me weirdly disappointed. At least death would have been an easy escape from this purgatory I've woken up to today.

'What the hell are you playing at?' Ronan grumbles as he picks himself up and dusts himself down. 'You almost got yourself killed.'

He helps me to my feet as the van driver, a man with dark, sun-kissed skin and a muscular physique, climbs out of his vehicle, ranting at us in Turkish. I have no idea what he's saying but I get the gist of it. I must have scared the life out of him. With his dirty jeans and a sweat-stained vest top that looks two sizes too small, I guess he's a gardener or maintenance man.

'Sorry.' Ronan holds up a hand in apology.

The driver continues to shout at us, animatedly gesticulating with both hands.

'She's having a tough day.' Ronan talks over him, slowly and loudly in that patronising way Brits abroad tend to do when they can't speak the language. 'But you shouldn't have been driving so fast. You need to keep your eyes on the road.'

Whether or not the man understands Ronan, his words seem to infuriate him further.

'I'm so sorry,' I say, trying to calm him as he eyes me up and down. I'd forgotten I'm still in my pyjamas. I must look a real sight, with my hair loose and matted, my clothes scuffed and my arms and legs covered in dirt.

After a few moments, he finally cools off and, with one final violent gesture with his arm, hauls himself back into his van and drives away.

'Let's get you back inside and cleaned up,' Ronan says, but I'm not listening. I push him away angrily. I can't even bring myself to thank him for saving me.

I'm not injured, just a little embarrassed. What I need to do is find Jacob. If he's wandered off on his own, he might not be far away.

I scan the complex looking for clues or any evidence he might have been out here on his own. A short distance away there's a wood that descends sharply down a hill, and in every other direction, there's just more woodland and olive trees. Jacob could be anywhere. I don't even know where to start.

Unless he's not wandered off at all but something terrible has happened to him in the villa that Ronan's not telling me about. What if there was another accident while I was sleeping and Ronan's covering it up, trying to make me think I'm mad to bury what's really happened?

It's some conspiracy theory, but I'm so desperate, any explanation seems half-plausible right now.

I turn slowly through three hundred and sixty degrees, taking in the entire landscape, forcing my brain to slow down and think. That woman from the villa opposite is watching again. Always watching. She thinks she's hidden in the shadows, but I can see her in the door by her pool, loitering. Maybe she's seen something. Maybe she knows what's happened to Jacob.

She slips back inside her villa as she spots me staring.

*Too late, I've seen you.*

'I'm begging you, come back inside,' Ronan pleads. But I'm not going anywhere with him. Not until I've found my son. *Our* son.

'No,' I hiss, before pulling away from him and running towards the neighbouring property.

Stones dig painfully into the soles of my bare feet but nothing is going to put me off.

I hammer frantically at the door with my fists as a bird of prey soars high overhead, its screeches echoing through the valley. The sun, already climbing high in the sky, warms my skin, burning it. I've not had a chance to put on any sun cream, but it's the least of my worries.

When there's no answer, I bang on the door again. I know she's in there and if that woman saw something, anything, I need to know.

Eventually, the door opens a crack.

The woman peers out. 'Hello?' she says with a broad southern English accent, looking at my pyjamas suspiciously.

At least she's English. I've never been good at languages, and if she was German or French or Turkish, I'd have no idea how I'd communicate with her.

'We're staying in the villa opposite,' I announce, 'but our son, Jacob, has gone missing. I can't find him anywhere. I woke up this morning and he was gone. I've looked everywhere and I wondered if you might have seen him?'

'Oh,' she says. 'No, sorry.'

'Are you sure?'

She's wearing a pretty dress adorned with pink roses, her hair tied back in a ponytail. I'm surprised she's applied a full face of make-up in this heat. Burgundy lipstick and a wash of sky-blue eyeshadow. She has a piggy nose, deep-set eyes and her dress rides high on the swell of her wide hips. She's what my father would have called buxom. Attractive in a wholesome kind of way.

'I've not seen him,' she says.

Ronan strides up behind me and places a protective hand on my arm. It's warm and clammy and I have to fight the urge to shrug him off.

'I'm Ronan,' he says, plastering a smile on his face and sticking out his hand. 'Sorry if we're disturbing you.'

The woman looks hesitant, glancing at me and then back at Ronan. She clears her throat. 'Polly,' she says. She shakes his outstretched hand. It's all weirdly formal and a bit unnatural.

'I hope Karina's not been bothering you with her nonsense, has she?'

'Oh, no. I don't—'

'She's just a bit upset, that's all. She's been through a lot of stress recently. This was supposed to be a break from it all, wasn't it, love?'

What *is* he talking about? He keeps saying I've been stressed, but no more than any other parent with a demanding four-year-old.

'Did you see or hear anything last night? I think someone might have taken him.'

To my surprise, Ronan laughs. 'Karina, stop it. We've been through this. I'm so sorry,' he says to Polly. 'She's not feeling well.'

'I feel fine,' I snap. '*Did* you hear anything, anything at all last night?'

'Well...' She glances at Ronan. The poor woman doesn't know what to say.

'Did you?' I coax. 'Anything might help.'

'Have you called the police?' she asks as she toys with her fingers nervously.

'No, not yet.'

'We don't need the police,' Ronan interjects. 'It's a misunderstanding, that's all.'

I could punch him. This really isn't helping. There's every chance Polly's seen or heard something, but Ronan's still being weird and now she doesn't want to say anything. Maybe it is time to call the police.

'Why don't you take yourself back inside and I'll explain everything to Polly.' Ronan tries to guide me back towards our villa.

'Get off me,' I yell.

He shoots Polly an apologetic smile as if I'm a child throwing a tantrum in the middle of a supermarket aisle.

'I'm sorry, I didn't see anything,' Polly repeats.

'He's about this tall,' I hold my hand palm down at the side of my thigh to indicate his height, 'with blonde hair.'

She shakes her head as if she doesn't know what I'm talking about. But she's seen him. She was watching us yesterday. She saw Jacob fall into the pool and nearly drown. I remember being worried what she'd think of us as parents.

'You saw him yesterday,' I say as Polly stares at me blankly. 'You were watching when Ronan dived into the pool to save him. He'd jumped in without his armbands.'

'I didn't see anything.'

What? Of course she did. I saw her watching.

Ronan grips my arm. 'I'm going to call a doctor,' he says to Polly in a stage whisper, as if I'm not there. 'I think it might be too much sun.'

'You must have seen him,' I repeat. 'He has fair hair and blue eyes.'

'I saw you and your husband arrive, but I'm sorry, I didn't see anyone with you. I'm sure you didn't have a child.' She grimaces. Apologetic.

'His name's Jacob.'

She stares at me with pity-filled eyes. This isn't happening.

'Karina's a little delusional. We don't have any children,' Ronan is saying, although his words barely register.

'Please, try to remember,' I beg.

'I'm sorry, I have to go.' Polly waves a hand in the vague direction behind her. 'I hope you get well soon.'

She shuts the door in our faces and I'm left staring at the paintwork in utter disbelief. There is no way she didn't see, or at least hear, Jacob yesterday when we were out around the pool. The villas are no more than twenty metres apart, and I could certainly see her clearly from our sun deck. So why's she lying?

My stomach flips. Unless she has something to do with Jacob's disappearance? What if she's one of those women who can't have children of her own? What if she's taken Jacob and he's in there with her right now? She was certainly keen to get rid of me quickly enough.

'Jacob!' I scream. I raise my hand to bang on the door, but Ronan catches it and stops me.

'Leave the poor woman alone,' he snarls. 'Let's not drag her into this.'

'But what if Jacob's in there with her? What if she's taken him?'

'Nobody's taken anyone. Now come on, back to the villa. You're going to burn in this sun.'

He has to physically pull me away from the villa as fresh tears fall from my eyes.

'I want to call the police,' I say. 'I think we need to get them involved. Jacob's in trouble. We need help.'

'No. Absolutely not. I really don't think that would be a good idea at all,' he says. 'I'm not letting you waste police time on this nonsense. And besides, you don't want them carting you off to the madhouse, do you?'

He laughs cruelly, but it's no joke.

# Chapter 11

Maybe I *am* going mad.

What if Ronan's right and everything I thought was real I've imagined? What if I don't have a son? What if my memories of him are false and he never existed?

I shudder. It's an utterly terrifying prospect and completely implausible. How could I have imagined it all? Yet even that woman in the villa opposite doesn't remember Jacob. I really should call the police, but Ronan's warning has frightened me.

*You don't want them carting you off to the madhouse, do you?*

I shake my head, chasing away my doubts. Of course I haven't imagined Jacob. He's as real as the fingers on the ends of my hands. A part of me. You can't create false memories as tangible as the ones in my head. And I don't need photographs or documentation to prove it. It's preposterous.

But there is something going on here I don't understand. Jacob is missing and my husband is going out of his way to make me believe he doesn't exist. And if I can't figure out why, I really am going to go mad.

Ronan sits me in the shade at the table on the sun deck and brings some coffee and bread. He's cut the bread into neat slices and stacked them in a basket. He heads back inside and brings out a jar of honey with two plates and some knives and sits with me, like we're an ordinary couple on an ordinary holiday in the sun. It's totally surreal.

'Have something to eat,' he urges as he slathers butter and honey onto a thick chunk of bread.

But I have no appetite.

I stare at the coffee, wisps of steam dancing from my mug, in a complete trance. Even before the chaos kicked off this morning, I wasn't feeling myself. There's a lethargy in my brain like it's trapped between being asleep and awake, my thoughts wandering, dreamlike. Too much sleep, I guess. I usually survive on five or six hours a night, if I'm lucky. It's all I need to function, but it must have caught up with me last night. Twelve hours was far too much.

If only we'd never come away. I should have seen the signs when we found out our villa in Crete was double-booked. It should have been a warning, but I couldn't see it.

'Do you have any memories of Jacob at all?' I ask, running a finger around the plate Ronan's put in front of me.

He's digging into breakfast like a man who's not eaten for a week. Honey dribbles down his chin. He wipes it away with a paper napkin, leans back in his chair and takes a deep breath.

'There is no Jacob,' he says.

It's like a spear being driven into my gut over and over again. I watch his face, the curl of his mouth, the twitch of his eyes, looking to read the lie he must know he's telling me.

'What time did you come to bed last night?'

He stops chewing. Eyes open wide. 'Why?' he mumbles.

'I didn't hear you.'

'It wasn't long after you.'

'Did you finish the wine?'

Ronan eyes me suspiciously. 'No.' I believe him. He's never been a big drinker. 'Why do you ask?'

'I wondered if something might have happened while I was asleep.'

'Like what?' His jaw tightens.

'Like you bumping your head?'

'What?' he laughs.

'If you banged your head, it might explain why you can't remember Jacob.' If I can at least persuade him to acknowledge the possibility it's his memory and not mine at fault, we can get on with calling the police. Time is ticking. Jacob's life could be in danger and every second we waste could be crucial.

Ronan sighs and his shoulders slump. He looks as disappointed as he did the day I broke his favourite mug while washing it up. The one he'd brought with him into the relationship that had the words, 'Coffee in one hand, confidence in the other,' printed on one side.

'I don't remember Jacob because he's all in your head.'

'But what if he's not? What if something's happened to you and you can't remember him?'

'Karina, don't.'

'Just listen to me. I think you might have had a stroke or something in the night, something that's affected your memory. It might even have been caused by you diving into the pool yesterday.'

'I haven't been in the pool,' he says, deadpan.

I resist the urge to scream. 'Would it hurt to get checked out? We could drive into town and find a hospital.'

'I don't need to go to hospital. I'm not the one losing their mind.'

'Please, just to be sure.' I reach under the table to stroke his knee. He flinches and I withdraw my hand.

'There's nothing wrong with me. But this is so typical of you,' he says.

'What's that supposed to mean?'

'Always deflecting. You can't help yourself, can you? I'm not the one with the problem, okay?'

'Ronan, please...'

He pushes his chair back angrily and stands. 'I'm getting another coffee. Want one?' he asks begrudgingly.

I shake my head. If he won't seek medical help, what can I do? I could call for an ambulance, but what if he refuses to be seen? They can't force him to have treatment.

This has gone on long enough. My husband is having some kind of breakdown and Jacob's missing. I need help, with or without Ronan's blessing. And if the police think I'm crazy, I'll have to deal with the consequences. I owe it to Jacob to try.

The sound of the kettle hissing and popping carries through from the kitchen. I've left my phone in the bedroom, so while Ronan's distracted, I rise silently from the table and creep inside. Ronan has his back to me, looking out of the window over the wooded hills.

My phone's on the bed, still showing that bland starscape on the lockscreen. I enter my passcode to unlock it and hesitate. What number do I call for the emergency services? Is it 999, like at home? Or 911?

Alerting the police suddenly seems like a big step to take. I'm not overreacting, am I? Of course not. My son is missing and my husband is potentially seriously ill.

'What are you doing?'

I jump so violently I almost drop the phone.

'I - I...' I mumble.

'Who are you calling?' Ronan asks, his voice laced with suspicion.

'No one.'

'Good.' He cradles his coffee mug in both hands, blocking the door. 'As long as it's not the police. I wouldn't want you wasting their time. And I'm serious, if you start telling them you have an imaginary son, they'll probably section you. Is that what you want? To be locked up abroad with no hope of ever getting home again?'

I laugh nervously. I'm not mad. They'll see that, won't they? All I need to do is prove that I do have a son and that Jacob is real. They can check with the airline. We had three seats booked in our names. And there must be CCTV of us arriving at the airport.

'I wouldn't be wasting police time. Jacob's our son.'

Ronan slams his fist against the wall. 'Karina, that's enough. No more! You're really beginning to freak me out.'

'I'm not imagining it. Jacob exists.'

'Only in your head.'

I stare at the phone in my hands. If only he'd let me make the call, we could sort this all out once and for all. Ronan could get the help he needs and we could launch a proper search for Jacob.

But there's another way. Of course! I should have thought of it earlier.

'What if I could prove to you that I'm not making it up?' I say. 'With one call.'

I scroll through my address book without waiting for Ronan to reply. There's one person who can put an end to this nonsense in a flash. A man who knows Jacob almost as well as I do.

I find the number for Sammy. I'll get him to talk to Ronan and explain to him that Jacob is as real as the ground under my feet.

'Who are you going to call?' Ronan throws up his hands, exasperated.

I dial the number and put the phone to my ear. I only hope Sammy's phone's switched on and that he answers. One word from him will prove beyond all doubt that it's not me who's losing their mind.

'Sammy,' I say. 'My ex-husband.'

# Chapter 12

The call connects and, to my amazement, Sammy picks up almost immediately.

'Karina?' He sounds shocked to hear from me, but I'm not surprised. We've not had any contact for almost two years, and we didn't separate on the best of terms.

Sammy was my best friend, as well as my husband. We'd been happy once, but it seems a long time ago now.

We met on a flight from the Middle East. I'd been photographing Asiatic cheetahs in the Kavir National Park, a trip fraught with danger, logistical issues and an incredible amount of bureaucratic paperwork. Sammy was returning to London for business. Fate sat us in the same row on the plane and after he struck up conversation, we didn't stop chatting for the entire journey. Two nomadic souls thrown together by chance.

We married not long after we'd met but our lifestyles simply weren't compatible and with both of us spending large amounts of time abroad, travelling for our jobs, it was inevitable we were going to drift apart.

The final death knell sounded when I fell pregnant. It wasn't something either of us had planned but it made us face up to what we both wanted from life. It had never even occurred to me that starting a family was something I'd wanted. I was loving my freedom, jet-setting off to exotic locations all over the world for shoots as my reputation and photographic career blossomed, while Sammy spent as much time in Iran as he did at home, building up his import-export business.

When Jacob came into our lives, it gave me a new purpose. It was as if I'd found my calling, that being a mother was what I'd always been destined to do. It's a shame Sammy didn't feel the same way. As his business expanded rapidly and he spent more and more time in Tehran, divorce became a sad inevitability.

We argued constantly. I was desperately sleep-deprived as I struggled to cope with a newborn, and Sammy barely lifted a finger to help, even when he was around. In the last few bitter months together, we hardly exchanged a civil word.

'Hey, Sammy.'

'How are you?' he asks stiffly.

'I've been better,' I reply, my throat tightening with emotion. 'But it's good to hear your voice.'

'Is it?'

'Yes, actually.'

We'd been in love once, thrown together by fate and circumstance, and you can't switch off those kinds of deep-seated feelings even if things didn't work out between us.

'What's wrong?' he asks with suspicion.

'Jacob's missing. He's vanished.'

I wait for a shocked intake of breath. A sigh of surprise. A gasp. Anything. He might not have been the greatest father in the world, but surely he's going to be concerned that his son is missing?

'Did you hear what I said? It's Jacob. We brought him on holiday and he's vanished. I don't know what to do.'

'Jacob?'

'Yes.' I rub my forehead, massaging away the tension. 'Things are really weird here. I feel like I'm losing my mind—'

'Who the hell is Jacob?'

I yank the phone away from my head as if it's suddenly turned red hot, and stare at the screen in shock.

Not Sammy as well. Surely not.

Tentatively, I bring the mobile back to my ear. 'What did you say?'

'Who's Jacob?'

*No, no, no. Please, don't let this be happening.*

My mouth opens and closes. I don't have any words.

'Karina? Are you still there? Are you taking your medication?'

'What medication?'

The only medication I ever take is a couple of ibuprofen for a pain in my knee I sometimes get when it's cold, and the odd antihistamine for my hay fever when it's warm.

'You know what the doctor said,' he continues. 'It's important you keep taking the tablets, otherwise there's a danger of a relapse.'

A relapse?

'I don't know what—'

'I can't help you if you're not prepared to help yourself. Look, I'm sorry, I don't have time for this. I'm due in a meeting in five minutes.'

'But Jacob... I don't know what to do.'

'Please, not this again. Are you trying to torment me?'

'What do you mean?'

'We've been through this a hundred times, haven't we?' he says. 'You know damn well we couldn't have children. So why do you persist with this fantasy? In constantly reminding me of what we could never have? You never fell pregnant and you never had a baby. I know it's sad and it's what you wanted more than anything in the world, but it's all in your head.'

I stare into space, his words swirling around my brain like misfitting pieces of a jigsaw that won't slot together.

'It's not all in my head,' I mumble. 'Why is everyone saying that?'

'There is no child, Karina.'

'You're his father!'

He sighs. 'I don't know how many times I can keep going through this. You're not well. You need to get yourself sorted out.'

'I'm not ill,' I scream.

'I'm sorry, I've got to go. Take care of yourself and please, don't call me again.'

He hangs up. A silence thrums in my ears. I lower the phone into my lap with the oddest feeling that my body is floating in space. Weightless.

*Am* I ill?

Have I really imagined it all?

'So, what did he have to say?' Ronan asks. I glance up to where he's still standing in the doorway, nonchalantly sipping his coffee. I'd almost forgotten he was there.

I lower my gaze. What the hell is going on? 'H - he was going into a meeting.'

'What did you call him for? I thought you couldn't stand him?'

I don't want to have this argument right now. I just want the ground to open up and swallow me whole.

'I'm sorry,' I mumble. 'I thought it would help.'

'And? Did it?'

I don't know what to think anymore. Nothing makes sense. My world is spiralling helplessly out of control.

'No,' I croak. 'Not really.'

# Chapter 13

Ronan puts his coffee on the side and hurries across the room towards me, his face crumpling with concern.

'Hey, don't cry,' he says, draping an arm around my shoulder and tenderly wiping a tear from my cheek with his finger. 'We'll get through this together.'

I nuzzle my face into his neck. I've never felt so completely alone and so utterly wrung out. I can't make any sense of what's happening to me. Everything I thought I knew, everything I believed to be true, has been thrown into doubt in a matter of a few hours. I don't know what to do or what to think.

Ronan rubs my back and makes soothing noises. It feels good to be held. We've had our problems of late, but his presence is reassuring. I can't remember the last time he held me. Hugged me. Told me he loved me. He's been such a different man to the one I fell in love with, the one who couldn't bear for us to be apart and who constantly showered me with gifts and notes of affection. I really don't know how it fell apart.

I'm still not ready to admit I'm wrong. There is no way on this earth that Jacob is a phantom child born of my imagination, as everyone, for some weird, inexplicable reason, wants me to believe.

If only there was someone else I could call to verify it. Someone who knows Jacob. Who'll put Ronan right.

Someone like my mother. Maybe if she's having a lucid day she'll remember, although her lucid days seem to be few and far between these days. The last time I visited, she didn't even recognise *me*. I doubt she'll remember Jacob. She's only met him a few times and even then, I'm not sure she understood he was her grandson.

But I can't think of anyone else. Since Ronan and I tied the knot and moved to Norfolk, I've lost touch with all my old friends, none of whom have met Jacob, anyway.

We spend most of our days at the house on our own. With my generous divorce settlement, I don't need to work. I prefer to spend my time making sure Jacob is ready for school next year. It's important he can read, count, even do some basic maths. So we spend our days exploring the beach for shells and rocks, counting them in piles, drawing, painting, reading. We build models out of egg boxes and spend hours constructing elaborate houses out of Lego. Making learning fun.

I probably should have encouraged him to make some friends his own age, but I never wanted to send him to preschool. I thought he was better off with me, knowing full well that when he heads off to school, I'll lose this precious time with him. It's not something I've been prepared to give up, but I had no idea until now how isolated it's left us.

I pull away from Ronan and pluck a tissue from the box on the side to dry my eyes. There's something else that's bothering me. It's been pricking at the back of my mind all morning. A deep-seated fear I've not wanted to think about.

'I'm terrified I'm going the same way as my mother,' I finally admit.

Ronan shrugs. 'I don't know,' he says. 'I suppose it's possible. I could try to reach the GP surgery and book an appointment for you for when we get back?'

I nod. 'Okay. Maybe it wouldn't harm.'

My mother was in her early fifties when she was diagnosed with early-onset dementia. In four years, her mental capacity has declined to the point I've had no choice but to move her into a care home where she can receive the proper attention and support she needs.

When she was first diagnosed, I read as much as I could about the disease and discovered some types of dementia can be genetic, passed on down the family line. I've been dreading ever since that I'll succumb to the same, sooner or later.

Is that what's happening to me? Is dementia ravaging my brain and creating all these memories of a son I don't have? I'm not a doctor, but I always assumed dementia meant you forgot faces and names, words and short-term memories. But could it also be responsible for creating false memories? I have no idea.

'Sammy said I was on medication,' I say, sniffing. 'And that this has happened before. Is he right?'

'Let's concentrate on getting you better, shall we?'

'So you *do* think I'm ill?'

Ronan casts his gaze downwards. 'Well, it's not normal to imagine you have a four-year-old son,' he says. 'Is it? Let's get you into bed. You should get some rest.' He pulls back the covers.

Reluctantly, I let him shepherd me towards the bed. I slide in between the cool sheets and rest my head on the pillow as Ronan drapes the duvet over me and kisses the top of my head.

'I'll bring you some water. Is there anything else I can get you?'

I pull my knees up to my chest and curl into a tight ball.

'No.' I just want to be left on my own to try to make sense of what's going on. My body and head feel as if they're two separate parts of me, disjointed and misaligned.

Ronan disappears and returns a few moments later with a glass of water which he places on the bedside cabinet, next to my phone.

'Try to rest. Get some sleep,' he says. 'Things will seem clearer when you wake up.'

But I don't think I can sleep. I've slept too much, and besides my heart is racing and my head spinning.

'What about Ja—'

I stop myself before Jacob's name spills from my mouth, but Ronan's expression grows dark, his forehead hooding over his eyes like a storm gathering over a perfect summer's day.

'Sorry. I didn't mean...'

'It's okay,' he says. 'Sleep now.'

I want to scream at him that I don't want to sleep and that what I really want is for all this craziness to end. For someone to explain to me what is really going on.

But before I can say anything, there's a loud knock on the door which makes us both jump.

# Chapter 14

I sit bolt upright in bed.

Someone's found Jacob. What else could it be?

'I'll get it,' Ronan says cheerily, as I snatch a breath. I clutch the duvet and twist the material between my fingers as he ambles out of the room.

The front door clicks open. The sound of cicadas grows louder. I hear a woman's voice. Ronan chatting casually. And then footsteps on the tiles in the hall.

Ronan ushers in a woman wearing a smart trouser suit and high heels.

'This is my wife, Karina,' he says.

'Hello, Karina.' The woman has huge black eyes and lustrous, long lashes. When she smiles, she flashes a row of perfect white teeth. 'I'm Doctor Akdash, but please call me Oya. How are you? Your husband says you've not been feeling well?'

The crush of disappointment hits me hard, and I slump back on the pillow.

'She's been under a lot of stress, but things took a turn for the worse this morning,' Ronan explains.

'You didn't tell me you'd called a doctor,' I whisper. It feels like a betrayal, sneaking around behind my back like that.

The doctor takes a step towards the bed, clasping a leather bag in one hand. I hate the way they're both staring at me, like I'm a specimen in a zoo.

'I'm fine, but it's my son, Jacob. He's gone missing.' Ronan won't listen to a word I'm saying, but maybe this doctor will take me seriously. 'You have to help us. We put him to bed last night but when we woke up, he'd gone. Please, I don't know what to do.'

Ronan rolls his eyes and shoots the doctor an I-told-you-so look.

'Would it be okay if I examined you?' the doctor asks.

Didn't she hear me? Or does she think I'm crazy too?

She opens her bag, pulls out a stethoscope and a blood pressure monitoring cuff, then sits on the edge of the bed and takes my arm.

'I'm afraid she experienced a miscarriage a few weeks back,' Ronan says.

In my confused state, it takes a moment for his words to register and to realise he's talking about me.

I've not had a miscarriage. We've not even been trying for a baby. Ronan has always been insistent that he doesn't want children of his own.

'That's not—'

'We'd been trying for a while so when Karina fell pregnant, we were over the moon,' Ronan says, with tears in his eyes. He lowers his head sadly. 'But I guess it just wasn't meant to be.'

'That never happened. He's lying,' I protest, but neither of them is listening to me.

'We were both pretty cut up about it at the time,' Ronan continues. 'That's why we thought a holiday in the sun would help us heal, but I can see now it was too soon. Karina took it hard and I think she's still grieving.'

The doctor nods as she listens, as if what Ronan is saying is the gospel truth, even though every word is a lie. She slips the blood pressure cuff over my upper arm and inflates it until it's cutting off my pulse.

'Just try to relax,' the doctor says, popping the stethoscope into her ears. She stares into the distance as she listens. 'Okay, so your blood pressure is a little on the high side.'

'Of course it's on the high side,' I grumble. 'My son's missing.'

'You see,' Ronan says, shaking his head, 'this is what she's been like all morning.'

'And has she ever had any episodes like this before?' the doctor asks. They're talking about me like I'm not even in the room.

'Not that I'm aware of. Do you think it's connected to the grief?' he asks.

The doctor shines a small torch in my eyes, asking me to look left and right.

'It could be,' she says. 'But it's not really my area of expertise. I would suggest you get her checked over by a specialist when you return home.'

'Of course.' Ronan moves to the bed and puts his hand tenderly to my cheek. 'We'll definitely do that. We just want you to get better, don't we, my love?'

My lungs are so tight, I struggle to breathe.

'I'm not making it up,' I say, grasping the doctor's hand and fixing her with a penetrating gaze. 'And I'm not crazy. I have a four-year-old son called Jacob and he's vanished. You have to believe me.'

She smiles sweetly and pats my hand. 'I do believe you,' she says.

My body softens, and I sink back into the mattress. At last. Someone who's taking me seriously. 'So you'll help me?'

'Of course, but you know grief is a powerful emotion and sometimes, to cope, our brains play tricks on us.'

My heart rate spikes. She *does* think I'm crazy. 'I'm not imagining it. You can check with the airport. They'll have a record of Jacob coming into the country and you'll see!'

'The good news is that you have the support of a loving husband, and I'm certain he'll make sure you get the rest you need. My guess is that this is a temporary episode. A reaction to a severely stressful moment in your life,' the doctor continues. Her tone is so warm and reassuring, I want to believe her, but it's not the truth.

'I didn't have a miscarriage.' I grip her hands more tightly in the hope I can convince her I'm not lying.

'In many ways, a miscarriage can be worse than losing a child. It's certainly as traumatic.'

*Oh god. Someone help me.*

'Do you have children?' I ask.

'Yes, three. Two boys and a girl,' she says, as lightly as if we've met for coffee in the local cafe and I'm not a patient desperately trying to prove my sanity.

'How old?'

She glances briefly at the ceiling. 'Three, seven and nine.'

I struggle to cope with one, let alone three. 'How do you manage, juggling them around work?' I need to make her see that I'm perfectly rational. Not hysterical. Maybe then she'll believe me about Jacob.

'I'm only part-time,' she says. 'Three mornings a week and the occasional weekend.'

'But your kids?'

'We have an excellent childminder.'

'Don't you feel guilty leaving them with a stranger?'

She laughs. 'Susana's hardly a stranger. And besides, it's good for them not be hanging on my coattails all the time. It gives them resilience.'

I'd never abdicate Jacob's care to a childminder. What's the point of having kids if you're going to palm them off on someone else? And anyway, after this is all over, I'm never going to let Jacob out of my sight again.

'The best thing for you now is to rest,' she says. 'Your husband's right, a holiday was probably a good idea. Try to make the most of the time to relax and take it easy.'

'Karina's mother has dementia.' Ronan has moved away from the bed and is leaning on the doorframe with his arms crossed. 'I think she's worried she may have inherited it.'

'I think that's highly unlikely, but as I said, do speak to a doctor when you get home.'

'And in the meantime?' Ronan asks.

'I'm going to prescribe some strong sedatives which will help your wife sleep and keep her calm,' she says. 'I can't promise they'll stop the delusions, but they should help.'

She dives into her bag and scribbles some notes on a pad, then rips off a sheet. She stands and hands the prescription to Ronan.

'Make sure she takes one of these twice a day,' she instructs. 'And keep a close eye on her. Call the surgery if you have any further concerns.'

That's it? That's her diagnosis? A quick assessment and a packet of pills? I'm speechless.

She's about to leave when she turns to face me again, smiling with well-practised and reassuring geniality. 'Let's see how the pills make you feel after a few days, shall we?'

My mouth hangs open in incredulity. I can't bring myself to thank her. She hasn't even listened to me.

Ronan shows her out while I'm still too numb with shock to move.

I hear them whispering. What are they talking about? Me? I strain to listen, but I can't make any of it out.

The front door clicks open, and rattles shut.

And once more I'm left alone in the villa with Ronan, a man I no longer know whether I can trust.

# Chapter 15

'Why did you tell that doctor I'd had a miscarriage?' I snap when Ronan returns to the bedroom.

'You heard what she said. You need to take it easy. Try not to stress yourself.'

'But I've not had a miscarriage. I haven't even been pregnant. I don't understand why you'd tell her that.' The more I think about the lies he's just told, the angrier it makes me.

Ronan pouts, his expression thick with sympathy. Puppy-dog eyes appraising me as if I'm nothing but a poor, deluded soul who doesn't know her own mind.

'We're going to get you better, okay? You trust me, don't you?'

Do I? I don't know who or what to trust anymore.

'I don't know, Ronan. I'm so confused. I don't know what's going on.' I rub my temples, the dull throb of a headache coming on.

'It's all going to be fine. Now, are you going to be okay here on your own for an hour if I pop out? I need to find a pharmacy to pick up these pills.' He waves the prescription in the air.

'Go. I'll be fine.' With Ronan out of the villa, it'll be a chance to think and get my head straight. To work out what I'm going to do next. I can't just lie here in bed and do nothing, not when Jacob's missing.

'Right. I won't be long.' He strides over to the bed and kisses my cheek as if everything is fine and dandy and that he's not just called a doctor behind my back and told her a pack of lies about me.

I wait until the front door opens and closes, the car revs into life and the tyres crunch over the dirt track before I snatch up my phone. I don't have long, but I know what I have to do.

I'm not going to risk calling the police. Not yet. Because if they suspect for a moment I've lost my mind, they probably will cart me off, just like Ronan said they would. And then what am I going to do? What's going to happen to Jacob if I'm locked up?

But if I can prove he was here in Turkey with us, that he arrived in the country yesterday, they'll have to take me seriously.

A quick Google search reveals a long list of local taxi firms. I pick the top one and make a frantic call. They promise to have a cab with me within twenty minutes.

That gives me just enough time to grab a quick shower, although I don't bother washing my hair. I tie it back with an elasticated band instead. I often get comments about my hair. I have long, corkscrew spirals of fiery auburn locks that tend to take on a life of their own and make me stand out in a crowd. Right now,

I'd shave them all off in a heartbeat. I can't be bothered with the hassle of it.

I throw on a loose cotton dress, slip on a pair of open-toe sandals and stand outside the villa in the shade, sweating, to wait for my ride. It must be thirty degrees or more and it's still only mid-morning.

The taxi, a battered old silver Mercedes, eventually appears, kicking up a dust trail. The driver is an older man grown fat by either years of inactivity or poor diet. Or maybe both. He's wearing mirrored sunglasses and appears to have the remnants of last night's meal down the front of his shirt, which is open too far, revealing a mat of wiry grey hairs.

I instruct him to head to the airport and to hurry. I'm in a rush. He nods sullenly as I climb into the back. I don't want to encourage a conversation with him, so I sit behind him, out of the view of his mirror. I need the time to think, not to chat.

To give him credit, he puts his foot down, speeding along with abandon, forcing me to hang on for dear life. He drives one-handed with an arm hanging out of the open window. A fierce blast of hot air washes over my face and causes my eyes to water.

As we hurtle along, dodging other cars, vans, coaches and lorries, my thoughts repeatedly return to my mother. I told her we were going away for the week, but I don't think it registered with her. I even tried to show her the photos of the villa online, but her misty eyes remained focused on the window overlooking the well-tended rose garden in the grounds of the care home where she now lives.

We've never been close, but now she's ill I have this inexplicable guilt that gnaws at my insides, like I should do more for her. That I should give her more of my time, because I know death is coming sooner rather than later and she'll be gone from my life.

Dementia is slowly turning her brain to mush and now I'm terrified the disease is doing the same to mine. That I'm in the early stages of a debilitating illness that's not only going to rob me of my senses but is the key to everything that's happened since we've been in Turkey. That because of it, Jacob exists only in my damaged mind.

Yet, I'm still not ready to believe it. It's too tical. Too outrageous.

The urge to hear my mother's voice, to talk to her about the hell I'm going through, tugs at my heart. Who else can I speak to? There is no one else.

I know it's probably a mistake, but I dial the number for the care home as the driver undertakes a coach at high speed on a busy dual carriageway, earning an aggressive horn-blast of rebuke as he swerves back into the outside lane with inches to spare.

It takes a few seconds for the call to connect. When the receptionist answers, I can barely hear her over the road noise and hot air rushing through the car. I stick a finger in one ear and yell down the line that I want to speak to one of my mum's carers.

I'm relieved when Andrea eventually comes on the line. She's been looking after Mum from the day she moved in. She has a soft, lilting Aberdeen brogue and a manner about her that always puts me at my ease.

'Andrea, it's Karina. How's Mum today?'

She pauses for a beat and I wonder for a moment if the connection's dropped.

'She's comfortable, aye,' she says.

'Comfortable?'

'She had a disturbed night. Got herself a bit upset, but she's fine now. She's eaten a good breakfast—'

'What was she upset about?' I hate to think of my mum abandoned in that care home all alone and getting agitated. Not that she ever worried about abandoning me.

I was cast off to boarding school at the age of six and rarely saw my parents during term time. My mother said it would be good for building my confidence, although the first few years nearly killed me. I was desperately homesick and dreadfully out of my comfort zone. And even when I was home during the holidays, my mother never spent much time with me. I don't ever remember her picking up a book to read to me or sitting down with me to draw or play. In fact, she never spent much of her time in the house at all. She was always out to lunch or meeting friends, leaving me to amuse myself at home alone. It's no wonder my father didn't stick around.

I've no idea what happened to him and I only retain the vaguest memories of his life with us. I remember he was tall, always seemed to be in a suit and tie, wore his hair slicked back and had a neat moustache that reminded me of a hairy caterpillar. I was never allowed to speak to him unless spoken to first, and have terrifying memories of him yelling at me, incandescent with rage for the most minor acts of bad behaviour. I felt nothing for him and no sadness when he wasn't with us anymore.

I suppose my mother may have been depressed by his sudden departure. It's not the kind of thing you notice when you're a child though. But I do remember there was a period when she seemed to be constantly knocking back pills and kept a glass of something on the go at all times. Gin, I suspect. And then there were all the men who came to visit or who were there in the mornings looking sheepish, hustling out of the door, when I came down for breakfast.

'Your mum often gets herself worked up at night. It's nothing to worry about,' Andrea assures me.

'Has she asked for me?'

The long pause is all I need to hear to know the answer.

'Your mother's dementia isn't getting any better,' Andrea says. 'You know that, Karina.'

I sigh. The thought of my mother slowly fading away, the last vestiges of the woman she was dissolving like rice paper left out in the rain, is soul destroying. 'Yeah, I know. Will you tell her I love her?'

'Of course I will.'

'We're in Turkey for a week. I don't know if they let you know. Tell Mum I'll pop in to see her when we're back.'

'Of course.'

I hang up and watch an olive grove flash past in a blur of green. I vowed never to be like my mother. I wanted Jacob to be at the front and centre of my life. It's why I gave up my job to care for him. I didn't trust anyone else to bring him up in my absence during the most important years of his life.

Not that it's been easy. It's been really hard. Especially when things didn't work out with Sammy and I walked out. Being a single mum with a toddler, with no emotional or practical support from a partner, is one of the toughest things in the world. It gave me a whole new appreciation for every woman who's been through the same. I was lucky I had money saved up from a good job, and then there was the divorce settlement which has left me comfortably off. How those women do it with nothing but meagre benefits from the Government staggers me. I have nothing but admiration for them all.

When I met Ronan, it was a blessing. A gift I never thought I deserved. He was so good with Jacob, treating him as if he was his own. And in return, Jacob loved him unconditionally. I don't think Jacob even remembers Sammy. He was too young. And he's certainly never asked after him. As far as he's concerned, Ronan is his father.

When we first separated, Sammy made a few noises about seeking custody, but I quickly knocked that on the head. Instead, we worked out an access arrangement so Sammy could spend time with Jacob every week. But I knew it wouldn't work out in the long run. Sammy was too often out of the country on business. Didn't care enough about his son. They certainly didn't have the same bond Jacob and I shared. Sammy liked the idea of having a child but didn't have the emotional maturity to be a father.

We tried it a few times. I arranged to meet Sammy in a park and he'd go off with Jacob for a couple of hours, but he never looked comfortable. Fatherhood just wasn't his thing. And the second time he failed to turn up for a pre-arranged access meeting, without even bothering to let me know, I called it quits. I told him he'd blown his chance, and to be fair, he didn't argue. He took it on the chin and let us walk away. I suspect he was secretly pleased. His life was his work. Having a family was a bind. And he couldn't reconcile the two.

How could I have made all that up? I'd have to have the imagination of a fantasy novelist to have dreamt up such elaborate false memories. Jacob *is* real, but for some reason, Ronan wants me to believe he's not. I have no idea why, and I still have no evidence to prove he's missing and in trouble.

My focus has to remain on finding my son. I'll worry about what's going on with Ronan later. Jacob is my number one priority.

The taxi driver winds his way skilfully through the airport approach roads, tooting his horn when anyone gets in his way, using his vehicle like a lance to spear a way through.

And eventually, he pulls up outside the terminal building.

There's a steady stream of holidaymakers coming and going, lugging heavy cases and gripping the hands of their children.

The driver turns around, tapping the meter on the dashboard, demanding payment. But in my haste to get out of the villa, I've forgotten I don't have any money with me. I gave Ronan all our lira to look after, and I didn't even think to bring my purse.

I hold up my finger. 'Can you wait here for one minute?' I plead. 'And take me back again?'

He scowls, uncertain. Do I look like someone about to scam him out of a fare?

'You pay me now,' he insists.

'No, I need you to wait. I'll pay you when we get back. I promise.'

He dips his head and looks over the top of his sunglasses. His eyes are glassy and dull. 'Money, now,' he says.

'Look, I'm really sorry. I left my money in the villa. But I promise you'll get paid. I just need to find my son,' I say.

And then everything comes pouring out. The whole sorry story I'm sure the taxi driver has no interest in hearing. 'He's disappeared, but my husband is saying I'm crazy and that we don't have a son. He says he's not real and it's all in my head, but I can prove it.'

Oh, god. Why am I telling him this? He's going to think I've lost the plot as well.

'We arrived yesterday and someone in the airport must have seen us. I just need someone to check the CCTV or something.'

The driver stares at me, obviously weighing up whether I'm telling the truth or simply spinning an elaborate yarn. Eventually he nods. 'I wait five minutes,' he says, holding up one hand and spreading his fingers wide. 'Five minutes. That's all.'

'Thank you.'

# Chapter 16

The airport is bustling with people milling around like ants, nobody really sure where they're supposed to be going. And noisy with it, a hubbub of chatter and the rumble of trolley and luggage wheels. I scan a long row of check-in desks stretching as far as the eye can see, until I spot the logo of the airline we flew with. They should have a record of the three of us travelling. Ticket details. Passport confirmations. CCTV footage. Proof that Jacob was with us. I just need to find someone who'll talk to me and give me that information so I can show Ronan and the police, but there are only three desks open and there's already a long snaking queue of passengers with piles of cases waiting to check in for their flights. If I take my place at the back of the queue, I could be here for hours, and I don't have the time.

Instead, I detour around it and sidle up to the desks from the side. I know I'm technically jumping the queue, but this is important. It could be a matter of life and death.

I wait patiently, watching each of the three desks until one of the check-in attendants comes free and I sneakily dart ahead of a family of four at the front of the queue while they are momentarily distracted.

'How many bags?' the woman behind the desk asks, looking up with a fake smile and dead, dull eyes. Not a woman enjoying her job from the expression on her face.

'I'm not here to check in.'

'Oh,' she says with surprise.

'I need to speak to someone about my son. He's missing.'

Her smile slips. She looks at me with uncertainty. 'I'm not sure how I can—'

'We flew in yesterday with your airline,' I lean closer, up on my tiptoes with my elbows on the desk, 'but now my son's vanished. He's only four and as you can imagine, I'm frantic with worry.'

The woman casts a concerned glance over my shoulder and then at one of her colleagues on the next desk along, but he's too busy attaching a label to the handle of a case on his conveyor belt to notice.

'There are lots of passengers waiting. So please, if you could step to one side for me. I'm not really the right person—'

'You're not listening,' I shout, my anger rising. Why does no one listen to me these days? 'My son has gone missing. We arrived on one of your planes yesterday afternoon and now my husband is trying to convince me we flew alone and that I don't have a son. I know that sounds crazy. Trust me, I wouldn't believe it myself, but I need your help.'

The woman's eyebrows shoot up in alarm. 'Please, Madam...'

'Don't fob me off. This is important.'

Someone taps me on my shoulder. 'Oi, you pushed in. We were next.'

I spin around. 'I just need a second,' I yell, spittle flying from my mouth.

'No, you can wait in the queue like everyone else, love.' The man I come face-to-face with is one of those men who thinks it's acceptable to wear a football shirt as casual wear. Tattoos creep from his chest up to his neck towards his chin and his fingers are weighed down with chunky gold rings. Behind him, his bleached-blonde wife, whose top is far too tight, bunching up rolls of fat around her waist and showing off too much cleavage, stares at me with evil eyes while their two obnoxious children bicker.

'I said I'll only be a minute.'

I turn back towards the check-in attendant. 'I just need to talk to someone who can confirm my son was on the flight. His name's Jacob. Jacob Shackleton. I'm sure there will be CCTV footage.'

Suddenly, I'm being pulled backwards by a hand on my arm.

I wheel around on my heel to face Football Shirt again. 'Get off me!'

'Back of the queue,' he snarls, his hands clenching into fists.

'Go away, you ignorant little man!'

'Don't you speak to me like that.'

'What the hell's wrong with you?'

'You jumped the queue.' He waves a hand angrily at the line of passengers, most of whom are staring at me with stony faces.

'I'm trying to find my son. Have a fucking heart, will you?'

I'm vaguely aware of the check-in attendant on the phone to someone. Hopefully she's calling her supervisor or someone who can help me. What I don't need right now is hassle from a Neanderthal.

'You could be trying to find the missing fucking city of Atlantis, for all I care. You jumped the queue,' he hisses in my face.

'Find another desk, asshole!'

'You find another desk,' he retorts, his wife tapping her foot on the floor, chewing gum and glaring at me.

This is getting childish. He puts a hand on my arm again but I bat it off and then shove him in the chest so hard he staggers backwards and trips over his cases, his arms flailing as he catches his balance. Passengers in the queue gasp.

'Oi, that's assault.'

'So sue me.'

I turn back to the desk, smoothing down my dress and wiping my brow, as the woman is putting the phone down.

'Can you help me or not?' I ask, thumping the desk with my fist.

'I've asked you several times, Madam. Could you please step away from the desk?'

'Why won't you help me?'

'Please don't raise your voice. Abuse of staff will not be tolerated.' She taps a laminated poster stuck on a concrete pillar on one side of the desk. It warns of fines for anyone swearing, making threats or behaving violently against airline staff.

'I'm not abusing you,' I say, doing my best to keep my tone measured, even though I feel like grabbing her by the stupid silk scarf around her neck and shaking some sense into her.

'Your behaviour *is* quite threatening,' she says with perfectly manicured eyebrows raised.

'Oh, bollocks.'

Her eyes focus on something to my left and a stern male voice commands, 'Stand still and keep your hands where I can see them.'

I pivot and encounter two tough-looking uniformed police officers with bulging biceps and tactical vests. One of them is actually pointing a handgun at me.

What the hell?

'Show me your hands,' the officer with the gun yells.

'Oh, come on. There's no need for—'

'Hands!'

'Alright, alright.' I do as I'm instructed, lifting my arms and showing them my empty palms, my face flushing with embarrassment. Everyone in the queue is watching.

'Now turn around.'

I have no choice, even though it's a total over-reaction. They actually have a gun pointed at me! What kind of tinpot country is this? As soon as I turn my back to them, they grab my arms, twisting them painfully. 'Ow, you're hurting me.'

They slap cuffs on my wrists and stand me upright. Order me to move like I'm a petty criminal. They'd never get away with treating someone like that in Britain.

'Where are you taking me?'

I don't get an answer, only a grunt of, 'Serves her right,' from Football Shirt as I'm bundled off. This is mortifying. I've never been spoken to by the police before, let alone arrested.

'You're making a mistake,' I argue. 'Please, let me go.'

But they don't listen. They march me on, past hundreds of people gawping, no doubt all forming the same opinion that at best I'm a troublemaker and at worst, a terrorist.

I lower my head, watching my feet and the floor, my cheeks flushed as they lead me the length of the building and finally guide me into a secure police station within the terminal.

We pass through several locked doors which slam shut menacingly behind us and head into a processing area where another officer is sitting behind a desk. They say something to him in Turkish and he asks me politely and in perfect English for my name, age and address. He taps the details into a computer.

'I don't know what I'm supposed to have done,' I complain. 'I'm just trying to find my son.' And then I burst into tears, but they're completely unsympathetic. Totally unmoved.

'Turn around,' the officer with the gun, which is now thankfully back in the holster on his hip, instructs.

'What's going to happen to me?'

He removes the handcuffs and, as I rub the feeling back into my wrists, he shows me into a small, windowless room with a table and four chairs. An interview room. Great. Although I suppose it could have been worse. At least it's not a cell. They haven't even told me what I've been arrested for. They wouldn't get away with it at home.

'Sit,' the officer orders. 'And wait here.'

'You can't keep me in here. I'm trying to find my boy. He's only four,' I yell as he heads out of the room, and the door shuts with an ominous click.

It's an absolute travesty. You'd think they'd be falling over themselves to help me, especially with a young child missing, instead of treating me like I'm a criminal.

It's the best part of twenty minutes before a stern-looking woman with a high hairline and a masculine face joins me. She doesn't bother to introduce herself, but I guess from the fact she's in plain clothes that she's a detective. She pulls out a chair opposite, drops a folder on the table and sits down.

She glances at a sheet of paper in the file, then closes it, folds her hands and glares at me.

'I'm sorry, I didn't mean to cause a scene, but I'm trying to find my son...'

The woman puts her finger to her lips and Ronan's warning comes back to me. I should be careful what I say. If they think I'm crazy, who knows what'll happen. What they'll do to me. Where they'll send me. But I can't sit here and not tell them about Jacob.

'Would you like tea? Coffee? Mrs...' She glances at the sheet of paper in the file again, '...Shackleton.'

I shake my head. 'Thank you. No. I'm fine.'

'What are you doing at the airport?'

'I was trying to tell the officers but they wouldn't listen to me,' I say, leaning across the table. Maybe as a woman, she'll take me more seriously. 'My son, Jacob, has gone missing from our villa. We only flew in yesterday and I was hoping someone might remember seeing him.' I consciously don't tell her that I was actually looking for proof of his existence and that my husband has been trying to convince me I'm losing my grip on reality.

'You were being aggressive with the check-in staff,' she says. Not a question. A statement of fact. 'Shouting. Swearing. Assaulting other passengers.'

'What? No, I didn't assault anyone. Look, I'm sorry. I'm a bit stressed at the moment. I didn't mean to cause a scene. Do you have children?'

'No.'

I didn't think so. 'Then you probably can't understand how I'm feeling right now. The pressure I'm under.'

'How old is your son?'

'Four.'

She raises an eyebrow and scribbles a note on the paper in the file.

'Have you reported him missing?'

I look at my hands in my lap, picking at an imaginary fleck of dirt under my nail. 'No.'

'Why not?'

'It's... complicated.'

'Why don't you try to explain it to me?'

I sigh, my gaze drifting to the ceiling. There's a dirty splodge on the white paintwork where it looks like a giant fly has been swatted. Oh, god, how do I explain everything without sounding deranged? 'My husband doesn't believe me.'

'He doesn't believe your son is missing?' Her eyes narrow as she tilts her head to one side.

'No.'

'Why not? I don't understand.'

I take a deep breath. 'He says we don't have a son. That's crazy, isn't it?'

The woman stares at me suspiciously. I don't blame her. I don't think I'd believe it either.

'Something has affected his memory, although he denies it, of course. That's men for you though, isn't it? I thought if I came to the airport, I could find someone who remembers Jacob and they could let me have a copy of the CCTV from when we arrived.'

The woman's face finally cracks into a sympathetic smile. 'What's your husband's name?'

'Ronan. Ronan Shackleton.'

'Are you currently on any medication, Mrs Shackleton?'

'No. Well, only antihistamine for my hay fever.' I laugh but she doesn't seem to see the funny side.

She makes another note. I wish I could read what she's written.

'And where are you staying while in the country?'

I give her the address of the villa as best as I can remember it. She appears to know it. She nods and makes another note.

'You do believe me, don't you?' I ask. 'About my son.'

She puts her pen down and looks at me earnestly, before laying a comforting, warm hand on top of mine. 'Of course.'

'Really?'

'Yes.'

'And you'll help me? Because I'm worried he might have been abducted. I mean, I've looked all around the complex but there's no sign of him, which means someone's probably taken him, doesn't it?'

'Not necessarily,' she assures me.

I guess she's employed by some kind of special airport police, but that she'll escalate it with the local force.

'So you'll start looking for him?'

She stands suddenly. 'Leave it with me, Mrs Shackleton. Are you sure I can't bring you a drink?'

'No, thank you. Am I free to go?'

'Not for the moment. But soon,' she says.

She walks out. The door clicks shut behind her and I'm left alone.

Maybe I was worrying unnecessarily and should have alerted the police sooner. If a four-year-old boy is missing, they're duty-bound to take it seriously, aren't they? Whether they believe me or not.

Hours have ticked by since I first discovered Jacob was gone. And if he was snatched in the middle of the night, he could be hundreds of miles away by now. A dangerous thought wheedles its way into my head. What if I never see him again? What if he's been taken and he's never found?

But I can't think like that. I have to stay positive.

And then another thought comes to me. One I really don't want to contemplate but that I have to face. What if something truly awful has happened and that's why I can't find him? What if he's already dead? If that's the case, my life is as good as over, and I'll never forgive myself.

Minute after minute passes and still I wait. What's she doing? And why's she taking so long? My foot taps impatiently on the floor, my thigh jiggling up and down.

Eventually, the woman who interviewed me steps back into the room.

'Mrs Shackleton,' she says.

There's something in her voice. A note of optimism? Cheeriness? I stand up with the sudden hope that maybe they've found Jacob. That he's about to walk in looking lost and confused.

She steps to one side, holding the door open. 'Come in,' she says. 'She's in here.'

I hold my breath, on the verge of tears.

But it's not Jacob. It's Ronan. He marches into the room with a face like thunder.

'Your husband's here to collect you,' the detective says.

'Karina, what are you playing at?' Ronan looks me up and down with disgust. 'What are you doing here?'

'I - I was looking for...' But what's the point in trying to explain?

'Come on, let's get you out of here before you cause any more trouble.'

'Okay,' I whisper, my head bowed. And then I find myself apologising, even though I've done

nothing wrong. 'I'm sorry. I didn't mean to worry you.'

# Chapter 17

'Are you utterly insane?' Ronan yells, slamming his keys on the kitchen worktop when we're back at the villa. 'What on earth did you think you were playing at? Do you know how embarrassing it was to get a call from the police telling me you'd been arrested? Honestly, I don't know what the hell's got into you today.'

He hadn't said a single word on the drive back, although I could tell how angry he was by the way he was gripping the steering wheel, the bony knuckles on both hands standing out, prominent and pale.

'That's rich. You're the one who's forgotten we have a son.'

'I'm not the one who's lost the plot, Karina. And to be honest, you were lucky they didn't lock you up and throw away the key. Fancy telling the police this imaginary child of yours has been abducted. How did you even get to the airport?'

I chew my bottom lip. I've completely forgotten about the taxi I left waiting outside.

'I took a cab. The driver was going to bring me back, but I forgot to take any money. Do you think you'd be able to pay?' I grimace. It's not the best moment to be asking for favours.

'Brilliant.' Ronan throws his hands up in the air. 'Not content with getting arrested for public disorder, you thought you'd add fare dodging to your list of misdemeanours.'

'I was flustered. I didn't do it on purpose.'

'That's your problem, Karina.' He takes a stride towards me until he's right up in my face. He taps the top of my head with his fingers. 'Your head is all over the place. You're not thinking straight.'

'Of course I'm not thinking straight. Our son has vanished and you don't seem to care. No, worse than that, you don't even seem to remember anything about him.'

'We don't have a son,' he screams. 'How many more times?'

'Don't say that.'

'This nonsense has to end. I can't stand it much longer. As soon as we get you home, we'll get you some help, but in the meantime, do you think we could just enjoy the few days we have here without you totally losing the plot?'

I stare at him, at a loss for words. There's nothing I can say that's going to change his mind or make him see that it's *his* memory at fault. He's the one with the problem.

'I can't give up on him,' I mumble. 'I won't.'

'Karina,' he growls. 'Even your ex-husband told you it's a fantasy. Let it go.'

No matter how many times he repeats it, I can't accept it. One of us is wrong, and I'm sure it's not me, even if I can't explain all the weird stuff that's been going on. Why Jacob's clothes and passport have vanished, all the photos of him gone and even his own father denying him.

If I give in to Ronan's way of thinking, even for a second, it means accepting his version of the truth, which is even more terrifying than my son vanishing. Because the only other explanation for everything that's happened is that I'm unhinged. Certifiably crazy. And that even though I remember nothing about it, a horrific miscarriage has caused me to create a fantasy child who exists only in my imagination.

Ronan produces a packet from a white paper bag on the side by the microwave oven. He opens it, removes a blister pack and pops out two pills. Then he fills a glass with water from a bottle chilling in the fridge and hands it to me with the tablets.

'They'll make you feel better.'

'What are they?'

He shrugs. 'Whatever the doctor prescribed. Sedatives, I think. She said they'll help you calm down and get your thoughts straight.'

I don't want to calm down, although thinking straight would help. What I really want is to find my son.

Reluctantly, I toss them into my mouth and swallow them with a gulp of water.

'Show me,' Ronan demands.

'What?'

'Open your mouth and show me you've swallowed them.'

He's treating me like I'm a mental patient in an asylum, but I do as he asks to keep the peace, opening my mouth wide and lifting my tongue.

I don't want to argue anymore. It's not getting us anywhere.

'I'm going for a swim. Why don't you have a lie down  and take it easy for a bit,' he says, heading for the bedroom to change.

I don't want to lie down and take it easy. I want to be out looking for Jacob, but there's no way Ronan's going to let me do that. And actually, I am feeling a little tired. Maybe I'll have a short rest and try Ronan again later. Perhaps when he's calmed down, he'll be ready to see sense, or at least listen to my side and accept it's him who might have the problem.

I grip the kitchen counter with both hands, holding myself up. Numb. Confused. Scared. As much as I'm trying to keep a grip on reality, I don't know what's true and what's in my head anymore. Whether to laugh or cry. Trust Ronan or my instincts. Wherever the truth lies, all I know for certain is that in the space of twenty-four hours, my life has been turned on its head and everything I thought I knew is slipping through my fingers.

I'd been so looking forward to this holiday. A family break in the sun was just what we need-ed. An opportunity for the three of us to spend some quality time together. But now I wish I could turn back the clock and we'd never come.

Ronan strides into the lounge. He's changed into a pair of swimming shorts and a faded red T-shirt.

'Feeling any better?' he asks.

'A bit,' I lie. What's the point in telling him how I really feel?

'Come out with me and have a nap on one of the sunloungers while I'm in the pool,' he suggests.

I let him take my hand and lead me outside. He adjusts a parasol over one of the loungers to give me some shade. Reluctantly, I sit and swing my legs up, my body suddenly weak with exhaustion.

'If you need anything, just shout,' Ronan says.

He peels off his T-shirt, revealing his pasty white chest, and slips into the pool, gasping as the water comes up to his waist. I hope he's put on some sun cream, otherwise he's going to burn and will spend the rest of the day complaining about it, but I can't find the energy to call out.

My eyes are heavy and I'm having trouble keeping them open. Ronan floats in and out of focus as he launches himself through the water and begins a lazy front crawl.

I shouldn't be sleeping, not while Jacob is missing, but five minutes won't hurt, will it? A quick catnap, that's all. It's been such a hectic, emotionally draining day. I'm sure I'll feel much better for it.

The sound of Ronan splashing and the water lapping against the sides of the pool is hypnotic and soon morphs into something else in my mind. A distant rainstorm. The whisper of the wind in a lush forest. Curtains at a window flapping in a warm, summer breeze.

I'm carried into the depths of sleep, even as I try to fight it, while a part of my brain taunts me with guilt. Reminding me I should be looking for Jacob. But sleep, with its giant, soothing hands, drags me into the deepest, darkest depths of oblivion where I don't have to worry about my sanity. About Jacob. Or the state of my marriage. I don't have to worry about anything.


My legs are burning. A prickling, uncomfortable heat that spreads from my ankles to my knees and jolts me awake. I pull them out of the sun and into the shade, gazing bleary-eyed at the flimsy material of the parasol above my head and beyond it to the sky which is the deepest blue I've ever seen. It's utterly beautiful.

Jacob!

Panic explodes through my core like a firecracker as my memories come flooding back through the viscosity of sleep. His empty bed. His missing passport. A taxi to the airport. Handcuffed and questioned by the police.

Why the hell am I lying here by the pool as if nothing is wrong? I should be out looking for my son. But my arms and legs are as heavy as concrete and my mind a tangle of rambling dreams that keep pushing reality back into a dark hole.

*Focus.*

*Concentrate.*

But I can't think straight, one thought tumbling into another, knocking it off its feet and morphing into something entirely new.

I can hear voices. They're close by. Not quite shouting. But they're angry. Short, sharp words being exchanged. Where? Who?

I blink sleep from my eyes and stare at the pool where the clear waters ripple and sparkle, catching the sun.

Ronan was swimming, but he's not there now. How long have I been asleep?

Is that Ronan's voice I can hear? The other belongs to a woman. It's higher pitched. Urgent. Irritated.

I prop myself up on one elbow, my neck barely strong enough to hold up my head.

Across a patch of scrub, in the villa opposite, I can see two shapes. Two people. I'm sure one of them is Ronan. He's put his T-shirt back on, but his hair is wet and he's still in his swimming shorts. What's he doing over there? He's talking to that woman. What was her name? Pippa? Or Petra? No, Polly. That was it.

Ronan's gesticulating angrily, arms waving. And shouting. He's so cross all the time these days. The sound carries across the pool but his words are too indistinct to have any meaning.

Now she's shouting back at him, her pudgy fingers jabbing him in the chest. It's all so surreal. What could they possibly be arguing about? I didn't think they even knew each other. Whatever's going on, it's not good. I should get over there and broker peace, but my body feels so heavy and weak. I try to put my feet on the floor and stand, but my limbs don't want to cooperate, resolutely refusing to move.

It must be those sedatives the doctor prescribed. I don't know what's in them, but they've knocked me for six.

'Ronan?' I attempt to shout, but my mouth's gummed up and I can't form the word. All that comes out is an almost inaudible grunt.

He glances over his shoulder, straight at me, while that woman continues to rant on. What *is* her problem? No wonder his expression is as black and as brooding as a gathering storm. He's not happy at all.

I snap my eyes closed. I don't want him to think that I'm spying on them, but when I open them again, they've both vanished. I'm sure I didn't imagine it. I wonder what it was about. I'll ask him when he gets back, but for now I need to sleep.

My eyes are heavy again and my mind wandering into a jungle of dreams.

Jacob's laughter, a shriek of delight and unbridled joy, brings a smile to my face and I follow it down a long, dim tunnel to a place of safety, warmth and total calm.

# Chapter 18

When I wake again, it's cold. I shiver, the tops of my arms puckered with goosebumps as someone shakes my shoulder.

'Karina, wake up.'

It's an effort to crack open my eyes and I'm surprised it's getting dark already. The sun is setting and the sky is a stunning shade of purple.

'I think it's probably time you came inside now,' Ronan's saying to me, although his voice is dull and distant as if he's speaking down a cardboard tube. 'You've been out here all afternoon.'

'What time is it?'

'Gone eight. You must be starving,' he says.

Eight? I can't have been asleep for all that time. Groggily, I sit up, my head swimming. Ronan drapes a towel over my shoulders and leaves a hand resting on the back of my neck.

'How are you feeling now?'

How *do* I feel? Confused. Lethargic. Like I'm caught halfway between my dreams, which have been bountiful, and consciousness. A hazy middle-ground where I'm neither asleep nor fully awake.

'I'm fine,' I mumble.

'Here, take these.' He presses two more little white pills into my hand and I swallow them whole with another glass of chilled water which brings relief to my parched throat.

'I didn't mean to sleep all afternoon. I don't know what's got into me.'

He kneels and smiles, sweeping loose strands of hair away from my eyes. 'It's okay, you were tired. You obviously needed the rest. It'll do you good.'

In which case, why do I feel so terrible? My eyes sting and my brain feels as if it's been removed from my head, put in a blender and poured back into my skull. I most definitely do not feel myself.

'Fancy eating out tonight?' Ronan asks, jumping up and straightening his shirt. 'I thought we could drive into town and check out some of the local restaurants.'

He's actually put a shirt on. That short-sleeved one with the blue checks I picked up for him last year in the Next sale. And a pair of smart shorts.

But the last thing I want to do is go out. I feel a wreck, like I've been bulldozed by a train and my body trailed behind a tractor through a lumpy field. Surely Ronan can't really be expecting us to carry on as if nothing's happened?

'I'd rather eat in, if you don't mind.'

'Really?' He sounds disappointed. 'Okay, whatever you want. There's a nice-looking mezze restaurant not far from here I fancied trying, but if you're not up to it, we'll leave it for a different night.'

'Maybe tomorrow?' I suggest with a grimace, although I can't imagine feeling any better tomorrow night either. Apart from my general grogginess, I can sense a dark cloak of despondency descending.

'Yeah, sure.'

'Has there been any news about...' I stop myself finishing the sentence as Ronan raises an eyebrow in warning. 'It doesn't matter.'

'I know what would make you feel better,' he says, jumping up with a boyish grin. 'You should take a dip. You've not been in the pool yet. It's lovely.'

I shudder as another chill ripples down my body. It's not a cold evening, but after sitting in the sun all day, my body's reacting to the cooling temperature. It probably doesn't help that I've not eaten.

'You know I'm terrified of water.'

'Are you?'

'Yes, you know that,' I sigh. Is he deliberately trying to be obtuse?

'Oh right, yeah. Because of your parents when you were little.'

'I nearly drowned.'

'That's a shame. We're paying extra to have a pool,' he says.

'We did it for Jacob's sake...' The words are out before I can stop them.

Ronan's smile evaporates and he stares at me with a mixture of disappointment and anger.

'Karina,' he warns.

'I'm sorry.' Why the hell am I apologising?

'Stop this. It's not good for you. Or us. I wanted this holiday to be a fresh start, but if you carry on like this, you're going to ruin everything.'

I don't know what to say. I don't want to drive a wedge any further between us. God knows, our marriage has been under enough strain lately, but I can't deny my son. He's my world. My everything.

'Do you know what, I'm not actually hungry.'

'You have to eat something.' Ronan's face clouds with concern. 'We can't have you wasting away. And besides, you need to keep your strength up if you're going to get better.'

'Better?'

He sighs. 'All this insane stuff going on in your head.'

'You think I'm crazy, don't you?'

He sits on the lounger next to me and puts a hand on my knee. 'I think it's been a hard few months for you and it's your body's way of coping.'

I take his hand, and our fingers entwine. It's the most intimate we've been in months. 'The miscarriage?'

'I can't even begin to imagine how difficult that was for you. I mean, obviously, I was devastated, but it's your body. I thought you were fine about it at the time, but I can see now the toll it's taken on your mental health.'

It's strange, I still don't remember being pregnant, let alone losing a baby. Surely I'd remember something so profound. Unless Ronan's right and it's my mind's way of shutting out the pain and distress. Maybe I am in denial and I've created the illusion of having a child to compensate. I don't know what to think anymore.

'I might take myself off to bed. Do you mind?'

'Bed? Already? You've been asleep for most of the afternoon.'

'I'm sorry. I don't know what's wrong with me, but I'm sure I'll feel better tomorrow.'

As I attempt to stand, I almost fall flat on my face. My legs are like soft clay and Ronan has to catch my elbow to stop me falling. Since when did standing and walking become so difficult? Must be something in those pills.

Ronan helps me stagger into the villa where the air con has been set far too low. It's absolutely freezing inside, and I'm glad to roll into bed after Ronan has helped undress me and pull on my thin cotton pyjamas.

'Are you sure I can't get you something to eat?' he asks as he pulls the duvet over my shivering body.

'I'm not hungry.'

'Okay, well if you need anything, just shout. I'll be outside.'

'Ronan?'

'Yes?'

'What were you arguing about with that woman opposite?'

He frowns, deep lines furrowing his forehead. 'What do you mean?'

'I woke up earlier and saw you. You were arguing with her. What was it about? Was it about me?'

He shakes his head. 'I've no idea what you're talking about. You must have dreamt it.'

'No, I'm sure—'

'Rest now. I'll pop in and check on you later.'

I don't have the strength to pursue it further. Maybe I imagined that as well.

He flicks off the light and pulls the door closed. Within a few minutes, I'm drifting back to sleep. As if I've not slept enough for one day. I honestly don't know what's going on. It's either the medication or, if Ronan's right about the miscarriage, I'm emotionally exhausted and it's finally catching up with me.

At some point, Ronan returns with a bowl of pasta on a tray, even though I told him I wasn't hungry. He props me up with pillows behind my back and I spoon a few forkfuls into my mouth to keep him happy, before I drift off again.

I'm not sure it's particularly restful sleep. I toss and turn through the night, experiencing dreams so vivid they're almost real. They're mostly of Jacob, to the point they become barely distinguishable from my memories of him, until dream and memory tangle together like pieces of string at the bottom of a kitchen drawer that seem to knot together of their own will.

Time loses significance and meaning.

And even when the sun rises, I don't leave my bed. I don't have the strength nor the inclination, weighed down by a heavy blanket of depression and a soul-destroying lethargy.

Ronan brings me meals and a steady supply of chilled bottles of water that I keep by the bed. And every few hours, he comes with my medication. Two little white tablets to swallow that he's convinced are doing me the power of good.

It's a waste of a holiday. And the villa wasn't cheap, but I can't face getting up. It's as much as I can manage to sit up, eat or even use the bathroom.

'You should go out and explore. You don't need to worry about me. I'll be fine here on my own,' I tell Ronan during a lucid moment when he's clearing away a tray of coffee and pastries which I've barely touched.

He leans over the bed and kisses my head. 'Don't be silly. I'm not going anywhere until you're better.'

'When will that be?'

'Soon,' he says. 'You're doing the right thing. Resting and taking your tablets. In a few days, I'm sure you'll feel as right as rain.'

'I'm sorry I've ruined the holiday.'

'You've not ruined anything. I just want you to be well again, my love.'

*My love?* He's not slept in our bed for the last few nights. I assume he's moved into Jacob's room. I mean the spare room. Not that I blame him. I've not showered in days and my hair is a lank mess. Sleeping with me isn't exactly an enticing prospect.

Ronan never once mentions Jacob's name and the more time that passes, the less convinced I become that he ever existed at all. If he was real, and not just a fantasy I've conjured out of my desperation to be a mother, someone would have found him by now, wouldn't they? A four-year-old child can't simply vanish without trace. Which means the only other logical explanation is that he's an illusion, no matter how real he seemed to me at the time.

And if both Ronan and Sammy, two men who've never met, have independently told me there is no Jacob, I have to believe it's true even though it goes against every grain of my being. As Sherlock Holmes liked to preach, when you've eliminated the impossible, whatever remains, however improbable, must be the truth. It's impossible Ronan and Sammy have colluded against me, because why would they? What would be the reason? There is none. And so the truth must be that I'm delusional. Not well. Riding the crazy train right on through to lunacyville.

So as much as I don't want to believe it, what choice do I have? The brain's a complex organ but it's clearly been playing tricks on me. Constructing false memories. Deluding me into believing in a fantasy world. It's terrifying, really. If it's capable of deceiving me so spectacularly, what else is it capable of? And what other illusory truths has it conned me into believing?

Ronan's promised to arrange an appointment with a mental health specialist as soon as we return home so I can get the help I need. It's horrible having to admit I have a problem, like an alcoholic forced to admit he's always thirsty, but I can't go on like this, caught between reality and fantasy. It's the worst kind of torture.

Even so, it still catches me by surprise when Ronan announces we're going home.

'Get up. We have a plane to catch.' He throws open the curtains allowing bright sunshine to flood the room for the first time in almost a week.

A week! Has it really been that long that I've been in bed, unable to function?

'What time is it?' I groan.

'Six. Our flight's in four hours.'

'We're leaving already? But we can't go.'

'Why not?'

'Because we've not found...' I clamp my mouth shut. 'Sorry. He still seems so real in my head.'

'I know. We're going to get you better. But first, that means getting you home.'

# Chapter 19

Ronan helps me to shower and dress, before packing all my clothes in my case. Then he loads the car with our luggage while I watch. It's as if we're caught up in a dream where nothing is real.

He checks all around the villa to make sure we've not forgotten any of our stuff and orders me into the car.

'I can't,' I say. Not without Jacob.

'We're going to be late.'

I shake my head. I can't abandon Jacob. We brought him here. How can I leave without him?

'I'm sorry,' I mumble, my legs trembling.

'Karina, get in the car. Now. Or I'll leave you behind.'

I take three steadying breaths. In through my nose and out slowly through my mouth.

Of course we're not abandoning anyone. Jacob will always be with me in my heart because that's the place he resides. Not in the real world. And yet I still can't shake the fear that he's out there somewhere and that we're leaving him behind, thousands of miles from home. It's silly, I know.

I drag myself to the car, hiding the tears that spring from my eyes, and yank on my belt. Ronan hands me a bottle of water and two more pills.

'I wonder if we'll be back,' he says wistfully as we pull away and he casts one final glance back at the villa.

I hope not. I don't think I could bear it. It holds too many awful memories. And as we drive away, a hollowness opens up in my chest. A desperate ache of grief. It's taken a week, but I'm finally letting Jacob go.

We drive to the airport in silence, but then we've hardly exchanged a dozen words over the last few days. I sit with my head lolling from side to side, lost in my own thoughts.

After dropping off the hire car in an enormous car park filled with rentals, Ronan hurries off to find a trolley for our cases. With my body weak and fragile from a week spent in bed, it comes in useful to help me walk.

'Do you have the passports?' I ask as we shuffle slowly towards the terminal building.

Ronan produces them from his back pocket like a magician pulling a rabbit from a hat. If only he'd been so diligent when we'd left home.

Inside the terminal, bad memories come flooding back, especially when I catch sight of the snaking queues of passengers waiting patiently at the check-in desks and the teams of armed police officers on patrol. My cheeks flush with embarrassment. What if someone remembers me? The crazy woman ranting about losing her imaginary son.

We take our place at the back of a queue, both lost in a trance. I'm sure anyone watching would think we've had a row. The tension between us hangs thick and heavy. So much for the holiday bringing us closer. I've never felt further apart from Ronan in all the time we've been together.

We progress slowly, dragging our bags behind us until we finally make it to one of the desks and come face to face with the same check-in attendant I confronted earlier in the week. What are the chances?

I keep my head bowed and my eyes fixed on my feet hoping by some miracle she won't recognise me. My hands tremble and sweat dampens my clothes. I'm fairly sure she alerted the police and was responsible for my humiliating arrest. God knows what she must think of me.

I reach for my sunglasses which I thought I'd popped on the top of my head, but they're not there. As I pat my hair, wondering if I've dropped them on the way into the terminal, I remember putting them in the pocket of the door of the hire car when I thought I was going to doze off on the journey. How stupid. They were designer frames and cost a small fortune.

'I've left my sunglasses in the car. They were my expensive ones. I'm going to run back and see if I can find them.'

Ronan looks panic-stricken as he hands over our passports and lifts our cases onto the conveyor belt. 'No, don't run off,' he says. 'I'll come with you. I won't be a minute.'

'It's fine. You check in the cases and I'll meet you back here in five minutes.'

The woman behind the desk finally clocks my face. Her eyebrows shoot up in surprise, but I don't hang around to see if she'll have the nerve to say anything.

'Karina! Wait!' Ronan yells after me as I turn and battle my way through a wall of people heading in the opposite direction.

I half walk, half jog back towards the car park feeling much better for a little exercise and a change of scene, even if my head's still woolly.

I find a man and a woman in matching company polo shirts hanging around a small office, clutching clipboards. When I explain what's happened, they're kind and understanding. She looks up the paperwork, identifies our car and tosses her colleague a key. It's parked amongst dozens of other dusty vehicles, I guess waiting to be valeted for the next customers.

'Thank you so much,' I say as I take the key and throw open the passenger door.

Inside, the scent of Ronan's aftershave still lingers, along with the hint of stale cigarette smoke. It's supposed to be a non-smoking vehicle, but somewhere along the line someone's obviously ignored that rule.

I dive into the pocket in the door and rummage around.

But I can't find my glasses. Strange. I'm sure that's where I left them. Unless they fell off my head and somehow landed in the back. They're a decent pair of Oakleys I treated myself to for the holiday and I'd hate to lose them.

The rental agent stands watching patiently with his hands in his trouser pockets. I shoot him an apologetic smile as I close the passenger door but as I dive into the back, I spot something that catches me by surprise. The child seat we hired for Jacob, still covered in crumbs from the bag of crisps we gave him to keep him quiet on the drive from the airport, has been there all the time, but I'd not registered it earlier. It begs the question, why's there a child seat in the car if we don't have any children?

'This seat,' I say, turning to the agent, my voice faltering. 'Does it come as standard with all your rentals?'

He looks at me blankly. 'No, it's extra,' he says.

'Thanks.' I thought so.

So if I only imagined we had a child, why would we need a child seat?

'Did you find your glasses?'

'Not yet.'

I crouch down to peer under the front seat, wondering if they've been accidentally kicked there where I can't see them. But I'd need to be a contortionist to get my head low enough to see into the dark recess. Instead, I shove a hand in, right up to my shoulder, and fish around. The carpet's covered in crumbs and sand, but there's no sign of my sunglasses. There is something else though. It's plastic, with a rough surface and pointy edges.

I pull it out and hold it up to the light. It's a toy dinosaur. A T-rex, to be precise. I should know. Jacob's told me enough times. Its jaw is wide open as if caught mid-roar, with red paint on its teeth to represent blood. I'd know it anywhere.

It *is* Jacob's. The last time I saw him playing with it was on the flight.

My breath comes in short, ragged pants.

I'm not imagining this, am I? This is real. I can see it. Feel it.

'Karina, I told you to wait!' Ronan comes bounding up to the car, sweating and red in the face.

When he sees the dinosaur in my hand, his eye twitches and he becomes very still. Almost statue-like.

'What's that?' he eventually asks.

'I found it under the front seat.'

'And your sunglasses?'

I shake my head. 'Ronan, why does the car we hired have a child seat?'

'What? Dunno. I think they supply them with all the cars because they get so many families,' he says.

'No, you have to pay extra. I checked.'

He swallows. 'I guess it was an oversight.'

He's lying to me. I can see it now.

'Did we pay for a child seat?'

'No, of course not.' He laughs nervously. 'Why would we need one? We don't have any kids, remember?'

I squeeze the plastic T-rex between my fingers. 'So you keep saying. It's funny, in my dreams, the boy I thought was ours had a dinosaur just like this one,' I say, choosing my words carefully. I'm already learning not to provoke Ronan by using Jacob's name or pretending he's anything other than a fantasy.

'It's just a toy dinosaur. Now come on, we're going to miss our flight. I'll buy you a new pair of sunglasses in duty-free.'

There's no point arguing with him. And it's not exactly incontrovertible proof of Jacob's existence. It could have been dropped by another child. And the child seat *could* have been left in the vehicle by mistake. Nonetheless, it leaves me with an uneasy feeling.

I slip the dinosaur into my pocket, hand the key back to the rental agent and follow Ronan sullenly back into the airport, my mind churning again.

# Chapter 20

When I was ten, my cat, Maisy, was knocked down and killed by a car outside our house. She was spiky and unpredictable, but always slept on my bed, loved to rub her head on my chin, purred loudly at the slightest show of affection, and I adored her. Her death, despite my father's cold indifference towards her untimely demise, was devastating. I've never felt anything close to the pain I experienced losing her. Until now.

For the entire flight home, I'm on the verge of bursting into tears while my insides echo with an empty, hollow feeling as if a huge chunk of my being has been ripped out and discarded.

Ronan's not even noticed how upset I am. He's spent most of the flight asleep, either reading his book, or preoccupied looking out of the window. He's not once asked how I'm feeling or how I'm coping. If Jacob did only exist inside my head, it's still a massive wrench to let him go. Not that he can appreciate that.

When we finally arrive back at our shabby cottage by the sea almost twelve hours after we left the villa, I'm tired and emotionally wrung out. The house looks almost exactly as it did when we left a week ago, and yet there's something odd about it. It's like pulling on a pair of stranger's shoes that look identical to your own comfy pair. They look the same, but they feel different. I guess I'm not the same woman who was here last.

It was Ronan who suggested we leave London and find a place by the sea when we were first married. We both agreed it would be wonderful to escape the rat race and put down roots somewhere we could reconnect with nature and live a simpler life.

We fell in love with the house with its crooked white-washed walls and mottled roof, because of its proximity to the beach and its bleak remoteness. We didn't have to worry about neighbours or integrating into the community. We could do what we liked. Live life as we wanted to live it. It was also the perfect place to bring up a child. I guess the child we thought we were going to have.

As we pull up outside and Ronan kills the engine, a million memories flood my brain. Of Jacob digging up worms in the garden. His eyes lighting up at the sight of the rocket-shaped cake I'd baked for his birthday. Dressing up in welly boots and thick coats to play on the beach in mid-winter. Sand in our socks. Salt in our hair. Jacob helping decorate his room and ending up with more paint on his clothes than on the walls. Lying in his bed, his head tucked into my shoulder and his thumb wedged in his mouth, as I read him *Room on the Broom* for what seemed like the millionth time.

These can't be false memories. They're too real, too vivid, too inherently part of my life to be something I've imagined. But how can they be true, because if they are, it would mean we've abandoned my son in Turkey, and what kind of parent would do that?

'Put the kettle on. I'll bring the cases in,' Ronan instructs gruffly.

The house keys are buried at the bottom of my bag. I hook them out and approach the front door with trepidation, as if the house might be haunted or there's something hiding inside the thick stone walls. It's silly. I don't know why I'm being like this. It's our home. Our refuge. Or at least it used to be.

The door creaks open like it's been sealed shut for seven years rather than seven days. Inside it smells damp and musty and feels cold. It's never been a warm house but after the heat of a Turkish summer it's particularly notice-able. But worse than any of that, it feels... emp-ty. Deserted. As if the soul of our home has been uprooted and there's nothing left but a barren shell.

A seagull screeches overhead, shattering the silence inside. I take a moment to stand in the hall, listening. Feeling. The sound of Jacob playing drifts down the stairs. The thud of his feet hammers across the ceiling. I close my eyes and press my lips together.

*It's not real. It was never real. It's only in my head.*

There's another feeling, hovering at the edge of my consciousness. A strange sense that the house hasn't been entirely empty while we've been away. A sensation that someone's been here, prying through our things. Touching stuff that doesn't belong to them.

I shudder but dismiss the idea. Just my crazy brain making nonsense up again.

Something draws me to the stairs. An unseen force. I watch myself as I climb, like a detached observer, my vision tunnelled and all the colours around me muted and faded like an old sofa that's been left in the sun. Behind me, Ronan huffs and grunts as he struggles with the cases and dumps them in the hall.

I'm on the landing now. One foot stepping in front of the other. All the doors are shut and it's dark. At the far end of the corridor is our bedroom with its delightful views across the beach. The family bathroom to the left. And to my right the room I used to think of as Jacob's.

I ease open the door. I have a memory of us decorating the room together, creating an accent wall in matt black that we turned into a night sky with a hundred glow-in-the-dark stick-on stars to match the space-themed duvet cover I'd ordered online. I can see it clearly in my mind, along with a bookshelf full of Jacob's favourite books. A wooden box we painted in red and blue and orange where he kept all his puzzles. A set of plastic boxes under the bed to store the thousands of Lego pieces he loved to build into amazing spaceships and rockets.

The room is filled with light blazing through a window that should be framed by a pair of astronaut-themed curtains. Dark blue with stars and men in spacesuits floating above the earth that I picked up for a steal online in the John Lewis sale.

But there are no curtains at the window now at all.

There's no black accent wall with stuck-on stars, or planets adorning the duvet cover. No bookcase crammed with Jacob's favourite bed-time stories or any of his Lego models lined up on a wooden shelf above the radiator.

There's nothing of Jacob's in the room at all.

The walls are painted in neutral tones. The bed is stripped of its covers and the duvet and pillows piled up on one end. The wooden book-case is empty. The Pokemon posters I remember hanging on the wall with drawing pins are gone. Three dusty model wooden fishing boat are on the shelves where the Lego toys should be. Even the lampshade, a moon globe which glowed sepia in the dark, has disappeared.

Disappeared? Or was it never there at all?

I fall to my knees as my insides tighten, squeezing the emotions up and out in an out-pouring of grief and regret. If ever I needed proof that there was never any Jacob, this is surely it.

Maybe it's punishment for what I did. The de-cisions I took when I found out I was pregnant. The road I travelled. It's time to accept Jacob is nothing more than a ghost and that finally I have to let him go.

Below, I can hear Ronan pacing around, look-ing for me.

'Karina?' he shouts, his voice sharp with anx-iety.

I sniff and dry my eyes, holding my face up to the ceiling as if to draw the tears back inside.

'Where are you?'

'Up here.' I climb to my feet. Brush the dust off my knees. Pat down my hair and try to make myself look respectable.

He bounds up the stairs and catches me coming out of the room. 'What are you doing?' There's an accusation in his question. He scowls at me.

'Nothing.'

'Why were you in there?' He nods at Jacob's room. No, not Jacob's room. The guest room. I can't keep hanging onto this fiction.

'I thought I heard a noise.' I force a smile. 'Guess I'm a bit jumpy being back.'

'You were looking for him, weren't you?' His face creases with displeasure.

'What? No, of course not.'

'Let me guess. You thought this was his room.' He kicks open the door, grabs my shoulders and spins me around violently.

'Ronan, please...'

'What did you think you were going to find, eh?' He's shouting now. I've not even said anything to antagonise him. 'Look! It's just an empty room.'

I lower my head and stare at my hands. 'Yes, I know,' I whisper.

'There is no child. Do you see?'

'Yes.'

'Go on, then. Say it.'

'Say what?'

'I want to hear you say there is no child. We have no son.'

I take a deep breath and clear my throat. It's the hardest thing to admit, especially to myself, and after all this time. 'There is no child.'

'Louder.'

'There is no child,' I say, lifting my head and looking Ronan defiantly in the eye through a blizzard of tears.

'Right,' he says. 'There is no child. There never was. It's always been in your head. And I don't want to hear any more about it, got it?'

He's in a foul mood, but I can hardly blame him.

'I'm sorry. I didn't mean to upset you.'

'Try harder,' he snaps.

'Everything felt so real and I have so many memories, it's difficult to accept that none of it happened.'

'Whatever you think you remember, it was only ever in your head. There's only you and me.'

'But I remember painting this room with Jacob and letting him have his own paintbrush and him getting covered in paint. It was all over his clothes and his nose. Don't you remember, you came in and found us laughing hysterically?' The memory brings a weak smile to my face until I remember none of it really happened.

'Stop it.' Ronan growls like a dog with his back against the wall. 'I don't want to hear that name again, do you understand? You're not well. It's weird that you constantly talk about him like he's a real person. I can't stand it.'

I know I'm ill, but the memories, if that's what I can call them, are so comforting. They bring me such happiness, what's wrong with clinging to them, even if they're only in my imagination?

'I'll do my best,' I promise. And I mean it. I don't want this thing to drive us further apart.

Ronan has been distant and moody with me all week. We've not even shared a bed. But I don't want to destroy the marriage. That's absolutely the last thing I want, because I need him now more than ever.

'You'll do more than promise if you want this marriage to survive.' It sounds like a threat.

'Of course I do.' I raise a hand to touch his cheek, but he flinches and takes a step back.

I've not noticed how tired and fraught he looks lately. There are dark bags under his eyes and his face is pinched and grey. I've been so wrapped up in my own misery, I hadn't seen the effect it was having on my husband.

'First thing on Monday morning, I'm going to book an appointment with the GP,' he says. 'I hoped you might be getting better, but I think it's time to get you back on your medication.'

What? I've never been on any medication. At least, not that I recall. But what's strange is that it's exactly what Sammy said when I called him from Turkey. I dismissed it at the time because my head was all over the place, but now his words come back to haunt me.

*You know what the doctor said. It's important you keep taking the tablets, otherwise there's a danger of a relapse.*

My head throbs like it's a ticking bomb about to explode.

'What medication?'

Ronan scans my face, as if he's trying to work out how to break bad news to me. 'After you lost the baby,' he says, 'you had a breakdown. You were understandably upset. We both were. But you became convinced the baby was alive and that it had been taken away from you.'

'No,' I gasp. 'That's not true.'

'You even gave it a name.'

*Jacob.*

'We had to take you to see a psychiatrist. Do you remember?'

I dive into the depths of my memory but I have no recollection of seeing a psychiatrist.

'No,' I protest.

He sucks in his lips. 'It is true. I can prove it, if you'd like? Wait here.' He strides off, down the stairs. Along the hall. I hear him in the kitchen, rifling through the drawers.

And then he's back, clutching a letter.

He hands it to me. I scan the letterhead. It's from the local health authority, addressed to me and dated two years ago. It's full of technical language but appears to be an assessment of my mental state. How I coped with the grief of losing a child at twenty-two weeks of pregnancy. My eyes blur with tears of sadness and frustration, while two phrases swimming on the page float to the surface and take on a prominence of their own.

*Delusional.*

*Psychotic disorder.*

I glance over the top of the letter. Ronan's standing chewing his nails, waiting for me to digest what I'm reading.

'I'm sorry,' he says. 'I honestly thought we'd put all this behind us. If I'd thought for one minute the holiday would rake it all up again, I'd have never booked it.'

# Chapter 21

First thing on Monday morning, Ronan drives me to the doctors' surgery. It's in a modern, bright building busy with old people and coughing children. The balding doctor who sees me is friendly and mild-mannered, his shirt sleeves rolled up to his elbows and a chocolate-brown tie tucked into an insipid beige shirt.

Ronan insists on sitting in on the consultation and does most of the talking on my behalf, which is just as well as I can't seem to get my thoughts straight this morning. I'm still on the pills the doctor in Turkey prescribed and although they've helped me to rest and sleep, they cloud my thoughts and leave my brain foggy.

Ronan explains that he's worried I've become delusional, telling the doctor how I had a breakdown while on holiday and started making up stories about an imaginary son being abducted. To my utter embarrassment, he even tells him I was arrested at the airport for making a scene after escaping from our villa.

The doctor nods sympathetically and asks me a few questions about how I'm feeling.

Whether I've had any suicidal thoughts, which I haven't, and suggests I see a psychiatrist with a specialism in my kind of mental health issues, whatever that means.

And that's it. We're in and out in less than ten minutes and I've barely spoken a word.

A few weeks later, an appointment comes through at a hospital in Norwich. Much to Ronan's irritation, the psychiatrist wants to see me alone and he has to wait outside in the car park. It doesn't bother me. Since we returned from Turkey, we've drifted further and further apart. I've moved into the guest room, the room I used to think of as Jacob's, and struggle most days to get out of bed, let alone function. Life seems to have lost its meaning.

The psychiatrist is old enough to be my mother with wild, grey hair, a colourful, spotted silk blouse and bright blue glasses that perch on the end of a pert nose. Far bubblier and idiosyncratic than I imagined she would be, but I'm immediately drawn to her. She's upbeat and caring and listens attentively as I relive what happened in Turkey as best I can remember. I try to be straight with her, explaining how I'd become utterly convinced we had a four-year-old son and that on the first morning I woke and discovered he was missing. That's when Ronan first suggested he was a product of my imagination and that I'd created all these false memories of him that I'd now come to accept weren't real.

'I'm worried these delusions I've been having are destroying my marriage,' I say. 'My entire relationship with my husband, Ronan, is teetering on the edge.'

'The good news is that you've acknowledged you have a problem and that you're able to take an objective view,' she says, resting her hands in her lap. 'And trust me, most of my patients aren't able to do that. So I'd say you're already on the path to getting better. Now we need to give you the tools to ensure you can make a full recovery.'

'A full recovery? You think that's possible?'

'Yes, I would have thought so.'

'That would be amazing.'

She attempts to look up my medical records but apologises when she can't find them. 'We've been having terrible trouble with the computers,' she says, rolling her eyes. 'They're supposed to be transferring all our patient records onto a new system, but it's a bit glitchy. Not that you need to worry about that.'

Instead, she asks me lots of questions about my health which I try to answer honestly. I tell her I was on medication previously but I can't remember what it was, and also about the miscarriage I can't recall and how Ronan is convinced that's the source of my problems.

'Grief is such a powerful emotion,' she says. 'It can affect us in so many different ways, and losing a baby is a particularly tough experience for any woman.'

Eventually she prescribes some new medication and advises me to stop taking the sedatives I was given in Turkey.

'What is it?' I ask, gripping the prescription she hands me.

'Anti-psychotics. They should help stop the hallucinations and delusions. Let's see how you get on with these and we'll reassess in a few months.'

It feels like progress. Finally, I'm getting the treatment I need. Except this time, I'm determined to keep taking the drugs. Look what happened last time. I don't know what I was taking previously, but obviously I must have thought it was best to wean myself off them. Look at the hole I fell into when I did.

The change to my medication makes an almost immediate impact. After I stop taking the sedatives, my head is clearer and I have more drive and energy. It's like putting on a pair of corrective glasses when I've been scrambling around with short vision for months. Everything is suddenly sharp and in focus.

I still think about Jacob from time to time, but now when he comes into my mind, I'm able to label it properly. Not memories but fantasies, seemingly so real because I wanted so badly for them to be true, as the psychiatrist explained to me.

There are still times when I wake in the night in a cold sweat, thrown back to the horrifying moment when I walked into Jacob's room and found his bed empty. Although I know it's not real, my heart still aches for him, which I guess is only natural. My maternal instincts kicking in. But every day gets easier and I'm sure in time I'll be back to my old self. I need to learn to be patient and let nature take its course.

If only my relationship with Ronan could be repaired with a handful of pills. We don't talk anymore. We don't share a bed. We don't even eat meals together or sit and watch TV, like we used to when we were first together.

Ronan is often away and I'm invariably left home alone. He says he's working, but I'm not sure I believe him. He spends so many nights away, I can't help but wonder if he's seeing other women behind my back. I wouldn't put it past him. He's a charmer who's always had a wandering eye.

After a few months of living like strangers, I decide it's time to confront it head on. Things have to change or we're heading for the divorce courts. Neither of us is happy like this.

On a rare night he's stayed in, I pluck up the courage to talk to him. He's in the living room watching a football match on the TV with a can of beer and his feet up on the coffee table.

'Ronan, do you still love me?' I ask.

'I'm trying to watch this,' he growls, attempting to shoo me out of the way as I stand between him and the TV.

'I know, but this is important.'

Begrudgingly, he pauses the match. 'What's brought this on?'

'Because we're living separate lives. We don't do anything together. We don't talk. And half the time you're not even here.'

'What am I supposed to do? Hang around the house while you mope about pining for a child you never had?' he says. It's a cheap shot, but I let it go. 'I can't put my life on hold waiting for you to get better.'

'But I am getting better. I'm taking my medication regularly and the psychiatrist says I'm making real progress.'

He shakes his head and rubs his temples. 'I don't think you realise how hard it is living with you. You spend most of your time in your room. You're not interested in going out—'

'That's not fair! When was the last time you suggested going anywhere?'

'Why should it be down to me? Why is it my responsibility to save this marriage?'

'Because I thought you cared about us. About me.'

'This is the problem with you, Karina. You've always got to make a drama out of everything, haven't you?'

'Is that what you think I'm doing?' I ask, exasperated. 'The last few months have been really tough. You know that. And I'm doing my best to get back to normal. It would help if I had some support. But you're never here.'

'And why do you think that is?' The bitterness of his tone catches me by surprise. 'Who in their right mind would want to be with you?' He casts a disgusted eye up and down my body.

'Is that all you care about? How I look? Whether I've put on any make-up or brushed my hair? God, you can be so shallow.'

'We don't even share the same bed, let alone anything else,' he fires back.

'So that's what this is about? Sex?'

'Don't be stupid.'

'And because I haven't been putting out, you've been finding it elsewhere? How many have there been?'

'What? Don't be daft.'

'Come on. One? Ten? Twenty?' I fold my arms across my chest and raise an eyebrow.

What's happened to us? To him? We used to be such a good fit. I think back to those early days when he bombarded me with gifts. Chocolates. Flowers. Teddy bears. Jewellery. And how he'd constantly leave messages for me, telling me how much he loved me. How he couldn't live without me. Sometimes several times a day. Now, it all seems like a distant memory.

His jaw tightens as he picks up the TV remote and fingers the buttons, not looking at me.

'You haven't answered my question. How many?' I ask, a stone in the pit of my stomach hardening.

'Karina, don't.'

I always suspected it, but I thought he'd at least deny it. Lie to me. A lump forms in my throat and tears of humiliation prick my eyes.

'Bastard.' I turn and run out of the room, sprint up the stairs and throw myself onto my bed.

In a matter of months, everything I knew and trusted has been reduced to ashes. My life as I knew it is over. There is no Jacob and now I realise there is no Ronan and me. We're over. Done.

The next morning, my mind's made up.

I wait until Ronan leaves the house - he doesn't even bother to let me know he's going, let alone where these days - and then I pack a bag and call a taxi.

# Chapter 22

It took me a while to realise it, but there's nothing for me in Norfolk or that house. I don't know what we were thinking when we moved there. It's in the middle of nowhere. It's bleak. It's exposed. The house is always cold and in the winter the wind rattles through the old window frames. The nearest shop is a forty-minute drive away and there are no other houses around for miles. I have no friends there and weeks can often pass without seeing another soul. Since Ronan and I started living separate lives, I've never felt more isolated. I've no idea how he persuaded me it was a good idea to buy it. We must have been out of our minds.

My instinct is to return to London where I was living when Ronan and I met. It's where you can be alone and surrounded by people all at the same time. I miss the parks, the galleries and the museums. The architecture. The smells. The sounds. The bustle of a busy city where it feels anything is possible and life is at your fingertips.

Fortunately, I still have money from the divorce settlement with Sammy. I'm glad now I resisted the pressure from Ronan to put it towards the house in Norfolk. I guess I always had a feeling I might need it for myself one day. It's not a fortune but it's enough that I don't have to worry about working for a while.

Initially, I move into bed-and-breakfast accommodation in Earls Court with a kindly old lady and her cats. But that only lasts a few weeks until I find a delightful flat to rent on the first floor of an old Victorian terrace in Muswell Hill. It's small and the furniture's dated, but it's what you get for your money these days in London.

For the first few months, I spend my days reacquainting myself with the city, falling in love with it all over again. I spend time in the art galleries and cafes, wandering aimlessly through the parks and gardens, seeing everything through a tourist's eyes.

It's weird. I don't miss Ronan at all. It's Jacob who floats to the forefront of my mind in unguarded moments. A child who only exists in my imagination. Not my husband, which tells me everything.

We don't keep in touch. What's the point? We have nothing in common and clearly he was grateful I walked away. He's never tried to persuade me to return or begged for my forgiveness. Told me he can't live without me. And when I file for divorce, he doesn't fight me. It's not at all like when I divorced Sammy, who took it as a personal affront and battled me every step of the way.

So that's another husband chalked up, and I'm not yet forty. How depressing.

The following year, my mother finally passes away. I'd not seen her as much as I should, but it broke my heart every single time she couldn't remember me. And if she couldn't remember me, what was the point of visiting? It feels as though I'd lost my mum a long time ago.

Her funeral is a simple, low-key affair, attended by some of the staff at the care home and a few of her oldest friends. We have drinks and nibbles in a nearby pub, but it's all a bit strained and difficult. Within an hour, everyone's drifted away and I'm left to pick up the bar bill.

I need to think about going back to work at some point. My money's not going to last forever, but I can't countenance a return to my old job. It feels as though that's passed me by. A young woman's career. And anyway, I've lost all my contacts and I've not picked up a camera in years. Even if my confidence wasn't shot, I'm not the woman I used to be. The woman who would happily jump on a flight to the back end of nowhere at a moment's notice, not knowing where she was going to stay or how long she'd be away. I don't have it in me these days.

The problem is, I don't know who I am anymore. Karina, wildlife photographer? Karina, mother? Karina, wife and homemaker?

I don't have any transferable skills and I've never done a 'proper' job in my life. Photography is all I've known. But luck finally lands on my side when I spot a job advert in the window of a photographic studio not far from my flat. I only notice it by chance as I'm heading to my favourite cafe to grab an oat milk latte and a cardamom bun.

They're looking for an assistant to help run the studio and lend a hand with some wedding shoots. Nothing taxing. Running a diary. Organising schedules. Carrying equipment and setting up lights. And so before I can talk myself out of it, I walk straight in and speak to the owner.

Freida is lovely. She's full of energy and has a wicked sense of humour and an infectious laugh. We instantly hit it off.

She wants to know about my employment history but I deliberately keep it vague and thankfully she doesn't ask to see a CV. I think she's impressed by my knowledge of cameras and that I can happily chat about F-stops and aperture, lenses and filters, different types of lighting and the importance of post-production. It's like catching up with an old friend and by the end of the interview, if you can call it that, we're both crying with laughter. It feels good. I haven't laughed so much in years.

To my surprise, Freida offers me the job on the spot.

'When can you start?' she asks.

'Monday?'

'Perfect.'

And suddenly I'm back in full-time employment for the first time in almost five years.

The job takes some getting used to, but Freida is patient and understanding as she shows me the ropes, how the electronic diary works and how she'd like me to answer the phone. I'm much more at home helping to set up the lighting and preparing the cameras in the studio. And by the end of my first week, she even trusts me with a set of keys so I can lock up on my own.

Over time, my life slowly gets back on track. I have a job, a regular income, a flat to call my own and more importantly, a routine. The job's not exactly nine-to-five but that doesn't bother me, especially as Freida occasionally invites me to help with some of her wedding shoots at weekends.

Recently, she's even taken to giving me a camera to snap some candid shots of the guests while she's busy with the standard line-ups of the bride and groom, friends and family. Being able to take photographs again has done wonders for my confidence.

Freida becomes more like a close friend than my employer and we start seeing each other socially. Initially, drinks after work at the pub, but with increasing regularity she's been inviting me to her house to eat and we've spent a number of raucous evenings putting the world to rights over too much wine.

It helps that I'm still taking my medication religiously and my mind is on an even keel. I'm not going to fall into the trap of thinking I can handle coming off it again. Not after last time. And although I think about Jacob from time to time, I've finally accepted he was nothing more than a mental mirage. No more real than the fairies living under the bed or the trolls at the end of the garden.

As close as we've become, I've never confided in Freida about any of my mental health struggles. Although she knows about Ronan, I've not told her about what happened in Turkey, and I've been careful never to mention Jacob's name. I don't want to jeopardise our friendship or my job.

I don't think she'd judge me, but I'm not willing to take the risk. After all, if she finds out I need medication to function and I never mentioned it at the interview, she'd be within her rights to sack me on the spot. And where would that leave me?

So I keep it to myself.

And life is good. Everything is under control. I'm happy. I'm sane. And I have the best friend in the world.

But then I receive an email out of the blue which brings my world crashing down.

It's ten years since that holiday to Turkey where my life was turned upside down, and once again, everything I thought I knew is thrown into total and utter chaos.

# Chapter 23

It's been a long day at work and I've been on my feet for most of it, helping Freida with half a dozen studio shoots and coping with the phone calls that never seem to stop. Now I'm home, on the sofa, with the TV on in the background and my feet up, spooning forkfuls of reheated pasta bake into my mouth, glad I had the foresight to make enough for two nights. I couldn't have faced cooking this evening.

My interest quickly grows tired of the never-ending conveyor belt of cat videos on Instagram and Facebook, and instead I check my inbox on my phone in the vague hope that someone's messaged me with something of importance. Not that they ever do. My inbox is usually full of newsletters and promotions from organisations and businesses trying to sell me something.

I slide my finger across the screen deleting each of them methodically, one by one, until I reach a message which instantly grabs my attention.

It looks as though it might be a clever marketing trick with a subject line designed to provoke my curiosity and entice me into clicking on a link to a page selling me something I neither want nor need.

I'm about to delete it, but the sender's address is a Gmail account, girlwithregrets123@gmail.com, with the intriguing subject line, **Something you need to know.**

I'm sure it's spam, but I can't help taking a look.

The message is short and to the point and sends a shiver from the base of my neck down the length of my spine and brings goosebumps to the back of my arms.

> **I thought you had a right to know that your son, Jacob, is alive and well. Sorry I didn't find the courage to tell you before. I hope this gives you some comfort.**
> **Best**
> **The Girl with Regrets**

What the hell?

I drop the phone like it's a hot coal and sit bolt upright, almost knocking the bowl of pasta off my lap and onto the floor.

It's like being stung by a swarm of a thousand angry wasps.

With a trembling hand, I pluck my phone off the carpet and read the message again, my eyes flying across the words, trying to make sense of what it means.

It has to be a prank. A sick and twisted wind-up. But who would do that to me? There aren't many people who know about Jacob. Obviously, there's Sammy and Ronan, but I can't believe either of them would be so cruel. And there's no way this has come from my GP in Norfolk who I saw all those years ago. Or my psychiatrist. It's inconceivable that they'd break their professional code and disclose my mental health battles.

*Jacob alive and well?*

But I've believed all these years that he wasn't real and that he only existed as a ghost in my mind. Everyone said it. Ronan. And Sammy. The GP. The psychiatrist. How could they all be wrong?

Unless they've all been lying to me...

I jump off the sofa and race to the bathroom, making it to the toilet as my stomach retches painfully. The shock of it is all too much.

I wipe my mouth with my sleeve and fall back against the wall with my head spinning. I've put so much effort into getting better and moving on with my life, rebuilding my sanity and taking back control of my senses, and now this? It's been a long time since I last woke in the night screaming for Jacob, convinced he'd been abducted and that we'd abandoned him in Turkey. Now what am I supposed to think?

Is it really true? *Can* it be true?

No, I can't go there. It's the road to madness. And that's probably exactly what the sender of the email intended. There's no other explana-tion.

I haul myself to my feet and trudge back to the lounge. My phone's lying on the sofa. I pick it up and read the email once more. Slowly this time, taking in every word.

It was sent yesterday evening. July the fif-teenth.

There's something about that date. Why does it seem so familiar?

Oh my god, it's exactly ten years since I thought Jacob had gone missing. The first day of our holiday when I woke in a panic and found his bed empty. That can't be a coincidence.

But who's sent the message? Who is the *Girl with Regrets*? I assume it must be a woman. Or a man who's cleverly trying to cover his tracks. I just don't understand what they hope to achieve. It's not as though they've provided any details or any proof of their claims. Which begs the question, why send it at all, unless to torment me?

Jacob is alive and well. That's all it says, although the subtext is clear.

*Jacob is alive and well, and you didn't make him up.*

He was as real as the sun rising in the sky every morning. I was never insane. But someone wanted me to believe I was.

The message poses more questions than answers.

I take a deep breath and close my eyes, centring myself like I was taught in those mindfulness sessions I attended for a short while after I left Ronan.

I can't jump to conclusions and I mustn't get my hopes up. It's one email from an anonymous sender. The chances are it's nothing more than an obscene piece of mischief intended to upset and destabilise me.

But I keep coming back to the same question. Why?

There's only one way to find out.

I hit reply and compose a short message, my fingers so shaky it takes several attempts to type the right words.

> **Who is this? And why are you trying to mess with my head?**

I hit send and wait patiently for a response, my thumb repeatedly refreshing the screen, praying answers will come swiftly. My stomach turns somersaults with a mixture of anxiety, excitement and fear.

It's taken so much work over so many years to finally come to terms with what I thought was the truth, that Jacob was alive only in my head, conjured from my grief, and yet one short email is threatening to unpick it all. I know I have to be careful, though, because if this turns out to be a hoax, it will crucify me. If I allow myself to believe what this email is suggesting, and my hopes are dashed again, I'll be destroyed.

A minute passes.

Two.

Still no reply.

In frustration, I type another message.

> **How do I know you're telling the truth? What do you know about Jacob?**

I glance at the clock. It's gone nine. Not that late. Hopefully the sender, this *Girl with Regrets*, will still be up and pick up my emails.

I pace the room, my eyes fixed on the screen of my phone. A car rumbles past outside. A dog

barks in the distance. The credits at the end of
the drama I was half-watching on the TV roll.

And finally, another email arrives.

This time, it comes with an attachment.

A photo.

A solitary image that changes everything.

# Chapter 24

It's a photo of a boy. A teenager. With a spotty chin and an awkward smile.

I gasp, my knees weak with shock. My hand shoots to my mouth.

There's something painfully familiar about those eyes. The curve of his nose. The colour of his hair, shaved now around the sides and left longer, floppy, on the top. The shape of his face has changed. His jaw more pronounced. His brow sterner. But there's absolutely no doubt in my mind.

It's Jacob.

It's my son.

I slump onto the sofa, drinking in the image, gulping it down thirstily as my brain struggles to keep up with my emotions.

He's ten years older, but I'd recognise my son anywhere. I sob silently, tears rolling down my face, my shoulders rocking. The enormity of it hits me like I've been run down by a articulated lorry.

So it's true. Jacob *is* alive and well.

But how can that possibly be? There's a chance, I suppose, if someone really wanted to go to the trouble, they could have Photo-shopped the image. Taken a picture that looks a little like Jacob and doctored it. Or it could even have been generated by AI. Freida and I have been playing around with the technology at work and it's produced some frighteningly realistic results. But why would anyone go to the effort? And besides, I know it's him. I can feel it. Sense it. Call it a mother's intuition.

I knew it all along. I wasn't going insane.

But now I have so many questions rolling around my mind, exploding in my brain like fireworks in the night sky. If Jacob wasn't a figment of my imagination, what happened to him? Where's he been all these years? Does he still remember me? Is he back in the country?

It's so strange to see him again. He'd been thoroughly deleted from my life, existing only in my memories. I didn't even have any photographs of him to pore over in my darkest moments. It's the first time I've seen his face in a decade and it's nothing like I remember.

I need to find him. To hold him. Touch him. To see him with my own eyes.

He was only young when he went missing, but not that young. He must have memories of me. What was he told had happened to me? Does he think I'm dead? Or has he been brainwashed into believing I don't exist, like I'd been brainwashed into thinking he was only a ghost?

There's so much to process. So much to think about. I don't know where to start.

First things first. I need to find him. But how? There aren't many clues in the picture. In it, he's wearing a red football shirt with blue stripes and holding a football tucked under his arm. It looks like he's on a football field with out-of-focus green pitches stretching out behind him. It could have been taken anywhere. I guess it's a school or local team, but the badge over his breast has been deliberately blurred out. Whoever's sent this photo doesn't want me to find him.

In which case, why email me at all? Of course I'm going to look for him. I've not seen Jacob in ten years, and was told he was as good as dead.

I need to think. To clear my head. But it's hard when it's a blizzard of conflicting thoughts and emotions. I was made to think I was going insane, and all this time I've been tricked into believing something so outlandish it couldn't possibly be true.

But why?

Ronan has to have something to do with this. *Everything* to do with it.

He's the only one who could have engineered it, who could have made Jacob disappear from right under my nose and persuaded me my son was nothing but a fantasy. But why? They had a good relationship, or so I thought. Jacob wasn't Ronan's biological son, but so what? He treated him like his own. Jacob even called him Daddy.

For a while, in Turkey, I considered whether something might have happened to Jacob and it was Ronan's ham-fisted way of covering it up. I thought maybe there had been an accident and Jacob was dead. That Ronan had concocted an elaborate story to conceal what he'd done. But here, in my hand, is evidence Jacob didn't die. He's alive. And looking so well.

So, what then?

The only other possibility is... No, it's too abhorrent to even contemplate. Unthinkable. There's no way Ronan would have sold our son, would he? We always kept our finances separate, even after we were married, but Ronan never gave me any reason to believe he was struggling for money. And he would have had to have been pretty desperate to traffic Jacob.

Is that what really happened though? Is that why we ended up in Turkey instead of going to Greece? Had he found a family - or worse, a trafficking gang - willing to pay good money for our son? I imagine Turkey's exactly the kind of place you'd go to make an illegal transaction like that.

Jacob was always a good-looking little boy. Blonde and blue-eyed with a cheeky smile and a cute dimple on his chin. What if Ronan had auctioned him off to the highest bidder? I've heard about the dark web. I imagine that's the sort of thing that goes on there.

But he could have been selling him for anything. Forced servitude. Maybe even for his organs. His kidneys or his liver. His heart. Or even worse, for sexual exploitation.

Nausea blooms in my empty stomach. If I ever see Ronan again, I'll kill him.

I squeeze my eyes shut and cast my mind back to that first night in Turkey, when I slept like the dead. For almost twice as long as I'd normally sleep. And even when I woke up, I was groggy. I put it down to having too much sleep, but is it possible Ronan drugged me? I'd only had a couple of glasses of wine, and although I was tired, it wouldn't account for me sleeping for twelve hours.

Unless Ronan slipped something into my wine. That would explain why I slept through and didn't wake when he was smuggling Jacob out of the house. Because that's when he must have done it. In the middle of the night, when I was virtually unconscious.

I stare at the photo on my phone, unable to drag my eyes away from it, trying to imagine the young man Jacob's become. What he must have gone through. He looks happy, although through the awkward teenage smile it's hard to be a hundred per cent sure. He's not dead at least. But it doesn't mean he's not been abused.

My poor, poor baby. What has happened to you?

I've no idea how to reach Ronan. Since the divorce, we've not kept in touch. I deleted his number and I doubt whether he's kept the same email address. He was adamant he'd never use social media, so I can't stalk him there. I don't even know where he works. He'd set up a fire safety consultancy, but if he ever told me the name of the company, I've completely forgotten it. I don't even know whether he kept the house in Norfolk. I have absolutely no idea how to get hold of him, and no way of finding Jacob.

He's probably not called Jacob anymore. I bet they've given him a new name. A new identity. Everything from his past life erased. I don't even know if he's in the same country. For all I know he could be in France or Spain or even America.

Where do I start? What do I do?

It's torture. I almost wish I'd never received that email, that I was left in blissful ignorance. Almost.

It was bad enough when I thought Jacob had been abducted, but if anything, this is worse. Knowing Jacob is alive and not having the first clue where to find him is driving me crazy.

All around me, the walls of my tiny flat start to close in. The air feels stuffy. I can't breathe. I can't think. I need to clear my head. If I stay here, I'll end up tearing my hair out.

I slip on my shoes, grab a jacket and head out.

The warm air of a balmy summer's evening offers little relief. But it's good to walk. To get the blood pumping. Thoughts and emotions swirl around and around my head, all the streets and houses and gardens passing me in a fog of shapes and colours.

I don't know where I'm going or what I'm doing, but before I know it, I arrive at Freida's door. It's late but I need to talk to someone. Anyone. And Freida's the best friend I have.

I raise my hand, lift the knocker and tap lightly three times. Freida will know what to do.

# Chapter 25

'Karina, what on earth's wrong?'

Freida's smile falls when she sees I'm crying. She wraps me up in a motherly hug and pulls me inside. I bury my head gratefully into her shoulder and black lustrous hair that smells comfortingly of coconut.

'I'm sorry, I had nowhere else to go,' I mumble through my tears.

'Come on through. We need wine.' I follow her down the hall and into her modern, open-plan kitchen diner where we've spent hours chatting and laughing in the past. Although I have nothing to laugh about tonight.

Her teenage daughter is sitting at the table, hunched over a laptop, one knee pulled up to her chest, papers and pens spread out in a mess. A quick glance confirms she's not doing homework but watching videos on YouTube.

'Prisha, can you finish that up in your room, please,' Freida asks, pointing me to a chair.

When she doesn't respond, Freida waves a hand in front of her daughter's face. Prisha looks up and removes an earbud. 'What?' she grumbles.

'Can you take that up to your room?'

I can see Prisha's about to protest, maybe even throw a teenage tantrum, until she sees me. I raise a hand and wave meekly.

'Oh, hi, Karina,' she says. 'How are you?' Such a polite young girl. Well adjusted. She's about the same age as Jacob must be now. I wonder if he's anything like her.

'Fine,' I lie. 'Just needed a chat with your mum.'

'Wine o'clock, is it?' Prisha laughs and I force myself to smile as she gathers up her papers and flips the laptop closed.

'Don't be so cheeky,' her mother scolds jokingly, chasing her out of the room with a pat on her backside.

I envy their relationship. Prisha's a bright, sociable, beautiful young woman. Freida treats her more like a friend than a daughter. They're always going shopping together and the frank conversations Freida tells me she has with her make me blush.

It hasn't always been like that but Freida says they've grown closer since Prisha's father walked out. I can't decide whether it's healthy or not. Whether the mother-daughter boundaries ought to be more clearly defined. But who am I to judge?

Freida grabs two glasses from a cupboard and pours healthy measures of white wine from a bottle already open in the fridge.

She sits opposite me on the other side of the table, both of us taking up our usual positions. 'Are you going to tell me what you're so upset about or am I going to have to drag it out of you?' she says, handing me a glass and pushing a box of tissues closer.

Where do I start? I've never told Freida about Jacob. She's still my boss and I didn't want her thinking I was crazy. She doesn't even know about the anti-psychotics I've been taking for the best part of ten years. I've always worried she might sack me if she found out, not least because I've lied to her for all this time.

I run my fingers around the stem of my glass, watching a pebble-dash of condensation forming around the bowl. 'There's something I've not told you.'

Freida's eyebrow shoots up.

'I have a son. His name's Jacob. He's about the same age as Prisha.'

'Okay,' Freida says, eyes narrowing. 'Any reason why you didn't mention this before?'

'Yes.' I take a deep breath and glance at the ceiling. 'This is going to sound absurd, but it's because for the last ten years I was convinced he existed only in my mind.'

Freida stares at me blankly for a second or two. Then she blinks. 'What?' She laughs nervously. 'I don't understand.'

I poke my tongue into my cheek and my hand trembles. 'Ten years ago, when he was only four, I took him to Turkey with my then-husband, Ronan. It was our first foreign holiday as a family. But on our second day, Jacob vanished. I woke up and he wasn't in his bed. He wasn't anywhere.'

Freida puts a hand to her mouth. 'Oh my god.'

'But that's not the weird bit. When I told Ronan, he flat denied we had a son. He made me think Jacob was a fantasy and that I was losing my mind.'

'Why would he do that?'

I shrug. 'I wish I knew. He even convinced me to see a psychiatrist when we came home.' I don't tell her I'm still seeing her. That can wait. 'For the last ten years I've thought I was crazy.'

Freida's mouth hangs open. It's a lot to take in. 'You should have told me.'

'I know. I'm sorry. I lied to you.'

'No, no, that's not what I meant.' She reaches for my hand. 'I meant you shouldn't have kept this all to yourself. You poor thing, going through all that on your own.'

'I was worried you'd think I was totally insane.'

'I don't think you're insane,' she says, squeezing my hand tightly. 'I think you're brave for dealing with this on your own for so long.'

I wish now I'd told Freida before. I should have trusted her.

Freida bites her lip, her gaze fixed on me. 'But why are you telling me this now? Something's happened, hasn't it?'

'Yesterday was the tenth anniversary of Jacob's disappearance, and this evening I received an anonymous email.' I fish in my bag for my mobile, find the first message from *The Girl with Regrets* and nudge the phone across the table. I allow Freida a few moments to read the email and digest it all. 'Jacob's alive,' I whisper. 'It was all a lie.'

Freida shakes her head, confusion written across her face. 'Who's this from?'

'I don't know, but hardly anyone knows what happened. It's not the sort of thing I've gone around broadcasting. At first, I thought it was someone messing with me, trying to drag it all up again, but then they sent this.'

I take the phone back and find the photo of Jacob.

'Is that...?'

'I think so. It looks like him. He has the same eyes and shape of nose, although he's obviously grown up a lot in ten years.'

Freida takes a large gulp of wine. I can almost see the cogs in her head whirring. If this wasn't my life, I'm not sure I'd believe it either.

'I still don't understand,' she says. 'What happened to him?'

'I have absolutely no idea.'

Freida rocks back in her chair, eyes narrowed. 'But it had something to do with your ex-husband, you think?'

I shrug. 'I guess. I can't think of any other explanation, can you?'

'Were you having marriage difficulties?'

'No, nothing like that. We broke up later because of the pressure it put on us.'

'So what, then?'

'I've been running it around and around my head and there's only one conclusion I keep reaching, that he must have trafficked Jacob.'

Freida's eyes widen. 'Seriously?'

'How else can you explain it? I think he sold Jacob and that's why he took us to Turkey.'

'Who the hell sells their own son, for pity's sake?'

'Ronan wasn't Jacob's real dad. He was his stepfather, but he always treated Jacob as his own. That's why I find it so hard to believe.'

'And this email.' Freida points at my phone. 'Who's that from? And why get in contact now?'

'I wish I knew.'

'Oh, honey, I can't imagine what you're going through right now. I mean, if Prisha had vanished when she was small, I don't know how I would have coped.'

'A lot of drugs, mainly.'

Freida laughs, but I'm deadly serious. I think about those sedatives Ronan gave me in Turkey and continued to feed me when we'd returned home until I'd seen a psychiatrist and was put on different medication.

It all makes sense now. He wasn't trying to help me, he was trying to subdue me and convince me to believe the lies he told me about Jacob. That he was born from the grief after my miscarriage. God, was that even true? I've never had any recollection of losing a baby, but I let Ronan put the lie into my head and over time, like all the lies about Jacob, I believed it.

What a naive idiot I've been.

'What are you going to do?' Freida asks, heading for the fridge. She grabs the bottle to top up our glasses.

'I don't know.'

'Have you called the police?'

'No. They wouldn't believe me.'

'Of course they would.'

I shake my head, remembering my last experience with the police at the airport in Turkey. They didn't believe me then and I have no reason to think they'll believe me now. The threat of being sectioned and carted off to some grim mental health hospital still weighs heavily at the back of my mind.

'I don't have any proof of anything, other than a vague, anonymous email. What if they think I really am crazy?'

Especially if they discover I've been seeing a psychiatrist for years?

'What about Jacob's birth certificate?'

I blink slowly, too embarrassed to admit I've never thought of looking for it. But why would I? I didn't think he was real. 'I - I don't know where it is. I expect Ronan destroyed it.'

'It'll be online,' Freida says, as if it's the most obvious thing in the world.

'Will it?'

'Of course it will.' She jumps up and picks up a laptop from the floor where it's plugged in, charging. She brings it to the table, flips it open and begins to search the internet.

Within a few moments, we're staring at a government website. She registers an account in my name, clicks on a link to order a birth certificate and together we fill in Jacob's details. His name, date of birth, my maiden name and where the birth was registered, and in the click of a button it comes up. Jacob's birth certificate. Finally, clear and indisputable proof he *does* exist.

I mentally kick myself. Why didn't I think of that before?

'You can even order a physical copy, if you want,' Freida says. 'It doesn't cost much.'

'Maybe later,' I say in a daze.

'Okay, so now we know this photo of Jacob is genuine—'

'But we don't. It could have been Photo-shopped or generated by AI.'

Freida screws up her nose. 'I think that's un-likely, isn't it? Why would anyone go to the trouble?'

'I don't know.' I throw up my hands. 'Until a few hours ago, I still thought I'd imagined my own son and now I'm having to come to terms with the fact that I willingly took him abroad to be sold to the highest bidder, for all I know. How could I have been so foolish? How could I have abandoned him like that?'

Freida puts an arm around my shoulder and pulls my head onto her chest. 'You were manip-ulated,' she says. 'Tricked. You can't beat your-self up about it. You need to look forwards, not back. You need to work out what you're going to do to get your son back.'

'But what can I do? Other than that photo, I have no idea how to find him.'

'I reckon we start with Ronan and find out what he knows,' she says.

'I don't know how to contact him. I deleted his number from my phone years ago.'

'Do you know where he lives?'

'No idea. The last address I had for him was the house we shared in Norfolk.'

'Right,' Freida says, a calm determination in her tone. 'Let's see if he's still there. I think it's time we had a chat with him, don't you?'

# Chapter 26

Freida offers to drive and the next morning picks me up from my flat early. I've not slept a wink, nervous about confronting Ronan, my mind in turmoil, trying to piece together how and why my son was taken from me all those years ago. What if Ronan denies everything? Tells me he had nothing to do with it? What then?

'Right, I've postponed the three shoots we had organised for today and rearranged them for a couple of weeks' time. Everything else will have to wait,' Freida says as I clamber into her sporty, two-tone Mini. 'It's all sorted.'

'I'm so sorry. I totally forgot about the shoots. You shouldn't have to—'

She holds up a hand. 'This is important. Closing the studio for a day won't kill us.'

'Thank you.'

'You ready to confront your ex?'

'Not really. I couldn't sleep last night and I'm too nervous to eat.'

'We'll grab a coffee and a pastry on the road,' Freida says, patting my knee. 'Don't you worry. I'm with you every step. We're going to find Jacob and put everything right.'

I wish I shared her confidence, but if we can't find Ronan, we have no chance of locating Jacob. I'm glad Freida's coming though. I'm not sure I have the strength to do it alone.

Traffic's slow getting out of London and even when we hit the motorway, it moves at a snail's pace. Everyone seems to be going in the same direction. It does nothing to ease my nerves. My stomach's turning in on itself as I rehearse in my mind what I'm going to say to Ronan.

'Whatever you do, don't lose your temper with him,' Freida advises as we finally pick up speed and start making progress along the M11. 'He's bound to be defensive, but we're here to find Jacob, not to confront Ronan about how he treated you, okay? That can come later.'

I spent half of last night tangled up in my sweaty sheets imagining what I'd do to my ex-husband when I lay eyes on him. He destroyed my life. Convinced me I was out of my mind. And worst of all, he stole my son from right under my nose. I'd like nothing more than for him to suffer a slow, agonising death.

But Freida's right. My priority has to be finding Jacob.

My stomach winds itself up tighter and tighter the closer we get to our old house. Everything starts to look familiar, but feels different. New housing developments have popped up. The road layout has changed. New roundabouts and traffic lights. But when we finally arrive at the cottage, it looks exactly the same as it always did, except maybe with an even more pronounced look of neglect and desolation.

The whitewashed walls are grimy and the paint peeling, the roof tiles dark and tarnished. There's no car parked outside and all the windows are closed, despite it being a warm July day. It doesn't look good and I'm worried I've dragged Freida all this way for nothing.

'You weren't kidding, it really is in the back of beyond,' she says, glancing up at the house through the windscreen. 'Nice spot though.'

For a while, it was idyllic. Jacob loved being so close to the beach with its beautiful, fine golden sand where he could fly his kite and build sandcastles to his heart's content. He had a big garden to play in. Grassy dunes to explore. Next to no traffic to worry about. It was isolated and gave us the feeling of being the only people in the world. And for a time, that brought me a great deal of happiness.

It's funny how quickly I've embraced the memories again. Accepted them for what they are. The truth. Not the lies I told myself. I used to have to check myself when they seeped into my mind, reminding myself none of it was real. A mental torture of a different kind. Ronan has a lot to answer for.

'Are you ready?' Freida asks, taking my hand and squeezing it. She smiles and again I'm reminded how lucky I am to have her with me.

I throw open the car door and my senses are immediately assaulted with the familiar smell of brine and the earthiness of samphire and sea lavender. The sound of waves rushing onto the shore and the screech of gulls. The graze of the warm, salty breeze on my skin.

Although the house is tainted with bad memories, of days shut in my room trying to come to terms with what I thought was the disintegration of my mind, it still holds many happy recollections. An image of Jacob surfaces, chubby pale arms and legs poking out of his T-shirt and shorts, tottering down the garden path towards the gate that spilled out between the dunes.

I push it away. It's still painful, especially as there are so many memories stolen from me that I never had the opportunity to experience, and never will. Jacob's first day at school. Learning to ride a bike. Parents' evenings and school plays. Birthdays, Christmases and holidays together.

Freida locks the car and pulls me towards the house. 'I'm right here,' she whispers. 'Let's see if he's in.'

My legs are leaden as I swing open the squeaky gate and head towards the front door, which desperately needs a fresh lick of paint. It doesn't look as if the house has been touched in ten years.

I take a deep breath, remind myself why I'm here and knock. It echoes through the house almost as loudly as my heart is hammering in my chest.

Freida scoots through the overgrown garden and peers through a window.

I knock again.

An ominous silence follows.

The house is empty. Ronan's not here.

'I think he might have moved away,' Freida says, her hands cupped around her eyes as she stares inside. 'It's empty. Stripped out.'

My heart sinks. 'Really?'

'At least we know.'

Part of me is relieved. I was dreading confronting Ronan, even with Freida at my side. But it also means I'm no closer to finding Jacob.

So I guess that's it. A dead end. Jacob could be in Timbuktu for all I know, and if I can't find Ronan, my chances of locating him are next to zero.

'I'm sorry I made you come all this way for nothing,' I say, conscious of the work Freida's turned down today to help me.

'Don't be silly. We had to try,' she says generously. 'Fancy stretching your legs for half an hour before we head back?' She points towards the dunes and the sandy beach beyond.

'Why not?'

We pick our way through the dunes and tumble out on the white sand, arm in arm, like a pair of lovers. If there's one good thing to come out of the disaster of the last ten years, it's finding such a good friend.

'I can't believe what that bastard put you through. Imagine someone trying to make you think you were losing your mind,' Freida says as we kick off our shoes and amble along barefooted. 'It's unbelievably cruel.'

'That's an understatement.' I laugh bitterly. 'What would you think if you woke up one morning and Prisha was gone? All her clothes had vanished, along with all her belongings and any evidence she'd ever existed, and someone told you she was only ever a fantasy inside your head?'

Freida puffs out a mouthful of air and shakes her head. 'I can't even begin to imagine what it would be like.'

'You wouldn't believe it, would you?'

She glances at me. 'I don't think so, no.'

'But if you were told it often enough and all the evidence pointed to it, would you believe it then?'

'I don't know. I'm sorry, but I'm not sure anyone could talk me into believing Prisha didn't exist. I mean, how could they? I know what's real and what's not.'

'That's what I thought, but Ronan knew what he was doing. He must have been planning it for months.'

I tell her about my missing photos of Jacob and how he even managed to persuade the woman staying in a nearby villa to lie about him, denying she'd ever seen him.

'And then he plied me with sedatives strong enough to knock out a horse. I couldn't think straight and ended up in bed for the rest of the holiday, unable to do anything.'

'That's scary,' Freida says, but she thinks I was weak. She doesn't believe she would have been taken in, but she doesn't know what it was like. How could she?

'You think I'm a bad parent, don't you?'

'What? No, of course not,' she says.

'But I abandoned my son in a country thousands of miles away.'

'You didn't know what you were doing.'

'I should have been stronger and believed in my own convictions. I thought someone at the airport could help me prove Jacob had flown with us, but the police arrested me for kicking up a fuss. Instead of listening to what I was saying, they called Ronan,' I explain. 'So what do I do now?'

Freida stares ahead, thinking. 'There must be another way to find Jacob.'

'How?'

Freida strolls on, arm still locked in mine, eyes fixed ahead, strands of loose hair flapping in the breeze.

'That picture,' she says after a few moments. 'Where was it taken?'

'I've no idea. On a football field somewhere, but it could be anywhere. And the badge on Jacob's shirt has been blurred out.'

'Let me see.' We stop as the bright sunshine dulls momentarily behind a wispy cloud.

I find the email on my phone and show Freida again, clicking on the image so it fills the screen.

'Save it to your photos,' she says with a grin that makes me wonder what she's thinking.

I do as she asks, still not sure how this is going to help. 'Okay.'

'Now open it in the photo app.' Her grin grows wider.

The photo has dropped into the bottom of my pictures, alongside a series of images I took at the weekend in Highgate Wood as the sun was setting with a beautiful burnt-orange glow behind the trees.

Freida reaches across my chest and flicks the image of Jacob with her index finger, revealing a hidden treasure trove of information.

'Oh my god, the metadata,' I squeal. 'I didn't even think to look.'

My hand's trembling so much, I can hardly read the details. It tells me the date the picture was taken - only a few months ago - and that it was taken on an iPhone 14. It even tells me the aperture and shutter speed. Not that I care a jot about that.

What I'm far more interested in is the map, which reveals exactly where the photo was taken. I tap on it and zoom in.

We both gasp and stare at each other open-mouthed.

'He's in London,' Freida says.

# Chapter 27

There are nearly ten million people living in London. Locating Jacob among them would be like hunting for a grain of sand on a beach. Next to impossible. Except the metadata on the photo I was sent pinpoints the precise location, within a few metres, of where it was taken. Richmond, a leafy, affluent suburb in the west of the city. And even better than that, I can see it was taken in the grounds of a secondary school.

'What are the odds that's Jacob's school?' Freida says.

'It has to be, doesn't it?'

'Although, I suppose if he was representing his school, they could have been playing at an away match.'

'But it's a start. And we know when the photo was taken, so even if that's the case, it shouldn't be too difficult to work out which two schools were playing.'

It's amazing news. After the high of discovering Jacob was alive and then having my hopes of finding him crushed, this has restored my belief that I'm finally going to be reunited with him.

'Thank you,' I whisper, pulling Freida into a hug which seems to catch her by surprise. Her arms flail and eventually settle on my back as I nuzzle into her hair.

'We've not found him yet.'

'I know, but we will,' I say.


Freida drives fast, sounding her horn at anyone who gets in her way. I can tell she's as excited as I am.

'What are you going to do?' she asks, casting a sideways glance my way. 'You can't just march into the school and tell them you're his mother.'

I run my tongue over my bottom teeth as a lorry indicates to pull out in front of us. Freida accelerates, in no mood to give way.

'I don't know. I've not really thought about it.' I've been so caught up in the exhilaration of it all, I've not considered my next move.

'And you've got to think about Jacob. You don't know anything about his life for the past ten years. You don't even know if he remembers you. He was quite young when he vanished.'

'He was four,' I protest. He's not going to have forgotten about me. I'm his mother.

'Have you considered that he must have a new family now? How's he going to react when he finds out they've been lying to him? Everything he thought he knew, you're going to expose as a lie. I think you need to be careful. You're about to blow up his world.'

'But I'm his mother!'

'I know.' She rests a hand on my knee. 'But you have to think about Jacob and how this is going to affect him. You might both need some professional help.'

'But he belongs with me.'

'Yes, I agree,' Freida says. 'Just think carefully about the impact it's going to have before you go steamrollering in.'

'Steamrollering? Is that what you think I'm going to do?'

She glances briefly at me again. She doesn't know whether I'm being serious or not. My lips curl upwards. Of course, she's right. But I'm excited. Not only am I entirely sane and not delusional after all, but I'm finally going to find my little boy after all these years.

'Yeah,' Freida says with a nod, 'you do have the tendency to go steamrollering into things without thinking sometimes.'

'Is that right?'

'I'm your boss. I notice these things.'

We both laugh. I can be impetuous at times, but I'm not going to miss my chance to get my son back. I just need to think carefully about how I'm going to do it.

Freida has a good point, as much as I hate to admit it. I can't expect Jacob to welcome me back into his life with open arms as if nothing has happened. He might not even remember me. What if I've been written out of his life entirely? Whatever happens, my reappearance is going to have a psychological impact, and I don't want to do anything that causes him any more harm or trauma than he's already been through.

The more I think about it, the more convinced I am that Ronan must have sold him to a trafficking gang in Turkey, although why remains an utter mystery. If he was that desperate for money, why didn't he say anything? I never even had an inkling he had money worries. He knew I had a tidy sum in the bank from my divorce settlement. He could have asked for a loan. Or at least been honest with me and we'd have worked out a solution. Anything would have been better than this. I guess I never really knew Ronan, fooled like a teenage virgin by his good looks and charm.

It's a miracle Jacob's back in Britain, let alone living in London, of all places. He could have easily ended up in the hands of someone truly evil, with horrible, deviant intentions, anywhere in the world. But it looks, from the photograph at least, like he's well and that someone's adopted him as their own.

Part of me thinks they're victims in this mess too because I'm about to detonate a bomb under their lives and destroy everything. There's every chance they'll go to prison, because at some point I'm going to have to involve the police. Just not yet. I can't feel too sorry for them though. They must have known what they were getting into when they bought a child through the dark web, or wherever they found him.

Freida drops me off at my flat and I'm glad to get home, even though she's offered to let me stay at hers so I'm not on my own. I need the time alone to think. And to plan. I'm not going to steamroller in, like Freida thinks, but I am determined to find Jacob and tell him the truth. He deserves to know what happened, no matter how painful.

That evening, I go through my options, which are limited. All I know for sure is that a few months ago, Jacob was playing football at a school, which he might or might not attend, in Richmond. I have nothing else to work with. I have to start there. It's my best chance of finding him.

The next day, I hop on the Tube at Turnpike Lane and make the painfully slow journey to Richmond. Armed with a map on my phone, I walk the rest of the way. It's a forty-minute stroll but it's an interesting walk which takes me along the banks of the Thames and through several leafy green parks. The houses around here are amazing. Lots of lodges and mews houses, walled gardens and expensive extensions. Wide streets and wisteria-covered walls. It's so much nicer than where I live.

I arrive almost half an hour before the end of the school day. It gives me time to scout out the place and work out where the pupils are likely to emerge.

The main gates are opposite a row of shops and a small park, part of which is taken up by one of those adult play areas, with communal exercise machines. I don't see the point around here. I bet everyone's got private gym membership.

It's an obvious place to hang around, and from a bench in the park, I have a good view of the school. Of course, I don't know for sure whether Jacob is even a pupil here and if he is, whether he's in today. Whether he has an after-school activity or even if he's likely to come out through the main gates. All I can do is wait and watch.

As time ticks closer to half-three, my pulse quickens and my palms become sweaty. Will I even recognise him? Will he recognise me? Is he tall? Short? Will he be surrounded by a group of fun-loving friends or will he come out alone with his head in a book? There's so much I don't know about my own son.

I should have brought something to read. A newspaper or a paperback. Not that I have the bandwidth to read anything right now, but it must look a bit odd. A single woman sitting in a park opposite a school, watching. Not that anyone's paid any attention to me so far.

Eventually, students begin to appear with bags over their shoulders, chatting with friends. Some take their time as if they have nowhere to go. Others are heads down, motoring off as if time is their enemy.

The number of pupils swells until it becomes almost overwhelming to scan all their faces. It doesn't help that they're all wearing the same uniform. Blue blazers. Dark trousers or skirts. I stand for a better view and still they keep coming, pouring down the drive and spilling out onto the street, dispersing in all directions. Some jump on buses. Others run for cars parked on the verge.

It's hopeless. None of them looks like Jacob. I'm beginning to think I'm at the wrong school after all, but then there must be getting on for a thousand pupils. It's like hunting for a snowflake in a blizzard. I could easily have missed him. The boys in particular all look the same. They wear their hair in a similar style, close cropped at the back and sides, and in their uniforms they look like clones.

The swell reaches a critical mass but in less than five minutes, it subsides. Fewer and fewer pupils are emerging now. Just the stragglers. Among them a group of lean, tall boys. Six in total. Same haircuts. Same blue blazers. Two of them even have the same rucksack. Whatever happened to teenage rebellion?

And there, right in the middle of the cluster, with his floppy blonde locks and commanding the attention of the others who are hanging off his every word, is a boy who looks just like the boy in the photograph.

Jacob.

It's him. I'm sure of it. He's older, taller, more muscular, of course, but I'd recognise him anywhere. And if I had any doubts, they're instantly dispelled when I see the way he walks, slightly loping as if his left foot is fractionally heavier than his right and he keeps forgetting. He's always had a distinctive gait. Even after ten years, I'd recognise it. There's absolutely no mistaking it, the boy walking off down the road is my son.

Finally, after all this time, I've found Jacob.

# Chapter 28

I really wasn't sure I would find him. The chances were stacked against me. The odds too long. I came to the school on a whim, more in hope than in anticipation. But I've found him. My son. My Jacob. The boy I've thought for the last ten years was nothing more than a fantasy.

The shock of it, of finally seeing him in the flesh, stuns me momentarily into inaction. All I can do is watch and stare.

He looks happy and healthy, and he's obviously popular from the throng of friends surrounding him. It's more than I imagined in my wildest dreams.

But what am I supposed to do now?

He's already halfway down the street, moving away. Fading into the distance.

I hadn't thought this far ahead. I'd only come to look for him. To see him with my own eyes and to prove to myself that the email and photograph wasn't a cruel hoax. But now I've found him, I don't want to let him out of my sight. Perhaps, if I'm clever, I could engineer a chance meeting. Exchange a few words with him. Look for any recognition in his eyes. I'll have to hurry though. He's almost out of sight.

I dart across the street and follow from a safe distance. Not that I think there's any chance of Jacob or his friends noticing me. They're far too obsessed with themselves.

I'm desperate to tell Jacob the truth, but Freida's warning echoes around my head. He might not even realise I exist. Popping up and announcing myself as his long lost mother out of the blue might not be the best idea.

It's obvious what I should do. What any sane person would do. I ought to alert the police now I've found him. They'll know what to do. I should let them handle it.

But then what? It'll turn into a complete circus. Social services will have to be called. Psychiatrists. Child behaviourists, maybe. More professionals and experts than I think I could handle.

No, I'm going to do this my way, by myself. I won't rush it, but now I've found him, I'll work out a way of approaching him that doesn't completely freak him out. And only then, when we've spoken and I've explained the situation, I'll call the police.

Two of Jacob's friends peel away. Another disappears shortly afterwards, running across the road and down an alleyway. Jacob and the two boys who are left carry on until they reach a bus stop where they lean against the shelter, laughing and swearing. I'm no prude, but it's coarse language that makes me blush, especially because there are so many people who could overhear them. Mothers with young children. Pensioners. It's embarrassing. Whoever has brought him up should have clamped down on that.

I slow to a crawl, pretending to look at my phone. I glide past Jacob, barely a shoulder's width between us, my heart rabbit-kicking in my chest. He's so close, I could reach out and touch him. But I mustn't. Not yet. I snatch a quick glance, but he doesn't notice me. He's still engrossed in his friends. Typical teenage boy. Completely oblivious to the world around him.

There's a newsagent's up ahead. I could nip inside and wait until Jacob's bus comes. See where it's heading. Make an educated guess where he lives.

But then a big red double-decker pulls in, its brakes screeching. Jacob and his mates let two women on first and then follow them on board. Before I know what I'm doing and why, I hop on behind them and watch as they disappear up onto the top deck. The driver stares at me with bored detachment while I hunt for my debit card in my bag. I've no sooner paid for my ticket than he pulls off and I almost lose my balance.

There's a free seat on the ground floor next to an elderly man holding onto a walking stick. He smiles sweetly as I stumble down the aisle and sit, nodding a silent greeting.

Oh god, what am I doing? This is madness. I don't even know where we're going. But the desire to find out more about Jacob and his life, where he lives and where he's going, is over-whelming.

As the bus trundles on, accelerating between stops and pulling up suddenly at traffic lights, I occasionally bump shoulders with the old man. He smells of lavender soap, and tries to engage me in conversation.

'When I was a lad, that cinema was fields,' he says, pointing with a crooked finger.

I smile, but don't reply. I don't want to get into a conversation with him. I have far too much on my mind.

Stop after stop comes and goes, but Jacob and his mates show no sign of getting off. Eventually one of Jacob's friends disembarks outside a church. Two stops later, Jacob gets off.

The doors are already starting to close when I spring out of my seat to follow him.

He turns right, his attention on his phone. Head down. Earbuds in. Rucksack over one shoulder. He moves quickly, turning down a side street where there are cars parked on both sides of the road and the pavement is cracked and uneven. I follow from a discreet distance, but he doesn't turn around or glance over his shoulder. He has no idea I'm here.

Eventually, he turns into a smart street lined with plane trees top-heavy with green leaves. The houses here are bigger. More substantial. Set back from the road behind immaculate gardens. All of them stand detached, unlike in most parts of the city where long rows of terraces dominate. I couldn't even begin to put a figure on how much they must sell for. A million? Two? Prices in the capital have gone crazy over recent years and this is a particularly upmarket street. All the cars in the drives are Audis, Range Rovers and Porsches.

Jacob crosses the road without looking and I wince. With his headphones in, he wouldn't have heard if there was a car coming. Luckily, it's a quiet street.

He walks up to a beautiful house with pink roses in bloom in neatly tended round beds cut into a pristine lawn. There's a car in the drive and a woman leaning into the boot.

Jacob ignores her as he walks past, heading for the front door.

'Hey, Jacob,' she calls to him.

I slow my pace to a crawl, pretending to look for something in my handbag. At least they've not changed his name, which is something. Imagine if I had to break the news to him that his whole life, including his name, was a lie.

'What?' he grumbles.

'How was school?'

Jacob stops at the door and pulls out an ear-bud. 'Yeah, it was fine.'

I glance up from my bag and steal a proper look at the woman, using one of the trees for cover.

Is this the woman who stole my son? If it is, she's not what I expected at all. She's tall and elegant with honey-blonde hair that's cut in an expensive style and hangs just above her shoulders. She's wearing a striped blue and white top, matched with pristine white jeans. She looks moneyed. A lawyer or a hedge fund manager. Slim and toned, no doubt from hours in a gym with a personal trainer called Juan. I recognise her type. The sort of woman who makes running a family and holding down a successful career look like a walk in the park.

What was I expecting? Not this. She seems too respectable. Too ordinary to have been caught up in anything as grubby as child trafficking. What's her story? Maybe she couldn't have kids of her own, fertility treatment failed and she didn't want to run the gauntlet of the arcane adoption process.

'Would you give me a hand with these bags, love?' she asks, struggling with a bulging carrier bag from a posh supermarket.

Jacob rolls his eyes and groans. 'Mum! I've only just got home from school. I'm starving.'

*Mum?*

My knees turn to water. He actually called her 'Mum'. He might as well have taken a stake and driven it through my heart. She's not his mother. I am. Although with her blonde hair and blue eyes, they do look alike. I doubt anyone's ever raised an eyebrow or questioned that he's her biological son.

'Come on, it'll only take a second.'

Jacob's shoulders slump but he turns, shuffles to the car, takes two of the bags and heads into the house as two young children come charging out. They look nothing like Jacob. They have dark hair and olive-coloured skin. Cherubic faces.

'Amelia. Henry. Get inside now,' the woman chides.

I edge away, stepping into the road without looking, watching the scene of domestic normality playing out in horror. This isn't what I expected. It's so much worse.

I don't see the cyclist until she's virtually on top of me. I try to jump out of the way but she swerves in the same direction, brakes squealing. Her handlebars catch my hip and I'm sent flying as she tumbles to the ground. It all happens in a flash. Both of us screaming. Both of us falling. My elbow digging painfully into the ground. Her body sprawling across the road.

'I'm so sorry, I didn't see you,' I apologise as I drag myself gingerly to my feet. I've scraped my arm and bruised the top of my leg.

The cyclist pulls her bike up and dusts herself down. 'You stepped right out in front of me,' she says, adjusting her helmet, her eyes wide with shock.

'I know, I'm sorry. I wasn't looking. Are you okay?'

Poor woman. It wasn't her fault. At least she doesn't appear to be injured and her bike looks undamaged.

'I think so,' she says. 'Right, well, look before you step out next time. You'll end up getting yourself killed.' She remounts and cycles off.

I let out a long sigh and smooth down my hair.

'Oh my god, are you okay?'

The woman I was spying on only a few moments ago comes running from her drive, concern etched on her face.

'I'm fine, thanks,' I say, hobbling back onto the pavement.

'You're bleeding.' She points to my elbow.

'It's just a graze.' I angle my arm to assess the damage. She's right, there is a lot of blood, but it looks worse than it is.

'Let me wash it out for you. You might have some grit in it.'

'Honestly, I'm fine. Thanks.'

'At least let me find you a plaster.'

I want to tell her I don't want a plaster. I want to tell her to hand my son back and for him to stop calling her 'Mum'.

But instead, I allow her to shepherd me towards the house. Along the drive, past the rose beds and into her home. She's so gentle and caring, I can't bring myself to be rude to her.

'I don't want to cause any trouble,' I say.

'It's no trouble. Let's get you patched up.'

# Chapter 29

Inside, the house looks like something out of a magazine. It has high ceilings with original moulded cornices, stripped wooden floors and tasteful artwork on the walls.

The woman leads me through to an enormous kitchen which feels as if it's spilling out into the back garden through a set of bifold doors which are fully open, letting in the warm summer air. It's a massive garden, surrounded by a tall brick wall and planted with a display that wouldn't look out of place at the Chelsea Flower show. She must have a gardener. I can't imagine this woman toiling away in the mud, getting dirt under her immaculately painted fingernails.

'Take a seat,' she says, pointing to a large family dining table, on which there's a vase brimming with freshly cut roses.

I pull out a chair while she dives into a cupboard looking for a plaster. Blood drips from my elbow onto the floor, seeping into the wooden boards. I try to wipe it away with my foot but only manage to smear it and make it look worse.

'I'm afraid I've dripped blood on your lovely floor.'

'Oh, don't worry about that,' she says, waving a dismissive hand. 'It's seen worse.'

A loud thud comes from above. So forceful it makes the house shake. The woman rolls her eyes. Overly exuberant children?

'Honestly, it's enough to drive you to drink.' She laughs.

Isn't she going to check on them? One of them could have had an accident. Banged their head. Or broken an arm. But she doesn't seem to care.

She pulls out a chair and sits opposite me. I bend my arm and hold it up to the light. She dabs at it with a cold, wet cloth, dries my skin and applies a large, fabric plaster.

While she's focused on my arm, I take the opportunity to look around. My eye is caught by an American-style fridge covered in children's drawings and paintings and, in the centre, a laminated sheet marked with the days of the week and the children's names. Each child has a task, like washing up, emptying the dishwasher and taking out the rubbish, against their name and day of the week, alongside other notes such as piano practice, ballet, choir and football training. Under Jacob's name, there's a list of subjects. Maths, English, French, physics and history. A homework timetable? I'm glad to see it. At least this woman pretending to be my son's mother is taking steps to ensure he stays on track with his schoolwork.

'There,' the woman says. 'That should do the trick.'

'Thank you. I should get going.' I gather my bag from the table. As fascinated as I am to have this glimpse into Jacob's world and the life he now lives, I don't belong here. And I'm nervous that at any moment this woman is going to work out who I am and throw me out.

'Won't you stay for a cup of tea?' she asks, looking a little crestfallen. Maybe she doesn't have many friends, although I imagine someone like her is bound to have a large social circle. Girlfriends from Pilates and book club, the PTA and work. 'To be honest, I could do with the adult company. It's like kiddy daycare in here sometimes.'

'Really, I should be getting back.'

'Please?' She pouts like a child, making puppy-dog eyes at me.

'Well, I guess I could stay for five minutes,' I say, glancing at my watch.

'Great.' She hurries back into the kitchen and fills a trendy-looking kettle that glows an electric blue when she switches it on. While she waits for it to boil, she busies herself putting away the shopping Jacob helped carry in. 'I'm India, by the way.'

'Karina.' My name's out of my mouth before I can stop it. Should I have lied? I'm not sure it's a great idea giving away who I am. Although, it's only a name. It's not as if it's going to mean anything to her.

'It's very nice to meet you, Karina, although I'm sorry about the circumstances.'

'What?' My face flushes.

She points to my elbow. 'The accident. Hopefully there's no lasting damage.'

'No, hopefully not.' I stretch my shoulder, which is starting to seize up, and breathe out a sigh of relief. For a moment, I thought she was onto me. I need to relax. Try to act normally, whatever normal is when you've found yourself face to face with the woman who's stolen your son.

India pours hot water into a teapot with three teabags. It seems such a quaint, old-fashioned way of making tea. I usually just shove a bag in a mug.

'Biscuit?' she asks, bringing the pot to the table.

'I'm fine, thank you.'

A thud of feet thunders down the stairs. The two young children I saw earlier come bowling into the room. The boy looks slightly older than the girl, but not by much. Eighteen months? Two years, maybe? How anyone could have babies so close together baffles me. Coping with one was bad enough.

'Can *I* have a biscuit?' the boy asks, sidling up to his mother and leaning against her. She kisses his head and wraps an arm affectionately around his shoulders.

'No, it'll be tea soon. You can have one afterwards, if you're still hungry.'

'Can *I* have a biscuit?' the little girl asks.

'No, darling. You can have one after tea as well,' India says.

I shoot her a thin-lipped smile of sympathy as I sip my tea.

'Pleeeeaaaaase, Mum,' the boy whines. 'I promise I'll eat my tea.'

'I will as well,' the girl chimes in.

At first, India holds firm, but when they continue to badger her, she gives in too easily. 'Alright, alright.' She throws up her hands in defeat. 'One biscuit, but if you waste your tea, I'll be very cross.'

I frown. Any parent knows you have to stay consistent or they'll run rings around you. It's in all the parenting books.

'Anything for an easy life,' India says, raising her eyebrows at me.

I don't approve. Children need boundaries, or they're never going to learn.

India produces a packet of biscuits from a cupboard above the kettle and hands one to each of the children. They run off in triumph.

Children one. Mother nil.

'Do you live around here?' India asks when peace is restored.

'No, I'm over in north London. Muswell Hill.'

'Oh, we have friends out that way. Not that we've seen them for ages. Do you have children?'

'Me?' I put my mug to my lips. 'No,' I lie and immediately regret it. I've spent the last ten years denying Jacob's existence and now I'm doing it again. What kind of mother am I?

'It's not for everyone.'

'How many do you have?' I ask lightly, trying to sound as if I'm asking in all innocence.

'Well, there's Jacob who's fourteen, going on twenty-four.' She laughs. 'Henry who's eight and Amelia's six.'

'That's quite a big age difference.'

She slants her head. 'Is it?'

'I don't know. I suppose not.' I brush off an imaginary speck of dirt from my thigh. If I was hoping she was going to crack and tell me all about how she and her husband thought they couldn't have children and were lucky to adopt a four-year-old little boy from an illegal Turkish trafficking gang when they'd given up all hope, I'm sadly disappointed.

Maybe I should just confront her. What's to stop me telling her exactly who I am? I could find that copy of Jacob's birth certificate on my phone, hold it up to her nose and ask her what she thinks she's playing at. I could order her to pack a bag with Jacob's clothes and tell her he's coming with me, and that she should expect a visit from the police.

But I don't.

Instead, I sit awkwardly, looking around the room wondering what the hell I'm doing here.

'You have a lovely house,' I mumble, desperate for something to say.

'It's hideously expensive around here, but it's such a nice area to bring up children.'

I bet Jacob has his own room. It's probably bigger than my flat. And a double bed. They probably spoil him rotten. That's the thing about people with money. Most of them don't appreciate the value of it and then they end up bringing up over-privileged kids. I suspect if Jacob wants something, he gets it. Fancy phones. An iPad. An Xbox. Trainers for every day of the week. It's not good for him. He needs to learn to understand the value of money.

I'm not exactly broke, but on my wages, working with Freida, I can't afford any of those things. That doesn't mean he wouldn't be better off with me. I'm his real mother. This - I glance around at all the fancy fittings and fixtures - is all fake. It's not his real life. But I can't just march in here and drag him away. He needs time to come to terms with the lie he's living.

'Mum, when's tea?'

Jacob walks into the room, his looming presence catching me by surprise. He's changed out of his school uniform into shorts and a T-shirt, his phone clasped in one hand and an earbud in one ear. He strides into the kitchen and throws open the cupboards one by one, looking for food.

I swallow hard and half hide my face behind my cup, my pulse racing.

'Not for another hour,' India says.

'I'm starving.'

'Have an apple.'

'I don't want an apple.' He reaches into one of the cupboards and pulls out a bag of crisps.

As he closes the door, he glances at me, noticing for the first time there's a stranger in the house. Our eyes lock. A hard lump forms in my throat.

'This is Karina,' India says. 'And this is my eldest son, Jacob.'

*My son?*

I could rip her tongue out with my bare hands.

'Hiya,' he says. His eyes narrow a fraction as he stares at me.

'Hello, Jacob.'

He keeps staring, reading my face. He remembers me! I'm sure he does. I can see it in the narrowing of his eyes. The slight tilt of his head.

'Do I know you?' he asks. 'Are you like a teacher or something?'

Shit.

I laugh. 'I don't think so. I just have one of those faces.'

'Oh,' he says, but he's still looking. Can't drag his gaze away.

The urge to jump up, run across the room and hug him is overwhelming. I want to smother him in kisses and never let him go. Tell him that he's safe now and I'm never ever going to let anything bad happen to him again.

I look away as my eyes begin to water. I can't cry. Not here, in front of them both. Whatever would they think?

But he won't stop looking at me.

A heat rises from my chest to my neck and even though the bifold doors are wide open, it feels as though all the air has been sucked out of the room.

I slam my mug down on the table and snatch up my bag. I have to get out of here. It was a mistake. I should never have followed Jacob. Should never have been persuaded to come into the house.

'I'm sorry, I have to go,' I mumble, jumping up.

India frowns. 'Karina? Are you okay?'

'Thank you for the tea. It was nice to meet you, Jacob.'

I race to the door without a backwards glance, let myself out, and run.

# Chapter 30

It takes me ages to find my way back to the Tube station as I wander absentmindedly through a rabbit warren of residential streets that all look the same. My mind's not focused on where I'm going. All I can think about is Jacob. I never expected to get so close to him so soon. Until this afternoon, I wasn't even sure I was going to find him, let alone end up speaking to him. If it hadn't been for that photograph I was sent, I doubt I ever would have done.

I've still no idea who sent it. Someone who knows the truth, obviously. Someone who must know India, so maybe someone she's confided in. But how did they know about me, let alone track down my email address? Not that it matters. All that matters now is that Jacob is safe and well and he's back in my life.

In fact, he's really well. He's grown into a good-looking boy. And popular too. It could have been so much worse. He could have ended up anywhere. Abused. Neglected. Malnourished. He could have ended up dead.

He has so much more than I could give him. Materially, at least. The house is incredible. And actually, as much as I wanted to hate India,

I liked her. She was caring and friendly. Not at all snooty like I expected when I first saw her in her fancy clothes and that expensive haircut. She didn't have to take me under her wing when I hurt my arm or invite me into the house and offer me tea. And she clearly loves Jacob and has done a decent job bringing him up. It would be so much easier if she was an old dragon.

Maybe it's better if I walked away and left them to it. Jacob's clearly happy. He doesn't want for anything and has supportive adoptive parents. Although India didn't mention her husband, I assume there is one. She was wearing a wedding ring. A plain platinum band, and an impressive diamond solitaire with a rock the size of the nail on my little finger. Not dissimilar to the ring Sammy bought me all those years ago. I never liked it. It cost him a small fortune but made me feel conspicuous. I was always paranoid I was going to lose it or someone was going to try to steal it off my finger.

No, Jacob has a right to know the truth. He needs to know what happened, that his stepfather stole him from me and sold him to a trafficking gang. He has the right to know his own mother, no matter how difficult that's going to be for him to comprehend.

Now I've spoken to him, albeit briefly, I want more. I desperately want to get to know him better. To find out what's going on inside his head. And then I can work out the best way of breaking the truth to him.

So, after another sleepless night, I'm up early the next day and back on the Tube with the first commuters. I know where I'm going this time and head directly for the house in Richmond.

By seven, I'm outside loitering behind one of the spectacular plane trees that line the wide street. God knows what the neighbours must think, but I really don't care. I'm not doing anything wrong and nobody challenges me.

An hour has passed, and my back is starting to ache, when Jacob finally emerges from the house. He slams the door behind him and slides past two cars in the drive. India's Audi and another vehicle, a smart-looking black Porsche with an unusual number plate. **SMT 1.** God, I hate people who have personalised plates. Especially when they drive Porsches.

Jacob has a slice of toast in his mouth and his blazer hangs off one shoulder. He adjusts it as he walks, leaving his collar turned up and his tie hanging limply halfway down his chest. I duck behind the tree as he approaches and hold my breath, hoping he won't spot me lurking. Now he's seen me in the house, he's bound to recognise me if he sees me again.

I count to ten and step out from where I'm hidden. Jacob's about twenty metres ahead. Hopefully far enough away that even if he does turn around, he won't see me. And anyway, he seems completely absorbed in his phone and barely even glances up as he walks.

When he reaches the bus stop, there are two younger children already waiting. They're not from Jacob's school. They're wearing different uniforms. Different coloured blazers and ties. It's clear there's some kind of altercation going on between them. One of the kids, an overweight, round-faced boy is pushing and shoving the other, a bespectacled, academic-looking, skinny boy, whose uniform looks two sizes too big for him. The overweight kid is taunting him with names. Yanking at his bag, pulling it off his shoulder.

Jacob finally looks up from his phone.

'Hey,' he says, with an authority that surprises me. 'Leave him alone.'

My heart swells with pride.

The two younger boys freeze and stare at Jacob with wide-eyed wonder.

'Give him his bag back,' he tells the bully.

The kid, realising it's not an adult laying down the law but a teenager who's not even shaving yet, is emboldened. 'Oh yeah, and who's going to make me?'

Jacob pulls himself up to his full height and takes a step forward, eyes wide and his expression locked in determination. 'I said give him his bag back, you little prick.'

He looms over the boy, emphasising the point that they're no match physically.

'Alright, I was only having a bit of fun.'

The bully lets the bag go, throwing up his hands in surrender. The skinny kid clasps it possessively to his chest.

'Now, I don't want to see you throwing your weight around again,' Jacob warns as a bus rumbles to a halt at the stop.

The overweight kid picks up his own bag, hops on board and yells over his shoulder, 'Arsehole.'

Jacob doesn't rise to it.

'You okay?' he asks the skinny lad.

He nods nervously.

'You getting on this bus?'

The boy shakes his head. 'Think I'll wait for the next one.'

'Good idea.'

And then, as the bus rumbles off, Jacob returns to his phone as if nothing has happened.

I could hug him. I don't know how many other teenagers his age would have stepped in like that. I wonder if that's something ingrained from birth or whether it's learned? I like to think it's an attribute he was born with.

Another bus comes along a few minutes later. I can see a number of students from Jacob's school already on board. I hang back while he jumps on, shows his pass and heads for the top deck. Then I leap on and take a seat downstairs at the back.

This time, I know exactly where Jacob will be getting off, so I don't stress. Instead, I enjoy the journey, watching all the shops, houses and parks drifting past the window. It's much leafier than where I live, but I don't know if I'd want a house here. It's like an overgrown village, rather than living in the city with all its hustle and bustle.

It was a shock being reunited with Jacob yesterday, seeing how my little boy has grown up, hearing how his voice has deepened, his face changed. I never intended to speak to him. At least not so soon. I certainly never intended to speak to the woman he calls 'Mum' or find myself inside their house. Things moved much more quickly than I ever imagined, and I wasn't prepared.

Maybe I should have said something. Instead, I sat at their kitchen table like a fool, pretending to be a stranger. I know it's going to be a shock for Jacob, and that it's going to take time for him to come to terms with what I have to tell him, but he needs to know. He has a right to know. And the longer I leave it, the harder it's going to be. I can't put it off forever, although there's going to be no easy way of saying it. Like removing a plaster, it's going to be kinder to rip it off in one go than drag it out, hoping to lessen the pain.

At least thirty pupils in blue blazers, including Jacob, pile off the bus a short walk from his school. I wait for them all to disembark before hopping off at the last minute and following them.

Jacob's only a few metres ahead with some of his friends. Larking about. Playing the fool. Any second now and they'll be inside the school grounds and I'll have lost him.

I push and jostle through a crowd of girls and boys until Jacob's within reach. As he makes it to the gates, I stretch out my hand. Tap him on the shoulder.

'Jacob?'

He turns around with a puzzled expression on his face. His friends all come to a halt, curious. Half a dozen expectant eyes fall on me.

'It's you,' he says, frowning. 'You're my mum's friend.'

*I am your mum,* I want to scream at him.

Instead, I laugh. 'I guess you could say that.'

'What do you want?'

I've been playing this scene through my head all night, the moment I finally reveal to my son that I'm his long lost mother and how he'll react. And now I'm here, face to face with Jacob, with his full attention, I don't have the words.

'You see, the thing is,' I mumble, glancing at my feet.

Jacob hooks his thumb over his shoulder. 'I've got registration at nine,' he says. 'I can't be late.'

'I know, but this is important.'

His mouth curls upwards in an embarrassed smile. Oh god, this is a mistake. I should have chosen somewhere quieter. Not in front of all his friends, outside the school. Too late now. I have to say something or it's going to look weird.

'Is it about Mum?'

'No, it's about you. About us. Oh god, sorry this is really difficult.'

'I really should be going.'

'Wait, one minute, please.'

He sighs, but his friends have thankfully lost interest. They wander off into the school grounds without him.

'I don't want to get detention.' He looks nervously towards the school.

'The thing is, Jacob, I'm not your mother's friend.' I take a breath through my nose and deep into my lungs. 'I *am* your mother.'

# Chapter 31

I don't know what I expected would happen, but if I thought Jacob would fall into my arms, sobbing with joy at being reunited with me, I'm sadly disappointed. It's not like that at all.

Rather than hug me, he physically recoils, as if I've wafted a terrible smell under his nose. I reach out for him but he backs away with pure horror written across his face.

'You were stolen from me when you were only little,' I explain. 'From Turkey. Your step-father, Ronan, organised it all, and I've been looking for you ever since.'

I deliberately edit out the part where Ronan set about convincing me I'd lost my mind and I'd believed him over my own son. He doesn't need to know I gave up on him.

He shakes his head, edging backwards. I might as well have told him he was raised by a pack of wolves.

'Get away from me,' he growls.

'Jacob, please, I know it's a lot to take in—'

'I said, leave me alone.'

'I've been looking for you for so long, please don't be mad with me.' I grab my phone out of my bag. 'Look, I can show you your birth certificate,' I offer, my hand trembling so much, I struggle to unlock the screen.

'I've got to go,' he says, turning and hurrying towards the school buildings.

'No, wait, listen to me, Jacob. I'm not lying. I'm your mother!'

He stops suddenly, his rucksack falling off his shoulder and hitting the ground. 'No,' he says. 'You're not. And I don't want anything to do with you, do you understand?'

Could this be going any worse?

'Just listen to me,' I beg.

'I said I don't want anything to do with you. You're crazy. Not right in the head.'

'Don't say that,' I gasp. For such a long time, I thought I was out of my mind, but I'm not. I never was. I was tricked. Manipulated and controlled by that bastard of a husband of mine.

'Why not? It's true. Dad's told me all about you, how you only cared about yourself and how you walked out on us when I was little because you didn't want me.' He's shouting now. Yelling at the top of his voice.

I glance around. Most of the students have moved inside but there are still a few milling around, together with some of the teachers. I can feel their eyes on me. Staring at me. Judging me. What kind of a parent do they think I am?

'That's not right. That's not what happened.'

'Isn't it?' Jacob strides up to me with real hurt in his eyes. He's shaking.

'Of course it's not. I would never have walked out on you. I don't know what you've been told but it's not true. I would never have abandoned you. I love you. You're my son. '

'Don't say that!' he screams.

'Just listen to me for a minute, Jacob.' I reach for his arm but he tears it away violently.

'Don't touch me.'

From the corner of my eye, I see a man striding towards us.

'Jacob,' he says, 'is everything okay?'

'No, this crazy woman is trying to claim she's my mother.'

The man looks at me suspiciously. 'Do you know her?' he asks.

'Not until yesterday.' He glares at me, daring me to contradict him.

I sigh. 'Look, it's complicated, but it's true. I am his mother, but his father's been telling him I walked out on him when he was young.'

'Jacob, you're going to be late for registration. Why don't you hurry along. I'll deal with this,' the man says.

Deal with it? He makes it sound as if I'm an awkward customer in a restaurant complaining about poor service.

'He's my son. I have every right to talk to him,' I yell at the man as Jacob slopes off.

'I think you'd better move on,' he says. 'You're causing a scene.'

'Of course I'm causing a scene. Until yesterday, I hadn't seen my son in ten years. They stole him from me and sold him to child traffickers.'

He raises an eyebrow. 'Please, I'm asking nicely.'

'I know it sounds unlikely, but I'm telling the truth. I just need to speak to Jacob. He has a right to know.'

'And our students have a right to study in a safe environment,' he says.

God, he really is a pompous little twerp.

'So you're going to stop a mother seeing her son, are you? Don't you have any compassion?'

He puts a hand on my back and tries to turn me away, towards the gate. Pushing me out onto the street.

'Don't you dare touch me!'

'I don't want to have to call the police, Mrs...'

'It's Miss, actually. Miss McHugh.' I've taken to using my maiden name since Ronan and I split up.

'Miss McHugh, if you continue to cause a scene, I will have no option but to call the police.'

'The police?' I laugh sarcastically. 'You'd seriously call the police because I want to talk to my son. That's an offence, is it?'

'It's an offence to breach the peace,' he says coolly.

'Oh, fuck off.'

'Everything okay, Mr Tibbs?' Another man's approaching now. He's in a smart grey suit and has a fake Hollywood smile, his teeth unnaturally white. And his hair's far too perfectly combed to be a teacher.

'I was explaining to this woman that if she doesn't leave the school grounds, I'll have to call the police.'

'Oh?' The second man raises a quizzical eyebrow. 'What seems to be the problem?'

'It's Jacob, in Year 10—'

'That's my son. I want to see him.'

'Ah, okay,' the second man says. 'Why don't you leave this with me, Mr Tibbs. I'm sure your class will be wondering where you are.'

'If you're sure?'

'I'll handle it from here. Thank you.'

At last, someone reasonable. Someone who's going to take me seriously.

'I'm not here to cause trouble,' I explain, 'but I need to see Jacob. It's really important. It's going to sound unbelievable, but he's my son and he was stolen from me when he was only four.'

'Why don't you come to my office and we can discuss it over a cup of coffee,' he says with a disarming smile.

# Chapter 32

The man who's invited me into the school to chat about Jacob isn't just another teacher. He's *the* teacher. The principal. His name's Henrikson, but says I can call him Peter. As if being on first name terms is going to make our conversation any easier.

'Coffee?' he asks as he invites me to take a seat in front of his leather-topped, antique desk made of beautifully polished wood. It dominates the room, looking completely incongruous in the modern surroundings of the school. And a bit pretentious, if I'm honest.

'I'm not here for coffee. I'm here for my son.'

'I understand,' he says. 'Now, I'll just be a moment and then we can discuss it.'

He leaves me sitting in his office while he slips out, closing the door behind him. An anxious thought occurs to me. Does he intend to keep me prisoner here while he calls the police? Is his charm and politeness a cover to keep me compliant until I'm no longer his problem? No, I don't think he will call them. And even if he does, he'll look pretty stupid when the truth comes out. They all will. I am Jacob's mother, and I have the certificate to prove it.

I tap on the arms of the chair while I wait, wondering what he's doing. Surely he's not making his own coffee. He must have a secretary or a PA who could do that for him.

An absolute age seems to pass before the door creaks open and Henrikson returns.

'Sorry about that,' he says, unbuttoning his jacket as he takes a seat and pulls himself up to the desk. He folds his hands and sits up straight. 'A couple of urgent issues I had to deal with. Now, shall we start from the beginning?'

I put three fingers to my forehead, rubbing away the tension, and sigh. I don't want to start from the beginning. I want to see Jacob. I *need* to see Jacob, but I suppose if I can get the principal onside, that would be a start.

'Don't ask me why, but it was my ex-husband's idea,' I say.

He frowns in puzzlement.

'To steal Jacob away from me.'

The lines on his forehead deepen, but he listens attentively, like you might listen politely to the crazy ramblings of a madman without having the first clue what they're talking about.

'I know how this sounds and you have no reason to believe a word I'm saying, but I think my ex-husband, Jacob's stepfather, abducted Jacob and sold him. I don't even know why. I guess he must have had money worries I didn't know about. But then after he took Jacob, he started gaslighting me, convincing me I was the crazy one for thinking I had a son. He tried to make me believe Jacob didn't exist.'

I can tell Henrikson doesn't believe a word of it. But I push on, hopeful I can persuade him

I'm not completely out of my mind and that he should take me seriously.

'Jacob was only four when he went missing. We were in Turkey, on holiday. I woke one morning and he was gone. I haven't seen him since. At least not until yesterday. I don't know who these people are who claim to be his parents, but they're not. They're frauds, and they've taken my son illegally.'

'Right,' Henrikson says, drawing out the word into one long syllable. 'And you have proof of this, do you?'

'Yes!' I hunt in my bag for my phone and find Jacob's birth certificate. 'Here, see.' I shove the phone across the desk.

Henrikson looks down his nose at it and nods. 'Okay,' he says.

'So you believe me?'

He pushes the phone back with the tips of his fingers.

'It's quite an allegation,' he says. 'I assume you've been in touch with the police?'

'Well, no, I haven't yet. I wanted to speak to Jacob first, which is what I was trying to do when your colleague rudely stuck his nose in.'

Henrikson offers me a tight smile. 'Mr Tibbs was only doing his job. We take pride in offering a safe environment for all our pupils.'

'I'm his mother!'

'So you keep saying.'

'I demand to see him.'

'We'll see. Obviously this is an extremely delicate situation and we need to consider what's in Jacob's best interests and prioritise his well-being.'

'What could be better for his wellbeing than speaking with his mother? You can't stop me seeing him, you know,' I hiss.

'We can if he expresses a wish not to see you.'

'Has he?'

'I don't know. I've not spoken with him yet, but he didn't seem keen on talking to you outside.' He leans across the desk and adopts an earnest expression. 'Can I be honest with you, Miss McHugh? This is a highly unusual situation. Certainly not something I've ever come across in my twenty years of teaching.'

'I can imagine.'

'So we need to take caution. Not that I don't believe you, but you understand I've never met you before. Nobody in the school has. You could be anybody.'

I reach for my purse. 'I can prove who I am,' I say, searching for some identification. 'If that's what you need.'

He holds up a hand. 'There's no need for that, but you can appreciate we can't just let anyone into the school and allow them access to the students, even if they do claim to be a parent.' He laughs as if the idea is totally ludicrous.

'I'm not claiming to be his parent. I *am* his parent.'

'Yes, you said.'

This is hopeless. We keep going around and around in circles.

'Maybe you're right, we should call the police. Let them sort this out,' I say.

There's a knock at the door and it clicks open behind me. Henrikson glances up.

'Mr Henrikson, he's here,' a woman says in a deferential tone.

'Thank you, Sarah. Please, show him in.'

Hang on, we're supposed to be in the middle of a meeting here.

I swivel around just in time to see the door fly open and Sammy, my ex-husband, march in.

What the hell is he doing here? He's the last person I expected to see. He looks much older, with a lot less hair, and chubbier, especially around the jowls and stomach.

He strides up to the desk with his hand outstretched and a brilliant white smile plastered across his face. His skin is dark, almost the colour of mahogany, like when he used to return from Iran after a protracted stay.

'Peter,' he says, shaking the principal's hand. He's immaculately dressed in a beautifully tailored suit. 'I came as soon as I could.'

I blink several times, my head swimming, struggling to make sense of what's going on.

'Karina,' he says, turning to me. 'How are you?'

I stare at him blankly. 'Wh - why are you here?'

He gives me a sympathetic smile. 'Mr Henrikson called me. I hear you've been making a bit of a fuss.'

'Yes - but - what...'

What is going on? The last time I spoke to Sammy, I was in a blind panic in Turkey, when Jacob first went missing. And he told me flat we didn't have children.

'You're looking well.' Sammy looks me up and down. He's wrong of course. I left the house in a dither this morning, having not slept properly for the last two nights. I have bags under my eyes and I haven't had the chance to brush my hair. I'm even wearing the same top I had on yesterday.

'I don't understand what's going on.' If I thought I was going mad before, this is on a whole different scale.

Sammy turns back to Henrikson. 'I'm so sorry you've been dragged into this,' he says, rolling his eyes as if I'm not in the room. 'She's not well.'

What? Not this again.

'Don't worry about it,' Henrikson says. 'I'm just glad you were able to get here so soon.'

Sammy nods his appreciation. 'Fortunately, I wasn't far away when you called. I don't suppose it would be possible to have five minutes alone to talk to my ex-wife, would it? Would you mind?'

Henrikson jumps up from his desk like someone's rammed a hot poker up his arse. 'Absolutely. Use my office. Take as much time as you need.'

'Thank you so much. I really appreciate it. I'm so sorry to put you out like this.' I've never heard Sammy so fawning. It's not his usual style. He must have mellowed in his old age.

'Not a problem.' Henrikson trots out. He looks like a man given a stay of execution. I'm not sure he was enjoying our conversation.

The moment the door shuts behind him, Sammy's obsequious smile drops.

'What the hell do you think you're playing at?' he yells at me.

# Chapter 33

It hadn't exactly been love at first sight when I met Sammy, but we definitely had a connection. A meeting of minds. We didn't stop talking from the moment we took our seats on that flight from Tehran until we were finally forced apart when we landed at Heathrow.

*Two nomadic souls thrown together by chance.*

Everything about him fascinated me. His brain. His culture. His enthusiasm for life. His determination that nothing would stand in the way of his dreams. When he set his mind to something, it was clear nothing could stop him.

He was the child of an Iranian mother and a British father and spent his life between London and Tehran, eventually establishing an import-export business specialising in an eclectic mix of antiques, dried fruits, and seeds, negotiating complex sets of trade restrictions and sanctions to develop the company into a multi-million pound enterprise.

It couldn't have been any more different from my life as a photographer. About the only thing we had in common was that we were always travelling for our jobs.

He had a car waiting to collect him from the airport and offered to drive me home, but it was miles out of his way and I was happy catching the Tube. As a compromise, I gave him my number, never in a million years thinking I'd hear from him again.

But he texted me that evening to make sure I'd made it home safely, and every night for the rest of the week. When he called, it was to ask me to join him for dinner. We went to an amazing sushi restaurant and picked up where we'd left off on the plane. He wanted to know everything about me and hung off every word that tripped off my lips.

When he kissed me at the end of the night, my stomach unexpectedly flipped and fizzed and I realised I was falling for him. It was the start of an intense and passionate affair. Whenever we were both in London, we'd spend all our time together, completely wrapped up in each other, blinkered to what was happening in the rest of the world.

Even then the strain started to show. He was back and forth to Iran all the time, and my job often took me abroad for weeks on end. It became more and more difficult to find time for each other.

Sammy thought the solution was for us to get married, but it didn't address the fundamental problem that we had incompatible lives.

He proposed a year to the day after we'd first met on that fated flight, dropping to one knee in the middle of a Michelin-starred Asian restaurant in Mayfair, a diamond ring that must have cost a bomb in his hand.

How could I refuse?

'There,' he said, sliding the solitaire onto my ring finger, 'and now you're mine forever.'

It was an odd thing to say, in retrospect, but I was too distracted by the rock on my finger and the prospect of becoming Mrs Karina Templeton to worry.

We were married six weeks later, at a small ceremony in a register office in Chelsea, where Hugh Grant, Marc Bolan and Pierce Brosnan had all declared 'I do' before us, with the promise of a larger celebration in Iran with Sammy's family at a later date, although that never happened.

The cracks that had already appeared in the relationship before he'd proposed quickly developed into fissures. Impossible differences. We seemed to spend most of our time when we were together engaged in angry, resentful stand-up rows, mostly about Sammy's demands that I give up my career and stay at home now we were married, but it was a compromise I wasn't ready to make. For his part, he would often be moody, unnecessarily difficult and uncommunicative. It was clear things weren't working out.

And then I fell pregnant.

That complicated things. For a start, having a baby meant giving up a job I loved. I could hardly travel the world, loaded up with camera equipment, crawling around in the desert or the tundra, waiting for the perfect shot, while I was pregnant.

It's not as if we'd planned it. We hadn't even discussed starting a family. It came as a total shock to both of us. Sammy took it better than me, mainly because I think he saw it as a reflection of his masculinity, as I'd fallen pregnant despite being on the pill. Not because he had any interest in becoming a father.

Sammy stands glowering at me, his hands in his trouser pockets, eyes burning with fury.

'You shouldn't have come here,' he yells. 'You had no right.'

I shake my head, hoping all the pieces of the puzzle will conveniently slot into place. I'm so confused, so completely spun out, I can't think.

'You kept in touch with Jacob,' I croak. 'But how?'

The anger drains from his face, and he looks at me with pity. 'Oh, come on, Karina, wake up.'

'What's that supposed to mean?'

But he doesn't explain. He doesn't lay it all out in easy-to-understand words of two syllables or less. He just perches on the edge of the desk and waits for me to work it out for myself.

'It was *you*,' I say at last, the mist in my brain finally evaporating. '*You* took Jacob.'

'With a little help, yes.'

'But how?'

'Did you really never work it out?'

I cast my mind back to Turkey. To that awful morning I woke up late and found Jacob was missing. How Ronan swore to me that we didn't have a son. That I had imagined him.

'You and Ronan,' I gasp. 'You were in it together.'

He pulls his hands out of his pockets and slow claps. Patronising bastard.

'Frankly, I was gobsmacked you fell for it,' he says. 'We just wanted you confused long enough that I could get Jacob out of the country without you kicking off. Who would have guessed you'd have genuinely thought your only son was a ghost in your own mind?'

I lower my head and stare at my hands, numb. It was all Sammy's idea?

'But you don't even know Ronan. How the hell did you persuade him to go along with it?'

He raises an eyebrow and another chunk of my life falls away, like the ruined ramparts of a castle under siege.

'Oh my god. You've known Ronan all along,' I say, the enormity hitting me like a thunderbolt.

'He was part of the plan from the start,' he smirks. 'And you had no idea, did you?'

'What do you mean from the start?'

'I mean, we engineered everything, from the day he first met you to the day you walked out and divorced him.'

'What?'

'Oh, come on, Karina. Don't be so naive. Didn't you ever stop to think it was all too good to be true, that a man like Ronan would really come along when you were at your lowest ebb and sweep you off your feet?'

'No, don't say that.'

'He didn't love you. He was a professional. He worked for me. I paid him to trick you into believing he'd fallen in love with you.'

That can't be true. It just can't. I fish around in my memories for the day I first met Ronan. After the acrimonious split with Sammy,

I'd vowed I was off men for good. Until Ronan catapulted into my life.

He'd approached me as I'd been sitting in the park. Asked for directions to the library, casually dropping into conversation that he used to be a fire fighter. Was that a lie as well?

It's a happy memory. Or at least it was. He'd made me feel good about myself, listening so attentively to what I had to say and paying me so many compliments. But as I start to unpick the memory and see things for what they really were, I feel sick.

All those messages he used to leave on my phone telling me how much he loved me. All the presents. The chocolates. The flowers. An aerial bombardment of love. Except it wasn't. It was a careful, cruel, callous campaign to make me fall for him. And it worked.

At least that's what Sammy's trying to convince me. But why would he lie?

Ronan and I were together for almost two years. Was none of it real? All of it fake? It can't be. It's almost as fantastical as denying to yourself you have a child.

Sammy's enjoying my discomfort. I can see it in the sparkle in his eyes.

'I don't believe you.'

He shrugs. 'I don't care what you believe, but I thought it was time you knew the truth. It's pathetic how weak you are, always falling for everything you're told.'

'How did you know him?' I ask.

'Ronan? He was a small-time con artist. I discovered him after his conviction for defrauding two women he'd dated out of a few thousand pounds. You didn't know about that either, did you? He got away with a fine and a suspended sentence, but I knew a man like that wouldn't be deterred from doing it again. So I made him an offer he couldn't refuse. Helped him to turn his skills to a good cause.'

'You paid him to con me,' I say, the true horror of what he's saying hitting me squarely between the eyes.

'It wasn't cheap but it was worth every penny.'

I think of all those romantic dinners we shared. The nights of passion when we couldn't keep our hands off each other. All my darkest secrets I told him. And it was all make-believe. I shiver as a cold finger runs down my spine. He never loved me. He was only ever interested in money. His job. No wonder he grew so cold so quickly after we returned home from Turkey. His job was done and he didn't want anything more to do with me.

'You did all that just to get to Jacob?' I ask, incredulous.

'You left me no choice. You took him from me, but I don't let people who steal from me get away with it,' he growls. 'I'm not weak like you.'

'That's not true,' I protest. 'You had the chance to see Jacob whenever you liked, but you were always too busy.'

'I wasn't prepared to accept I could see my own son only when you decided I could see him. I'm his father. He deserves to be with me, not you. What could you offer him?'

'You couldn't even be bothered to turn up to the last contact day we arranged.'

We'd planned to meet in Hyde Park, somewhere public where I could keep an eye on
Sammy. I still didn't entirely trust him with
Jacob on his own, and until we were divorced
he hadn't shown much interest in him anyway.
He never played with him. Or read to him. Or
wanted to help feed him. Or change a nappy.
He liked the idea of being a father, but didn't
know what it meant to be a dad.

'And then you disappeared with him,' Sammy
says with a scowl. 'You walked out and I never
saw you again. You stole my son and I had no
idea where you were. You had no right to do
that to me.'

'Don't you dare lecture me,' I scream. 'You
didn't care about Jacob.'

'He's my son. Of course I cared about him.'

It's all too much. The weight of everything
he's told me bears down on my shoulders like a
rockfall, crushing me. If what he's saying is cor-
rect, there's nothing about the last twelve years
of my life that's true. It's all lies and fiction. A
total fabrication.

'How did you do it?' I ask, still reeling. 'How
did you take him from right under my nose?'

'A sedative in your wine before you went to
bed. Ronan said you were out like a light.'

It's what I've always suspected, but hearing it
confirmed makes it no easier to swallow. My
own husband drugged me and conspired with
my ex to steal my son. I wouldn't believe it if I
didn't know it was true. It's too outrageous. Too
fantastical.

'Then he put Jacob in the car with all his
clothes and toys, and drove to meet me,' Sam-

my explains. 'It was a good day's drive to get to the Iranian border and I was afraid you might raise the alarm, but I knew that once we were in Iran, you couldn't touch me or Jacob.'

'You made me think I was going crazy. That I didn't even have a son!'

'Who'd have guessed you'd be so gullible?' he says.

'Bastard!' I spit. 'I thought I was going out of my mind.'

'Ronan was great. He ran with it without needing much encouragement. If you ask me, I think he enjoyed the challenge. You know, it was his idea to delete all the photos from your phone and your cloud storage. I wouldn't have thought of that. Apparently he was up half the night.'

I can't believe the lengths they've gone to, all to make me question my sanity.

'What about our house? When we got home, every trace of Jacob had gone. Even his room.'

Sammy nods. 'Ronan thought about that too. When he realised you'd swallowed the whole story, he made arrangements to have it redecorated while you were away, and everything that belonged to Jacob removed. You can achieve anything if you're willing to pay for it. He even had some false paperwork drawn up to convince you that you'd been having treatment for your mental health.'

'The letters from the hospital?' But they looked so real. So professional. And I fell for it without question. 'But why go to those lengths? You'd got what you wanted. You had Jacob.'

'I thought I'd have to keep Jacob in Iran, at least until he turned eighteen, but when you bought the lie and we were confident you weren't going to go to the police, there was no reason not to bring him back to Britain,' Sammy explains.

It's all slowly making sense. Twisted, depraved, contemptible sense. I still can't believe he went to such lengths to kidnap his own son. Was it out of vengeance? Power? Did he really take Jacob just because I'd said he couldn't have him? After all, Sammy is a man who always gets his own way.

I want to punch him. Drive a knife through his heart. Hurt him as badly as he's hurt me.

'I was at your house yesterday. India seems nice,' I say through gritted teeth.

Sammy jolts with surprise. 'What?'

'Didn't she tell you about the woman who cut open her arm? She invited me in for tea and gave me a plaster,' I say.

Sammy wipes a hand over his brow. 'No, she didn't mention it.'

'Oh, really? It's a very nice house, Sammy. Amelia and Henry, are they yours?'

'Stop playing games, Karina. How did you find out about Jacob?'

'That's my secret. Anyway, does it really matter?'

'You shouldn't have come looking for him,' he says. 'You should have let things be and now you're going to upset him and it's an important time of his life.'

'Me upset him?' I laugh. 'After everything you've done, you're worried I'm the problem.

What did you tell him had happened to me, anyway?'

'Nothing.'

'Sammy, I know you better than that. He told me I was crazy and to keep away from him. Why would he say that?'

'We told him you walked out when he was small and that you'd needed some treatment for your mental health.'

'Seriously?'

'I did it to protect him,' he shouts.

'You're not interested in protecting him. You're only interested in protecting yourself. It's always been the same.'

'Keep away from him, Karina. I'm warning you.'

'I want him back, with me, or I'm calling the police.'

'You're not a fit mother,' he says. 'You're washed up, drugged up and not to be trusted. He's staying with me, where he's happy.'

'Happy? Let's see what he has to say about that when he finds out the truth. When I tell him what really happened to him.'

For a large man, Sammy moves surprisingly quickly. He jumps off the desk and has his hands around my throat before I know what's happening.

'Walk away, Karina. I'm warning you,' he snarls in my face.

I gasp for breath, my fingers trying to prise his hands away. I can't breathe. Panic swells in my chest.

'You should be thanking me. I could have had you killed. It would have been so much easier.

And then I'd have had custody as a right. But no, I let you live. So don't you dare start causing trouble now.'

In desperation, I reach for his face. Dig my nails into his skin and drag them down his cheek.

He yelps in pain and recoils, releasing his grip around my throat.

I'm pleased to see I've drawn blood. As I gasp for breath, he dabs at the wound with a hand-kerchief.

'Bitch,' he hisses.

'I want my son,' I rasp. 'He needs his mother.'

'He has a mother. A better one than you could ever be.'

'Do you seriously expect me to walk away and agree to never see my son again? It's not going to happen, Sammy. Jacob deserves to know the truth and he deserves to know his mother.'

Sammy's jaw tightens and his nostrils flare. 'Look, I'm telling you for the last time. Stay away from Jacob. Do you hear me?'

'Or what?'

He inspects a spot of blood on his handker-chief and puts it back in his pocket. Unfortu-nately, I've only inflicted a superficial wound and it's already stopped bleeding.

'Or I tell him you thought the pregnancy was a mistake.'

Cold hands grip my body.

'Maybe I'll show him the emails. You know the ones, when you were planning the abortion. Because believe it or not, I kept them all as a little insurance.'

I feel the colour draining from my face as he watches my reaction. 'You wouldn't,' I say.

'Try me.'

# Chapter 34

It had never even crossed my mind that one day I might want children. I was young and carefree with an amazing job that offered me so many incredible opportunities. I was seeing places I never imagined in my wildest dreams I would have the chance to visit. The Qinling Mountains in China to shoot snub-nose monkeys. South Africa to snap elephants in the wild. Colombia to capture images of Amazonian river dolphin. The Maasai Mara in Kenya to see hunting lions in the wild.

It was an unreal life. Exciting. Exhilarating. Fun. Children simply didn't factor into the equation. It's not as though I'd made an active choice not to have them, it just never even occurred to me that it was something I'd ever do.

And then I met Sammy. We fell in love, and we were married, for better or for worse. And I fell pregnant. It was an accident. A mistake. I'd been busy. Rushing around. Planning a trip to the Brazilian Pantanal wetlands. I forgot to take my pill at least twice that week. Sammy had made a surprise visit home, one thing led to another and the next thing I knew...

I found out three weeks later in a hotel in São
Paulo, crouched over the basin in a cramped
bathroom with sterile white tiles, staring at two
distinctive blue lines on a little plastic stick. At
first, I was in denial and buried my head in
my work, unable to face the enormous impact
being pregnant and having a child would inevitably have on my life.

It was only when I was back in Britain and
I'd finally worked up the courage to confess to
Sammy, that I made up my mind.

There was no way I could keep it. I didn't
know the first thing about being a mother. And
it wasn't really a baby yet anyway. More a col-
lection of cells and blood vessels. Not a sentient
being. And if I went ahead with the pregnancy,
I could kiss goodbye to my career, for at least
the next eighteen years.

I booked an appointment at a clinic in Ful-
ham to discuss my options and immediately
felt a huge sense of relief. It was the right thing
to do. I was still only thirty-three. There was
plenty of time to start a family later, if that's
what Sammy and I decided.

I didn't consult with Sammy. It was my body.
My decision. And he'd not shown a great deal
of enthusiasm when I told him I was pregnant.
He was pleased, but he'd have been equally de-
lighted if I'd announced I was buying him a new
Rolex for his birthday.

The clinic was in a modern building on the
ground floor of a trendy block of flats with
glass-enclosed terraces and mauve cladding.
Not some grotty backstreet dive off a dingy
alleyway with an anonymous steel door as I'd

imagined. The staff were lovely. So warm, caring and sensitive, it immediately put me at my ease. It was no more scary than going to the dentist.

It was at the clinic that I met Michaela. She was loitering outside, all alone, hunched up and looking lost, tears streaming down her face.

I couldn't ignore her. She was in such a state and so young. Jeans that hung off her skinny hips. A scruffy coat that didn't look warm enough to fend off the chill in the air.

'Are you okay?' I asked.

She glanced up at me like a frightened mouse, shocked that someone had actually spoken to her. She was playing with her fingers, shoulders rounded inwards as if she was trying to cocoon herself from the world.

'Yeah,' she whispered. 'Thanks.'

'Can I buy you a cup of tea?' There was only one reason a young girl would be hanging around an abortion clinic in tears. If that had been me, I'd like to think someone would have looked out for me.

'Oh no, I'm fine.' Her eyes opened wide in terror.

'Come on, one cup of tea. You don't even have to talk to me if you don't want to.'

Reluctantly she agreed. We found a quiet corner in a coffee shop down the road and over Danish pastries and lattes, she told me everything. How she was only sixteen and had found out she was pregnant by her boyfriend of six months and how terrified she was about her mum finding out, which is why she'd come alone. She couldn't see any other option than a termination, even though the idea of it appalled her.

I liked her. She was sweet and innocent and had had an unlucky roll of the dice. She didn't deserve to be facing something so enormous on her own. And that's how I found myself offering to go with her back to the clinic.

We sat and listened to her options together and, in those few hours we spent in each other's company, we developed a strong friendship, as meaningful as any I've experienced in my life, even though I was almost old enough to be her mother.

When she was done and she walked out clutching various leaflets of advice, I gave her my number and email address, and told her to call me at any time, even if it was just for a friendly chat. At that point, I think she was still minded to have a termination, but I hope I made her realise she had a choice. She didn't have to go ahead with it if she didn't want to. We talked about the positives of being a mother, the joy unlike any other it would bring, the miracle of delivering a new person into the world, as well as the negatives and how she might feel in the days and weeks after an abortion. The sense of guilt, the shame and regret.

I had no idea of the profound influence those conversations would have on me until later, and how it completely transformed my opinion about being a mother. But without meeting Michaela that day, Jacob would never have made it into our lives.

It would destroy Jacob if he knew the truth. Or at least that truth. The poor kid. So much of his life has been based on a lie. If we're not careful, he's going to end up really messed up.

I run a hand around my neck which is burning from the grip of Sammy's fingers, my throat tight and uncomfortable when I try to swallow.

I stare him down, challenging him, but I know what's he's like. If he says he's going to do something, he never lets anything get in his way. He's a human bulldozer. It's probably why he's been so successful in business.

'Don't say anything to Jacob. It would destroy him,' I plead.

'It would destroy him if you came back into his life and spun him stories about how he was spirited out of the country by his father.'

'But that's true.'

Sammy shakes his head and looks down at his feet. 'He's been through enough as it is, Karina. He's happy now. He's doing well at school. He has a good life. You want to ruin all that?'

'Of course I don't but—'

'Then walk away and forget about him. Carry on with your pitiful life.'

A surge of anger brews in my stomach and percolates through my chest. 'You want me to walk away from my son? And forget what you did? That you abducted him and almost had me sectioned?'

'That's exactly what I'm saying,' he spits.

'You don't deserve him, you worthless piece of shit.'

He grabs the back of my head in one swift movement and slams it onto the desk, smashing my forehead against its leather-bound top.

The pain arrives fractionally after the shock and the stars that float across my eyes.

'Don't you dare talk to me like that.'

I'm too dazed to reply, stunned by his violence. He never once raised his hand to me while we were married but I always suspected he was capable of it.

The door clicks open, brushing against the thick carpet.

'Everything alright in here?'

Henrikson must have heard the commotion and wondered what the hell was going on in his office.

Sammy transforms in an instant, all smiles and sickly charm.

'We're just finishing,' he says. 'Thanks so much for the use of your office. It was good of Peter, wasn't it?' he says to me.

I nod, still dazed.

'No problem at all. Everything sorted now?' Henrikson says.

'Absolutely. You won't be hearing from Karina again, will he, Karina?'

Dutifully, I nod my head.

# Chapter 35

'What are you going to do?' Freida tops up my glass but doesn't bother putting the bottle back in the fridge. The chances are we're going to get through it all tonight.

'What can I do?' I shrug. 'He has me over a barrel.'

I spent most of the rest of the day wandering aimlessly around Richmond. I don't think Sammy ever thought I'd go looking for Jacob, but he was clever enough to have a contingency plan, just in case. He knew exactly how he'd stop me going to the police. Of course, he could be bluffing. He might not have copies of those emails, but I can't take the chance. I'd rather never see Jacob again than for him to find out the truth and hate me.

Almost inevitably, I ended up at Freida's house. I have no one else to talk to and I couldn't face going back to my empty flat.

'Why do men have to be such bastards?' Freida grumbles.

She's still getting over her divorce from Dev, who had multiple affairs during their twenty-year marriage. It's no wonder she's so bitter.

'It's in the genes.'

'Don't you think it's time you went to the police?' Freida says.

'Absolutely not.'

'But why? If Sammy took him without your consent, even if it was in Turkey, they have to do something, surely? You're his mother.'

'It's not that simple. He's threatening to tell Jacob I planned to have an abortion when I was pregnant.'

'So? What's the big deal? He'll understand. The main thing is that you came to your senses and went through with the pregnancy.'

I take a deep breath and let it out slowly through my nose. 'You don't get it, do you? You don't know what Sammy's capable of.'

'I think I get the picture.' Freida takes a large mouthful of wine. 'He tried to convince you that you were going insane. That's pretty twisted.'

'Maybe Jacob would be better off without me. He has a good life. He's obviously doing well at school. What's it going to do to him if I waltz in, drag him away and tell him what really happened with his father? That could screw him up.'

'He has a right to know what Sammy did.'

'I don't know, Freida.' I drain my glass, welcoming the numbing effect of the alcohol.

'You could always give it a few years until he's an adult and knows his own mind. When he's eighteen, he'll be able to make his own decisions. That's less than four years, and you've waited this long already.'

'And miss even more of him growing up? I've already missed out on ten years.'

'So what's another four? All I'm saying is that it's not an either or decision.' She takes the bottle and empties it into our glasses. Chews her lip for a moment. 'Look, there's something else I wanted to talk to you about. I wasn't going to say anything but it seems like an opportune time.'

'Oh yeah?' What's she going to say now? That the business is struggling and she needs to lay me off? Oh god, I hope she's not ill. I don't think I could cope with that on top of everything.

'It's not that I want to get rid of you or anything,' she says, looking sheepish.

It *is* the business. She can't afford to keep me on. And I thought she was doing well. The diary's always full and there have been occasions recently when she's had to turn business away.

'You're letting me go,' I say with resignation. I won't make this any more difficult than I'm sure it must be for her.

'What? God, no. It's nothing like that. It's an opportunity, actually. You've been saying for a long time that you wanted to get back into wildlife photography—'

'Oh, no, Freida, I can't think about anything like that with all this business with Sammy going on.'

'Just hear me out,' she says. 'A friend of a friend needs an assistant for a trip she's planning to Brazil to document a family of jaguars for a book she's co-authoring. She needs someone with experience. Someone she can trust. I immediately thought of you. I know it would be a step down from what you were doing previously but I thought you'd be perfect for it. I can put in a word for you if you'd like?'

'Wow, I don't know what to say.' I've never photographed jaguars before, although I've been to the Pantanal a few times on other assignments. It sounds like an amazing opportunity.

'You don't have to give me an answer straight-away. They're still planning the trip, but I think it would be great for you.'

'I can't. I've got too much going on and besides, I can't leave you in the lurch,' I protest.

'I'll manage. This would be great for you, Karina. Just what you need to get your confidence back.'

I'm sure she's right and once upon a time I would have leapt at the chance without a second thought, but how can I contemplate something so reckless, right now? And anyway, my skills are too rusty. I'd hate to show myself up.

'Promise me you'll think about it,' Freida says. She peers at me earnestly over the top of her wine glass.

'Fine, I'll think about it.' I can't help the excited grin that curls my lips. Even if I know I can't do it, it's nice to be asked.

'Just let me know.'


A few weeks later, I'm sitting in a coffee shop that sells the most delicious-looking and smelling chocolate muffins arranged temptingly on a cake stand on the counter, watching Jacob through the window kicking a ball about with friends in the park opposite.

He's just attempted an ambitious scissor kick and has landed flat on his stomach having missed the ball entirely. It brings a smile to my face.

I have been thinking about the photography job in Brazil, but only fleetingly. It's a fantasy that I catch myself dreaming about at odd moments. Most of the time, my mind's preoccupied with Jacob and how motherhood has been stolen from me. Even if by some miracle I can win back custody of my son, nothing can replace those missing ten years. I can't leave it for four years until he's eighteen. That would be another four years lost. Another four years for Sammy to poison Jacob's mind against me.

I could take my chances, of course. Call Sammy's bluff and hope I can persuade Jacob that despite everything his father has told him, I love him more than words can express. But if Sammy does have copies of those emails, and shares them with Jacob, there's no way of knowing how he'll react. If Jacob finds out the truth, he'll want nothing to do with me.

But he doesn't want anything to do with me now. So what do I have to lose? If only I could make him understand I didn't abandon him and that I'm not out of my mind.

I've been watching him like an obsessed stalker ever since my run-in with Sammy at the school. It's a way of spending time with him, even if I'm not really with him. I can't think what else I can do. I've been up early and across London every day to wait for him to leave the house. It was easier during term time when he'd leave at the same time every day, but there are some days during the holidays when he doesn't leave the house at all.

I've been wearing my hair tied back and have sported a variety of hats and head coverings to disguise my appearance. I've even taken to wearing spectacles with clear glass, and he hasn't spotted me once, although I know I'm taking a risk. If Sammy finds out what I'm doing, any chance of being reunited with Jacob will be over.

I recognise most of his friends now. They are almost all boys of his age, although I've noticed there is one girl he spends time with. She's a pretty girl with a severe black bob and stunning blue eyes. She's quiet and studious and I'm not sure how impressed she is with Jacob playing the fool around her, like a gaudy peacock desperate to win her approval. It all seems innocent enough, but a reminder he's growing up fast.

He seems happy. He's always laughing and larking around. He's sociable and, according to his father, is doing well at school, so I guess Sammy and India must be doing something right. But the better I get to know him, the more I realise I don't know him at all. I don't know his favourite food, his favourite movie, or even which subjects he excels in at school. I don't know what he plans to do after school, if he's going to go to university or travel the world or if he wants to become an electrician or an electrical engineer. I don't even know what football team he supports, whether he's shown any interest in photography, like me, or is an entrepreneur in the making like his father. And it kills me.

The yearning to be a bigger part of his life grows stronger every day. I want him to be happy and psychologically grounded, but if I tell him the truth about how his father abducted him, how's he going to take it? It's a lot for a teenager to deal with when there's already so much going on in his life. The alternative is allowing him to live with the lie and maybe finding out the truth one day and blaming me for not being honest with him.

All I know for sure is that I can't rush things. I need to bide my time and wait for my opportunity.

At the weekend, I followed him to the cinema and observed from the safety of a bus stop as he hung around with some of his mates outside a row of shops, disappointed when I saw them all passing around a vape, puffing out clouds of sweet-smelling smoke. At least he's not doing drugs, I suppose, and all kids experiment, don't they? He just seems so young.

I've even had the chance to watch him on the athletics field after the school website helpfully revealed it was the end of term sports day. I had no idea if Jacob would be competing, but he seems to be a sporty boy and I took my chances.

It wasn't difficult to sneak into the school. There were so many parents, I blended in easily, although I kept a look out for Henrikson, the principal, and wore my hair tucked up under a baseball cap. Typically, there was no sign of Sammy, or India.

It gave me such a thrill when I got to watch Jacob running the four hundred metres, which he won comfortably. He celebrated by punching the air and casting a sly smile at the dark-haired girl I've seen him hanging around with.

While Jacob picks himself up off the floor and rubs the grass stains on his knees, I check my phone.

To my surprise, there's another email from *The Girl with Regrets*. It's the first time I've heard from her since she sent me the picture of Jacob that set off this incredible journey back into his life. I never expected her to ever message me again.

Curious, I put down my coffee cup and swipe open the email.

It's brief and to the point, but I have no idea what to make of it.

> **Hi Karina,**
> **I was wondering if you'd like to meet up?**

I don't know. Would I? What purpose would it serve? I'm not sure I have anything to gain, and possibly everything to lose, but curiosity eats at me like a maggot chewing through rotting flesh. Whoever *The Girl with Regrets* is, they know something about what happened to Jacob and decided I needed to know.

And so I type out a quick reply and we make arrangements to meet at a motorway service station in a couple of days.

It's as easy as that. And finally, I'm going to find out who sent those emails - and, more importantly, why.

# Chapter 36

Freida insists on driving me. She says there's no way she's going to let me go on my own.

'They could be a serial killer, for all you know,' she says in all seriousness.

'Are you kidding?'

'All I mean is that you don't know who you're meeting or why,' she says.

I guess she has a point and anyway, it will be good to have some support. Not least because I don't have a car and without Freida's help I'd probably have to take a taxi which would cost a small fortune.

We arrive early and park according to the instructions I was sent, close to a drive-through coffee cabin, in a lay-by off the main slip road into the service area.

As I wait, my leg jiggles up and down with a mind of its own. It's the first day in as long as I can remember that I've not spent trailing Jacob. It feels weird not seeing him. I think about him all the time, wondering what he's doing. Who he's seeing. What he's thinking. I'm not obsessed. I'm just making up for lost time.

'Are we supposed to wait in the car?' Freida asks, turning on the radio.

I switch it off again. I'm too nervous to have it on and I want to concentrate.

'That's what it said.' I constantly check my wing mirror, assuming that whoever's meeting us plans to follow us in and park behind us, ready for a quick getaway. Not that they have anything to worry about. I just want to talk.

There's a regular stream of lorries, white vans and cars. But nobody pulls in behind Freida's Mini.

I check the clock on the dashboard. It's three minutes past eleven. They're already late and a niggle of doubt gnaws at my gut. Are they even going to bother to turn up or are they going to stand me up?

Another agonising five minutes pass.

'Are you sure it was eleven?' Freida asks.

'Yes,' I snap.

'I'm only asking. Maybe they got cold feet.'

I feel bad. Freida's given up another day to help me out, to look after me, and I can't even be civil to her.

'I'm sorry, Freida, I'm—'

Movement catches my attention from the corner of my eye. I glance out of the side window to see a figure appearing through the bushes from a large car park on the other side.

I sense Freida stiffen. 'Is this our man, do you think?'

'It's - it's Ronan,' I gasp.

'What, Ronan as in your ex-husband Ronan?'

'What the hell is he doing here?'

He strides confidently towards the car with his hands in his pockets, craning his neck to see through the glass. When he confirms it's me, he raises a hand in an apologetic wave.

I throw open my door and jump out. He looks much older than when I last saw him. And thinner. Gaunt around the face, his cheeks hollowed out and his skin mottled by a rash of broken blood vessels. Age hasn't done him any favours.

'You bastard,' I scream, flying at him. It's the first time I've seen him in ten years since I walked out of the house in Norfolk with all I could carry packed into one rucksack.

His eyes open wide with surprise as my fists pummel his chest, spittle flying from my mouth as I scream obscenities in his face. He puts his arms up to protect himself and turns his head away.

'Karina, that's enough.' Freida, who's followed me out of the car, grabs me by the arms and pulls me away.

My hair's come loose from its ponytail and strands of it fall across my eyes as I stand there huffing and puffing, trying to catch my breath. 'I could kill you,' I scream.

Ronan holds his hands up, palms facing me. 'Look, I'm sorry, Karina. I didn't mean to hurt you. I came to apologise.' He lowers his gaze deferentially. 'I can't imagine the pain I must have put you through.'

I go for him again, but Freida holds onto me tightly, stopping me from gouging his eyes out. Scratching his face. I don't believe a word that comes out of his mouth anymore.

'You made me think I was out of my mind!'

He shakes his head sadly. 'It wasn't my idea.'

'I thought you loved me. I thought you wanted to be with me. But you used me. You kidnapped my son and you convinced me I was crazy.'

'I know I don't deserve your forgiveness, but I was doing what I had to do to survive,' he says.

'Get off me,' I yell at Freida, whos fingers are digging into my arms.

'Not until you calm down,' she says.

'I *am* calm.'

'You sure?'

'Yes,' I huff.

She lets me go, but stays close.

'Everything you ever said to me was a lie, wasn't it?' I say, fixing Ronan with a stare that could kill. 'Every note claiming your undying love. Every voicemail telling me how much you missed me. Even your wedding vows, you worthless piece of lowlife shit.'

'You have to realise it was just a job. I needed the money.'

'You needed the money,' I repeat, hardly able to believe what I'm hearing. 'And that's what you came here to tell me?'

'No, of course not.'

'What, then? And why now after ten years?'

'I wanted to say I'm sorry. To let you know how much I regret what I did,' he snivels.

'Oh, that's fine then. You're sorry. And I'm supposed to forgive you, am I? You ruined my life, Ronan. You convinced me to fall in love with you, to marry you, and then you told me I was deranged. You stole my son, my sanity and my life. You drugged me. You manipulated me. And you lied to me.'

'I know,' he says so quietly, I can barely make out the words above the roar of the motorway traffic behind us. 'But I was desperate. It was all Sammy's idea. I didn't really know what I was getting into.'

'Oh, right, so you're a victim too? You should have said.'

He sighs and rolls his eyes. I wonder if I hit him hard enough I could break his nose or knock out a couple of teeth?

'I'm not after your sympathy.'

'Good, because you're not going to get it. Why are you here, Ronan? I don't believe you've come here to apologise. I know you better than that. What do you really want?'

His Adam's apple bobs up and down. Freida's at my side, arms folded, staring my ex-husband down. Now I'm really glad she insisted on coming. If I'd known I was going to be meeting Ronan, I'd have brought an army with me.

'Don't go to the police,' he says. 'I'm begging you.'

I can't believe my ears. 'I'm sorry, Ronan, the only reason you're here is to save your sorry arse? That's it?'

'I can't go to prison. It'd kill me.'

'And I'm supposed to care?'

'Think about it this way, if it hadn't been for me, you'd have never seen Jacob again,' he says, pulling his shoulders back and lifting his chin. 'You owe me.'

'What?' I splutter. 'I don't owe you anything.'

'I did the right thing. I came clean. All I'm asking is that whatever you do, don't tell the cops I was involved. Please?'

'Because they might lock away the key this time? It wouldn't be the first time you'd landed in trouble with the police for conning women into believing you're something you're not, would it?'

'Sammy told you, then? I'm not proud of it,' he says with a shrug. 'But it is what it is.'

'Just doing what you had to do to survive?' I grunt. 'Defrauding all those innocent women out of their life savings.'

Over his shoulder, in the car park beyond the bushes, a woman climbs slowly out of a car and stares in our direction. It's not the passing glance of someone checking what's going on, but someone who's watching us.

Her face is familiar, but I can't place it. Don't I know her?

'It wasn't their life savings. It was a few thousand quid, that's all.'

'You're a lowlife petty crook who preys on vulnerable women and who deserves to be locked away for a long time,' I say. 'Why shouldn't I go to the police and tell them everything? It's what you deserve.'

'Please.'

I narrow my eyes, trying to make out the face of the woman across the road.

Ronan turns his head, looking to see what's distracting me.

Something's not adding up about this meeting. If he was so worried I'd go to the police, why did he confess to me in the first place, after all this time? Did he email me in a drunken, guilty stupor? Or did he have a moment of genuine repentance, waking the next day regretting what he'd done? I just don't believe he's been wracked with remorse all this time. So something's either forced his hand, or...

I know where I've seen that woman before. It was in Turkey. She was staying in the villa opposite. I spoke to her when Jacob first went missing, hoping she might have seen or heard something.

What was her name? It began with D. Or was it S? Sally. Or Holly. No, I remember. It was Polly. It reminded me of that silly children's nursery rhyme I used to sing to Jacob.

*Polly put the kettle on, let's all have tea.*

What's she doing here? It's some coincidence that she's appeared at the precise moment and at the exact location where Ronan asked me to meet him.

Ronan's body tenses. And then he yells, 'Get back in the car!' He waves a hand at her, but she doesn't move. She's standing clutching a bag to her stomach, her mouth turned down, watching us. That's weird. So she's with Ronan?

'Is that—?' I ask.

'What did I tell you?' Ronan's getting agitated now. 'Get back in the fucking car and stay there.'

She gives an almost imperceptible shake of her head.

'Polly! Do as I tell you. Now!' he screams, turning away from us.

She edges away with what looks like fear in her eyes.

'Polly!' he shouts again.

It looks as if being in the car is the last place she wants to be. But what's she doing with Ronan in the first place? Don't tell me he kept in touch with her after Turkey and they got together. Or worse, something happened between them while they were both out there and I was drugged up to my eyeballs unable to even work out what day of the week it was.

It makes my skin crawl and my stomach fold over on itself. I knew he was a bastard, but this is a new low, even for Ronan.

'Don't make me come over there,' he cries.

His attention is entirely focused on Polly now, almost as if I don't exist. She glances at a squat, low building where the restaurants, coffee shops and toilets are located. It looks as though she's going to make a run for it.

Ronan's obviously drawn the same conclusion as he breaks into a jog, running across the slip road, back towards Polly and the car park behind the bushes.

Either he doesn't see or he doesn't hear the van approaching at speed. It should be slowing down, but it's not. It's belting along. Far too fast.

And in a flash of white, it hits Ronan with a deadening thud like nothing I've heard before.

And in a split second, Ronan disappears.

# Chapter 37

For a few awful seconds, everything goes quiet and nobody moves. The white van has come to a halt a few metres further down the road, the smell of burning rubber pungent in the air.

'Oh my god,' Freida gasps, clamping a hand to her mouth, horrified.

I take a few tentative steps towards the vehicle on trembling legs. When I peer into the van, the driver is gripping the wheel, frozen in shock, staring out of the windscreen. For a moment, I wonder what he's looking at, until I see Ronan's crooked body sprawled across the tarmac, arms and legs sticking out in all kinds of abnormal directions, his head angled away as if he's watching the traffic.

'Ronan?' I whimper, hurrying to his side.

He groans and tries to move.

Thank god, he's still alive. I might hate him more than anyone on the planet, but even I don't wish him dead. Not like this.

'For fuck's sake, don't just sit there. Call an ambulance!' I scream at the bald-headed driver who hasn't moved an inch. His eyes are wide and black, but he makes no attempt to get out of his cab.

Freida hurries up to me, phone clamped to her ear. 'Ambulance. Please hurry. A man's been knocked down,' she says with surprising calm. 'He's not moving.'

She crouches at my side. I've never been so grateful to have her with me. 'Freida,' I cry, numb with shock.

'Is he breathing?' she asks, still holding the phone to her ear.

Ronan groans again. I think he's trying to say something but it's incomprehensible. Garbled words. Weird, strangulated sounds.

'Yes, he's breathing, but there's a lot of blood,' Freida says.

A pool of crimson liquid is seeping into the road in a deepening puddle around Ronan's head. Scraps of his hair have been pulled out and, in places, bone is visible. His face is a mess too. A sickening pulp of blood and gristle that looks inhuman.

'No, I won't move him. I understand,' Freida's saying into the phone as I battle with nausea.

Ronan's clearly in a bad way, but I dare not touch him or move him. All we can do is wait for an ambulance and pray that his injuries look worse than they are.

Finally, the driver of the van stumbles out of his cab and staggers around the front of his vehicle. 'I didn't see him,' he moans. 'He ran out in front of me.'

'Quick, give me your jacket,' Freida demands. He stares at her blankly.

'Your jacket,' she repeats. 'Give it to me.'

He does what she asks, moving slowly, deliberately, showing no sign of hurrying. The poor guy's obviously in shock. It wasn't his fault. Ronan ran out in front of him. He stood no chance of stopping, although if he'd not been travelling so fast, things might not look so bad.

Freida snatches his jacket and lays it over Ronan's back. 'An ambulance is on its way,' she soothes. 'Hang in there, Ronan. You're going to be okay.'

'Is he going to die?' The woman, Polly, has appeared from around the side of the stationary van, not coming too close, craning her neck to see.

I stand up to meet her eye. 'I don't know. Help is on the way.'

As her legs buckle and she breaks down with a pitiful wail, I catch her. Help her to the ground and sit her on the kerb.

'Don't look,' I tell her.

'Is he going to die?' she repeats.

I take her hands in mine. They're cold and clammy. 'I don't know. I'm sorry.'

When the paramedics arrive in a fanfare of blue lights and wailing sirens, there's nothing we can do but watch and hope. They spend some time working on Ronan on the floor. Talking to him. Shining a torch in his eyes. Attaching drips. Covering him with a blanket.

A kindly police officer with a weather-worn face who's turned up asks us all what we saw. Sits the van driver in the back of his patrol car and makes him blow into a breathalyser. Takes all our details. Names. Addresses. Phone numbers. It's a blur, like being in a lucid dream where you have no control over your own body while everything happens out of your control around you.

Eventually, they lift Ronan into the back of the ambulance. Polly climbs in the back with him and I promise we'll follow on and meet her at the emergency department at the hospital.

'Are you sure you want to do this?' Freida asks as we clamber back into her car and the police wave us through the cordon they've set up around the scene.

'I'm not doing it for Ronan's sake. I'm doing it for Polly.'

# Chapter 38

We find Polly sitting quietly in a waiting room at the hospital. She's clutching her handbag in her lap, her eyes reddened with tears, staring at a blank wall.

'They're still assessing him,' she says, her voice flat and emotionless.

I want to assure her that everything is going to work out fine and that Ronan is going to make a full recovery, but it's an empty promise I can't deliver. Instead, I take her hand and offer a grim smile.

Freida and I sit with her in an uncomfortable silence, all of us lost in our own thoughts. I keep replaying the scene over and over in my head, how Ronan was right there in front of me one moment and gone the next. The sound of his body as it was hit by the van. The screech of tyres. The smell of burning rubber. The stillness that followed. The look of sheer horror on Polly's face.

'I didn't realise you and Ronan knew each other. Are you together?' I eventually pluck up the courage to ask.

Polly dabs her eyes with a scrunched-up tissue and nods.

'Oh, I didn't know.' I'd love to ask her how and when their relationship started. Whether they were carrying on under my nose in Turkey, although even that wouldn't be the worst thing Ronan's done to me, or if he kept in touch with her and they started seeing each other later. I'd like to hope it happened after we split up, but then I think of all the times Ronan was away, supposedly working. Was he with her? Is that why he was hardly ever around, because he was having an affair with Polly?

'You don't understand,' she says.

'It's fine. You don't need to explain.'

'We were together before the two of you met.'

'Excuse me?'

She bites her lip and glances at her hands which are tearing the tissue into strips. 'Ronan and I have been together for fifteen years.'

'That can't be right,' I say, shaking my head. 'I remember you. You were staying in the same resort in Turkey. You had the villa opposite. I came to see if you knew anything about my son, Jacob. Do you remember?'

'I know all about Jacob,' she says. 'Who do you think sent you those emails? The photo?'

My mind flips, turning dizzying cartwheels. I thought Ronan was the *Girl with Regrets*. A clever pseudonym to throw me off the trail.

'You?'

She nods. 'The girl with regrets. Like Sinatra said, I've had a few.'

'I'm sorry, I don't understand.'

'It's complicated. And this probably isn't the time, not when Ronan might...' She starts cry-

ing again, her chest and shoulders rocking with
emotion.

'It's okay. We can talk about this later.' Whatever I think about Ronan and Polly, there's a
time and a place to get to the truth. It's not
in a hospital where doctors are fighting to save
Ronan's life.

'You deserve to know.'

'We can do this later.'

'No, it needs to be said. I need you to understand. I know what he's like, what he is, but I've
always loved him. Or at least I thought I did. I've
tried to leave before, but I couldn't do it. Every
time I've ever come close to walking out, when
he's hurt me one too many times, he'd shoot me
that smile, tell me he was sorry and that he was
going to change, and I'd be putty in his hands.
He's had a hold on me like no one else has ever
had,' she says. 'Do you know what I mean?'

I know exactly what she means. For a while,
Ronan had the same effect on me. That charm.
The way he looked at me and listened to every
word I said, as if I was the only woman in the
world. He knew how to play women like me and
Polly, who were vulnerable and lonely, and who
were all too happy to dance to his tune.

'Are you saying you were already together
when I met you in Turkey?' I ask. The truth is
torture but I have to know.

'We'd been together for a couple of years by
then. He walked into the pub where I was working one night and after half an hour chatting,
I thought he was the one. The man I'd been
destined to meet all my life. Unfortunately, it
turned out I was just one of many for him. He

couldn't help himself. One woman was never enough. *I* was never enough for him.

'I should have left him the first time, but it's not that easy with him. Once he gets his hooks into you, it's so hard. And then I found out he wasn't only having affairs, he was fleecing women out of money.'

'Were you together when he was arrested?'

'I should have left him the moment the court found him guilty, but I didn't. Stupid me, I thought he'd need me more than ever and so I stayed. I genuinely thought he'd have learnt his lesson.'

'Did you know about me?' I ask.

She nods and swallows. 'After he was sentenced, he promised he'd find a job and said he wanted to start a family. I know now he was telling me things he knew I wanted to hear. Then a few weeks later, he told me we were going to be rich, and that he'd met a man who'd offered to pay him half a million to do a job.'

'Sammy? My ex-husband?'

'He said the catch was that he was going to have to go away for a while. When I pressed him, he explained how you'd run off with Sammy's son and were denying him rightful access, and Ronan was going to help sort it out.'

'No,' I protest. 'Sammy didn't want anything to do with Jacob until I took him away and he couldn't have him.'

'I don't doubt it. I'm just telling you what Ronan told me. He said he was going to have to seduce you, but worse than that, he had to marry you. You know, to make it believable. It's what Sammy wanted. We'd never even talked about marriage. He'd always made it clear it wasn't something that interested him, but suddenly he was planning to marry a complete stranger.'

It's an extraordinary story and if I didn't know Ronan like I do, I'm not sure I'd believe it. He seemed so genuine. So ordinary. So totally charming. But it was all a lie. Every word he uttered carefully chosen to manipulate and control. I can't believe I fell for it, but I was in a strange place. My divorce hadn't long been finalised and I was vulnerable.

'He told me he used to be a fire fighter.'

Polly laughs bitterly. 'Yeah, I bet he did.'

'It's not true?'

'Not much of what Ronan says is true. You learn that after a while,' she says.

How could I have been so naive? 'When he told you he was going to seduce me, didn't you try to talk him out of it?'

'It was a life-changing sum of money. And I knew he'd do it anyway, with or without my support. He didn't really give me much choice. Ronan said it would only be for a year. Maybe a little longer. Just long enough to reunite Sammy with his son.'

'And almost have me sent to the lunatic asylum.'

'I swear, I never knew that was what they were planning. I'd have never gone along with it if I had.'

I study her face, looking for a tell, an indication that she's lying to me. 'When did you find out?' I ask through gritted teeth.

'In Turkey,' she says. 'I couldn't bear to be apart from Ronan for even a week, so he booked a flight and the villa next to yours just for me. Of course, he had his own reasons. He thought it might be useful to have me close when it came to removing Jacob from the house. I'm so sorry. I was so young at the time, I didn't really appreciate what I was doing.'

'You helped Ronan abduct my son,' I say, spelling it out in black and white. 'You could go to prison for a long time.'

She lowers her gaze and sniffs. 'Yes, I know. It would be nothing more than I deserve.'

'So why reach out to me now? After ten years?'

She takes a moment to compose herself and stares at the wall on the other side of the room. 'Because I finally understood the pain we'd put you through and I realised you deserved to know the truth about what happened to your son.'

'You couldn't possibly understand the pain of what you put me through,' I hiss, momentarily forgetting where we are.

'We lost a child when he was only three,' she whispers. 'He had meningitis and there was nothing they could do. He died five days after we rushed him to hospital.'

Now I feel really bad. 'I'm so sorry. I didn't know...'

'I was devastated. My whole world fell apart,' she continues. 'I couldn't believe he was gone. It left my life so... empty. That's when I started to think about what Ronan and Sammy had put you through. My little Max wasn't much younger than Jacob. At least we had a body to bury.'

'Ronan told me *he'd* written the emails,' I say.

Polly shakes her head. 'Did he also beg you not to involve the police?'

'Eventually, although he tried to pretend that the only reason he wanted to meet was to beg my forgiveness. He tried to tell me he regretted what he'd done.'

Polly moistens her lips with her tongue and glances at me. 'He never regretted anything.'

'I know.'

'I found that photo of your son on Ronan's phone. It was from Sammy with a note about how Jacob had won a medal for being the top scorer in his school football team. I had no idea they were still in touch,' she says.

'Sammy sent it to Ronan?' It seems highly unlikely they maintained contact, but I suppose it's not impossible.

'I was as surprised as you. He never talked about Jacob to me.'

It's extraordinary. Ronan had developed what I thought was a strong relationship with Jacob, stepping easily into the role of stepfather, but I'd assumed like everything else it was an act. Maybe he did care. Maybe he felt some guilt about what he'd done and he wanted reassurance that Jacob hadn't been affected by what they'd put him through.

'I'm gobsmacked,' I say. 'I wouldn't have thought he cared.'

'Unfortunately, when Ronan found out I'd emailed you, he hit the roof. I never thought he'd find the account I'd set up, but he did. And he wasn't happy. I couldn't go out for a week, at least not without a lot of make-up to cover up the bruises.'

I grimace. At least Ronan had never hit me.

'He couldn't cope with the prospect of going to prison, and he was worried if the truth came out, they might even try to extradite him to Turkey. He was terrified of ending up in a Turkish jail.'

As awful as it is to hear, everything she's told me confirms what Sammy said. Ronan never had any feelings for me. It was a confidence trick on a grand scale, motivated by nothing more than greed.

'Are you okay?' Freida asks, her brow furrowed with friendly concern. I'd almost forgotten she was here. 'That's a lot to take in.'

'I'm fine,' I assure her.

Am I? I've always wanted to know the truth, but now I do, what am I supposed to do with it? I've lost the best part of ten years of my life and although I now know Jacob is alive, I'm still nowhere near being his mother again. All I can do is watch him from afar. Where's the justice in that?

'What you did was wrong, Polly, and nothing can ever excuse the part you played in the abduction of my son,' I say, 'but thank you.'

She looks up at me, surprised.

'For having the bravery to write. For bringing my son back to me.'

Rubber-soled shoes squeak across the tiled floor. A doctor in scrubs, his sleeves rolled up and a stethoscope swinging around his neck, approaches us.

'Mrs Shackleton?'

Polly looks up awkwardly and gives the doctor a thin-lipped smile. 'It's Martel, actually,' she says. 'We're not married.'

'Okay, well I just wanted to give you a quick update. Mr Shackleton is stable now but he's not out of the woods. He's suffered some severe injuries. He has damage to his liver and spleen, fractures on both legs and multiple rib fractures. In addition, he's suffered severe facial trauma involving significant soft tissue lacerations and fractures of the facial bones.'

Polly's hand flies to her mouth in horror.

'They've prepped him for surgery and he'll be going into theatre soon.'

'Is he going to be... deformed?' Polly asks, her face pale.

The doctor smiles sympathetically. 'I'm afraid it's a little early to say, but we're doing our very best for him. We'll probably need to move him at a later stage to a hospital better equipped at treating maxillofacial trauma. They'll be able to give him the best possible care. As soon as we know any more, I'll let you know.'

'Thank you, doctor.'

As he disappears back onto the ward, I struggle to find any words of comfort. Ronan has relied on his charm and good looks his whole life. Maybe this is some kind of divine justice.

'I didn't want to come with him today,' Polly says, the colour coming back to her cheeks. 'But he insisted. I don't think he trusted me in the house on my own, but I realised it was my opportunity to get away. I was going to run. See if I could flag down a lift and disappear.'

'Where?'

'Anywhere,' she says. 'Far away from Ronan. But now how can I? He's going to need me. Who else is going to look after him?'

'It's not your job.'

'Of course it is. He has no one else.'

I should feel sorry for her, but there's a kind of poetic justice about Polly being forever tied to Ronan, and Ronan depending on Polly for care.

'You've been very kind, but don't feel you have to wait with me. It's going to be hours, by the sound of it,' she adds.

'Do you have someone you can call who can be here with you?' Freida asks.

Polly nods. 'My sister. I'll call her.'

'Well, if you're sure?' I didn't really want to spend my day hanging around a hospital waiting room, especially for someone like Ronan who's never done me any favours.

'Go.'

I glance at Freida who shrugs and nods.

'But before you do, there's something I want to show you.' Polly pulls a phone from her pocket. 'I hope this might help.'

She swipes the screen open and hands it to me.

It's an email, from Sammy, sent to Ronan, roughly around the time Ronan and I got together.

'What's this?' I ask.

'Read it,' she says.

So I do.

'Bloody hell,' I mutter to myself. It's not a smoking gun. It's a whole damn artillery.

# Chapter 39

It doesn't take long to locate an address on the internet for Sammy's firm. Their fancy website reveals they have airy modern offices in Central London. Not that I have any interest in visiting. All I need is a contact number. It's the only way I can think of to reach Sammy urgently. And this is urgent.

Freida parks up in a retail park on the outskirts of the city to let me make the call. She sits with her hands in her lap, watching the world go by through the windscreen. It's been a crazy day for both of us and Freida's not said much since we left the hospital. I think she's still in shock from the accident.

A woman answers the phone breezily.

'I need to talk to Saman Templeton. Can you put me through? It's important,' I announce, determined not to be fobbed off.

'Just one moment, please,' she says to my surprise.

Of course, it would be too much to hope I'd get straight through to my ex-husband. Instead, my call is diverted to another woman. An assistant or a secretary, I guess.

'Mr Templeton's office. How may I help?' she says gruffly, sounding as though the effort of picking up the phone is all too much for her.

'I need to speak to Mr Templeton.'

'I'm afraid Mr Templeton isn't—'

'It's urgent.'

There's a hesitation and the woman continues speaking, the irritation in her voice evident. 'As I was saying, Mr Templeton isn't available right now. If you'd like to leave a message, I'll see that he gets it,' she says.

Yeah, right. I'm sure you will. But I don't have a choice. I have no other way of reaching Sammy, especially as I don't have his mobile number these days. I could email him, but I'd prefer to talk.

What the hell.

'Okay, tell him that I have a number of emails he sent to my ex-husband, Ronan, that prove everything he did, and that we need to talk. He'll know what that means.'

'That's it?'

'Yes.'

'And who shall I say called?'

'You can tell him it's Karina. His ex-wife.' I reel off my number.

There's a pointed silence at the other end of the line and I have to check the screen to make sure we've not been disconnected.

'Was there anything else?' the woman asks.

'No, but make sure he calls me.'

She hangs up and I drop my phone in my lap, wondering how long she'll sit on the message. I'd like to hope she's immediately jumped up from her desk and scurried into a boardroom to interrupt a meeting, understanding the importance of getting the message to her boss. I imagine Sammy's smile fading as he reads it. Realisation dawning that he's going to have to hand Jacob back to me. Or face the police. Or both.

In reality, she'll probably put the message in a pile and deliver it to him when it suits her. It's the only real power people like her wield in big corporations.

'Don't you think it's time to involve the police?' Freida says, starting the engine. The air conditioning kicks in, blasting a welcome gust of cold air over my face. 'I mean, those emails are pretty damning. It proves everything.'

'Not yet.' I still don't trust the police to take my side and I'm not going to blow my one chance of getting Jacob back. If the police get involved and Sammy or Ronan convince them I'm still delusional and not fit to be a mother, I might never see him again. All they'd need to do is speak to my psychiatrist, who has a damning ten-year record of my treatment.

'So you're going to rely on Sammy finally doing the right thing?' she says.

'These emails are proof that he and Ronan conspired to kidnap Jacob. When he finds out that I have them, I can't see he has any choice other than to give up custody. Otherwise I *will* go to the police.'

The emails Polly gave me are remarkably specific, documenting the plans Sammy and Ronan made to abduct Jacob. There are details of the monthly payments Sammy agreed to make to Ronan, information about the villa

Ronan booked in Turkey and even the specifics of where and when Ronan was to make the handover of my son to Sammy. Sadly, they've been more careful about discussing how Ronan planned to drug me and then convince me I was out of my mind. Nonetheless, it should be enough to rattle Sammy into reacting.

She might not be my favourite person in the world, but I am grateful to Polly for having the sense to find the emails and the bravery to share them with me. It couldn't have been an easy decision but it changes everything.

Freida drops me off at my empty flat, turning down my offer to stay for a cup of tea. She looks exhausted. It's been a long and emotional day and I can understand her desire to get home to her daughter.

'Keep me posted if you hear from Sammy, yeah?' she calls as I climb out of the car.

'Of course. And thank you for today. I'm glad you were there.'

'Anytime. Are you back in work tomorrow?'

I bite my lower lip. I've not been into the studio for days and I'm conscious of abusing Freida's good nature. She's been so understanding, letting me have as much time off as I need to sort my life out, but I'm going to have to go back to work soon.

'I just need a few more days, if that's okay?'

'Yeah, sure,' she says lightly, as if it's no problem. But I can tell from the look in her eye that she was hoping I'd be back.

'I promise I'll make it up to you and I'll work all the weekends you need me in future.'

'Don't worry about it. I'd better get back and check the house is still in one piece. You can never be sure when Prisha's home alone,' she laughs.

I smile and wave as she drives off, then check my phone for what feels like the millionth time as I let myself into my flat.

Still nothing from Sammy.

It's gone five o'clock. I just hope he's picked up my message.

By the morning, he's still not called, which puts me in a terrible mood. Does he think that by ignoring me I'll go away? We need to talk about Jacob. He can't bury his head in the sand forever.

On the stroke of nine, I call his office again and get through to the same miserable assistant.

'I phoned yesterday and left a message for Mr Templeton to call me urgently. I've not heard back from him yet. Did he get the message?'

I can almost see the sour expression I know she's pulling. 'And the name?'

She knows who I am, but she's going to make me play the game anyway.

'Karina McHugh,' I say slowly and deliberately. 'Mr Templeton's ex-wife. It's vital I speak to him. It's about our son.'

'Yes, well, he's been incredibly busy.'

'But did he get the message?'

'Yes,' she says pointedly. 'He has your message and I'm sure when he has a spare moment—'

'Did you tell him it was urgent?'

She doesn't answer and I can imagine her rolling her eyes to the ceiling in exasperation.

'Well, can you remind him he's not called me yet.' I take a breath. I have one last string to pull. 'I'd hate to have to involve the police.'

If she's rattled, she disguises it well. 'I'll mention you've called this morning.'

'Do you want my number again?'

'No, I already have it.'

I spend the rest of the morning on tenterhooks, pacing up and down the flat, chewing my nails, not able to settle to anything.

Why isn't he calling? Does he think I'm bluffing? I *will* call the police, if that's what it takes. There's more than enough evidence in the string of emails to prove that Sammy and Ronan conspired against me to kidnap Jacob. Sammy might be Jacob's father, but it's still a breach of the law. It's child abduction and the authorities will take a dim view of it, I'm sure. Maybe I need to speak to a lawyer and get the courts involved. But how much is that going to cost? It would be easier all around if Sammy admitted what he'd done and returned Jacob to me without all the fuss.

By lunchtime, I'm on the verge of calling Sammy's office again and reading the riot act to his assistant. Sammy can't be too busy to pick up a phone, especially over something so important.

But then I have a better idea. Enough is enough. I've given him plenty of time to respond. If he doesn't think this is serious, or that he can ignore me, let's see how he likes it when I up the stakes.

I pull on a pair of Converse, grab a denim jacket, my bag and my phone and head out. The Tube is busy at this time of the day, packed with hot and sweaty bodies, the air thick and sooty, particularly as we cross Central London. It's a now familiar route, although with all the people crammed into the carriages like battery hens in a shed, it's not my favourite trip.

I'm glad when the train rolls up at Richmond and I have the chance to breathe fresh, clean air again. By now, I know my way to Jacob's house without having to rely on the map on my phone.

Jacob's street is quiet, the trees heavy with leaves. I've been here so often, I know the road almost as well as I know my own. I even nod an elderly man I've come to recognise over recent weeks. He's shuffling along the pavement with a cane, his slippers scuffing along the flagstones, plastic carrier bag in one hand. When he smiles, his eyes crinkle and his long, grey beard ripples.

There's only one car in the drive. India's Audi. The Porsche, which I now realise is Sammy's, with that ridiculous number plate, **SMT 1**, is nowhere to be seen. It would have been a bonus if he was home, but I wasn't expecting it. Not during the middle of the day.

I stride confidently up to the front door, hammer on the brass knocker and stand back to wait with my heart thrumming.

After a few moments, the door opens. India peers out from the shadows with a friendly smile on her face. It slips a fraction when she sees it's me.

'Oh,' she says, surprised. 'Hi.'

'Hello, India. May I come in?' I ask.

She frowns. 'Sure. Is everything okay?'

'No,' I say, glancing over my shoulder into the street to make sure no one is watching. 'Everything is most definitely not okay. There's something I need to tell you.'

# Chapter 40

India's appearance is so immaculate, it puts me to shame. She's wearing a claret wrap dress that looks stunning on her, and a full face of make-up. How do these women do it, looking like they've stepped off a film set when all they've been doing is pottering around the house all morning? It's not natural. Even her honeyed hair, lustrous and glossy, looks as though she's just back from the stylist. Money, I guess.

When I announce I have something to tell her, she looks more shocked than intrigued. I suppose she's only met me once and must be wondering what kind of bombshell I'm about to drop.

'Can I come in?' I ask. It's not a conversation I want to have on the doorstep.

She looks hesitant. 'Sure,' she says, eyeing me warily.

Thank god for middle-class sensibilities. She doesn't want the neighbours gossiping. She leads the way to the kitchen and stands with her arms crossed, leaning casually against one of the worktops.

'I didn't expect to see you again,' she says. 'It's Karina, isn't it?'

'That's right. You remember.'

'How's your elbow?'

'It's fine, thank you.'

'So, what can I help you with?' She forces a smile, but there's a nervousness behind her eyes.

I've had plenty of time on the journey across London to think about what I'm going to say and how I'm going to say it, but now I'm here, standing face to face with India, the words don't come as easily as I'd thought they would. How much does she really know? When she met Sammy, did he tell her the truth about Jacob? Or did he lie? I guess there's only one way to find out.

'It's about your stepson, Jacob,' I say, watching her face carefully.

She blinks a couple of times, but maintains eye contact, her expression neutral.

'What about him? Is he in trouble? Has he done something?'

'No, it's nothing like that.'

'So?'

'The thing is, Jacob is... I'm sorry, there's no easy way to say this, but Jacob's my son.' I pause to gauge her reaction. She stares at me blankly. 'He was taken from me when he was four years old, and I want him back.'

India's face clouds with confusion. 'What are you talking about?'

'Sammy is my ex-husband.'

Her eyes narrow but her forehead remains smooth and unfurrowed. She's probably Botoxed up to the eyeballs.

'And he kidnapped Jacob,' I continue.

The heavy weight of silence falls across the room as we stand, staring at each other. I wait for the dust to settle, for India to process what I've told her, watching as her eyes make micro shifts left and right.

'You're Sammy's ex?' she says at last, her body softening. 'Why didn't you say when you were here before? I had no idea.'

'Did you hear what I said? Sammy abducted Jacob when he was only four years old, and I've come to take him back.'

She purses her lips. 'Well, this is all a bit awkward, isn't it?'

'It doesn't have to be.'

'Would you like to take a seat?' She points towards the dining table and invites me to sit like she's talking to a child.

'No, I wouldn't, thank you.' I didn't come here to be civil. As far as I'm concerned, India is complicit in Sammy's crimes. Didn't she ever wonder about Jacob's real mother?

'Sammy talks about you with such great affection,' she simpers. 'It must have been really hard for you giving up Jacob.'

'Excuse me?'

'Sammy told me all about your...' She pauses for a beat as if she's trying to find the right word, '"issues."'

'Issues? What issues?' I hiss.

'It's nothing to be ashamed of. Lots of people struggle with their mental health.'

My jaw tightens and anger flares in my veins like hot acid. 'I don't have any mental health issues. I don't know what Sammy's told you, but it's all lies.'

'Oh,' she says, looking wounded. 'I'm sorry, I didn't mean to speak out of turn. It's just that Sammy always said it's why you had to give Jacob up. Because you couldn't cope. Not that I'm judging. I know how hard it is to bring up young children.'

'I didn't give Jacob up!' I shout. India visibly startles. 'He was taken from me.'

'Please, don't get upset.'

'I'm not getting upset.'

'If you're feeling better now and you think the time's right to get more involved in Jacob's life, I'm sure we can work something out.' There's a nervousness about her now. She's afraid of me. I can see it in the way she's keeping her distance, her eyes constantly flicking towards a phone on the counter, calculating if she can pick it up and call for help before I can make it across the room to stop her. 'We could perhaps come to an arrangement for you to see Jacob on a supervised basis. Why don't I give Sammy a quick call. I'm certain we can work this out between us.'

Her hand snakes across the worktop towards the phone. It's plugged into a socket on the wall.

'Don't touch it!' I snap, my arm shooting out as a warning.

She recoils, her eyes opening wide. 'Okay,' she says timidly. 'Whatever you say. No need to raise your voice. '

'You don't believe me, do you?'

Her eyes dart nervously around the room, as if she's looking for somewhere to run. An escape.

'I never walked out on Jacob,' I continue. 'Sammy took him from me and made me think I was losing my mind. He tried to convince me I didn't have a son, that it was all an illusion. Until a few days ago, I believed him.'

The way India's trembling, you'd think she'd let a serial killer into the house. God knows what poison Sammy's been dripping in her ear, but it's about time she found out the truth about her husband.

'In fact, he was so determined to have custody of Jacob, to make me pay for daring to divorce him, that he paid a man to seduce me and marry me. But he never loved me. It was a trick to steal Jacob. Crazy, isn't it?'

India nods but I can tell she's not really listening. All the colour has drained from her face and she's wrapped her arms defensively around her body. Her gaze shoots sideways towards a row of kitchen knives attached to the wall on a magnetic strip.

'That's some story.' There's a quiver in her voice.

'And every word of it's true.'

'Please, let me call Sammy and you can talk to him.' India forces a nervous smile. 'I think you probably ought to speak to him about this.'

'Believe me, I've tried. Why do you think I'm here? I've left messages for him, but he's not returning my calls.'

'I'm sure he'll answer if I call.' She makes another move for her phone.

'No!' I yell. 'Leave it alone. I've not finished!' I snatch it off the counter, yank out the cable and stuff it into my back pocket. 'I want you to hear my story first.'

'Okay. Just stay calm, alright?'

'I am calm. I'm not here to hurt you, India, but I want you to understand what Sammy did to me. I want you to know what kind of man he really is. And I want my son back.'

She blinks and nods, encouraging me to continue.

I tell her about the holiday Ronan booked to Turkey, Jacob's first trip abroad. How excited we all were about it. The beautiful villa set in a wooded hillside with stunning views to the coast.

'But it was all a trick planned by Sammy. Together, they plotted to drug me and when I was unconscious, they took Jacob. Ronan handed him over to Sammy who drove him across the border into Iran where he thought I'd never find him.'

India shakes her head, incredulous. 'Why would Sammy kidnap his own son?'

'Because I refused to give him access. He didn't care about Jacob, but he hated that I'd taken him away. He saw him as a possession that I'd stolen and he was determined to get him back at whatever cost.'

'I don't believe you.' India pulls her arms more tightly across her chest and lifts her chin defiantly. 'And if that happened like you say, why didn't you go to the police?'

'It's a good question. I wish now I'd tried harder, but between them, they convinced me I was going mad. Ronan swore blind that I didn't have a son. He removed all trace of Jacob from the villa and deleted every photo of him from my phone. They did everything they could to erase Jacob from my life. Ronan even arranged for me to see a psychiatrist and for the last ten years I've been taking anti-psychotic medication to help with my apparent delusions. But it was all a conspiracy.'

I can see India's still not sure whether to believe me or not. I don't blame her. It's a lot to process. And maybe exactly the sort of thing a mad woman would claim. It's up to her whether or not to accept what I'm saying. Ultimately, I'm not here to convince her of the truth. I'm here for my son.

'Look, I know how this must sound, but I'm telling you the truth.' I pull my phone from my bag and find the emails Polly shared with me.

When I offer it to her, India stares at the phone like it's a severed hand.

'These are some of the emails Sammy and Ronan sent to each other when they were planning it. Read them,' I order.

Eventually, India takes the phone and reads. I watch as she mouths the words silently to herself. Everything she could possibly want to know is captured in those emails. Dates, times, plans, instructions, updates, payment schedules. A damning dossier of evidence.

'What is this?' she asks.

'The truth.'

'No, not my Sammy. He couldn't... he wouldn't.'

'I'm sorry, I know it's hard to believe. I assume this is the first you knew about it?'

'Sammy told me you were crazy. He said you'd suffered post-natal depression and couldn't cope with having a baby. He said you walked out and he had to bring Jacob up on his own.'

I laugh bitterly. 'That's what he told you? Sammy wouldn't have had the first clue how to bring Jacob up.'

'He said you'd been admitted to a psychiatric hospital for treatment. He was worried you were going to hurt Jacob.'

*Bastard.* 'I would never hurt my son. Do I look insane to you?' I throw my arms out wide, inviting her to look at me. Okay, so my hair's a mess, I probably have a wild look in my eye, and I've stormed into her house with a story about her husband forcibly abducting his own child, but surely she can see Sammy's been lying to her all these years. 'I just want my son back.'

'Did he really do all those things?' There's a catch in her voice. A slight tremble of apprehension.

'I'm afraid so.'

Her chin falls to her chest and her shoulders slump. 'It's a lot to take in.'

'Yes, I know, and I didn't want to involve you, but I gave Sammy a chance. I've been phoning him at his office, leaving messages for him to call me back urgently, but he's not had the decency to ring. That's why I'm here. If he wouldn't face me, then I figured it was time you knew the truth.'

She nods slowly as if it's all starting to make sense. 'You know I love him.'

'Jacob?'

'Sammy. He's a good man.'

'I loved him once too. I'm not here to drive a wedge between you. I'm only here for my son. For Jacob.'

'I understand.'

'So you'll help me?'

She glances up, eyebrows arched. 'Help you?'

'I need to find Sammy, because my guess is that he's with Jacob right now, isn't he?'

'Oh.' She scratches the back of her head with long, red nails.

'Where are they, India?'

'They left for the airport a few hours ago. It was a last-minute decision,' she says.

My heart sinks. 'Where are they going?'

'Back to Iran, I'm afraid. Sammy wanted to take Jacob to visit family. The plane leaves at five.'

# Chapter 41

It's no wonder Sammy hasn't been answering my messages, but if he thinks I'm going to give up on Jacob now, he really doesn't know me. There's no way I'm losing my son for a second time, but it's already gone two and their plane leaves in less than three hours. Once they're on that aircraft, my chances of ever seeing Jacob again are virtually zero.

'Sammy's taking Jacob back to Iran,' I scream down the phone to Freida as I run out of India's house and into the street.

'Woah, slow down. What's going on?'

'I came to see Sammy's wife. She says they're flying at five. And if they make that flight, I can kiss goodbye to my chances of ever seeing my son again,' I wail, panic flooding through my body like a poison.

'Then we need to stop him. Where are you?'

'Richmond.'

'Can you grab an Uber back to your flat? I can meet you there and drive you to the airport. I presume they're flying from Heathrow?'

'I don't know. Yes, I assume so. But I'm already in West London. Doesn't it make more sense for me to head straight there? If I took a taxi, I could probably be there in half an hour.'

'If they're through security, you'll have to intercept them airside, so you'll need your passport. I take it you don't have it with you?'

'Shit, no. You're right.'

'Get in a cab and I'll pick you up at the flat. Okay?'

'Okay,' I say, uncertain. If Sammy pulls this off and robs me of my son again, it'll destroy me.

'I'll see you soon.'

The journey back to my flat is painfully slow. Every minute that ticks by is a minute that I'm closer to losing Jacob again, but although traffic is heavy on the North Circular, it still beats trying to navigate across London on the Tube.

Almost an hour after I called Freida, I finally make it home. She's waiting in the car outside. I motion to her that I'll only be a minute as I dive into my flat, race upstairs and pull out the cardboard box under my bed where I keep all my important paperwork.

My passport's under a copy of my rental agreement. A quick check confirms it's still in date, although my photo looks ten years old. I renewed it a few years ago when I thought I might be ready to travel again, but in the end I didn't bother. I spent a week in Dorset instead. In fact, I've not been out of the country since that trip to Turkey.

I shove the passport in my bag, fly down the stairs and slam the door behind me.

'Drive!' I yell as I climb into the car and yank on my seatbelt.

She doesn't wait to be told twice, flooring the accelerator and pulling out in front of a bus. She drives like a maniac, back around the North Circular, towards Heathrow, picking up countless speeding tickets along the way, I'm sure.

We're both too anxious to talk, the atmosphere in the car as taut as a drum skin. I tap my fingers on my thigh impatiently every time we're forced to slow down by traffic or roundabouts. But Freida's doing her best, driving like her life depends on getting me to the airport on time.

As we hurtle along, I check for flights on my phone. It looks as if the flight Sammy must be booked on is delayed by thirty minutes, departing from terminal three. That still only gives me an hour and a half to find Sammy and Jacob, and somehow stop them from boarding.

'Did you pick up your passport?' Freida asks. 'And is it still valid?'

'Yes, and yes.'

'Have you thought about booking yourself onto a flight so you can get through security? I had a look while I was waiting. The cheapest ticket I could find was to Germany. There were still some seats available when I checked.'

'That's a good point. I'll do it now.'

Ten minutes later, I'm booked on a plane to Nuremberg, although I have no intention of getting on the flight.

Freida navigates expertly through the spaghetti network of roads around the airport and drops me off right outside the terminal entrance.

'Go,' she instructs as I unclip my seatbelt and scramble out of the car. 'I'll find somewhere to park and meet you later. Good luck!'

I sprint into departures with my head spinning. It's been so long since I've flown from Heathrow, everything's changed. It takes what feels like an age to work out where I need to go, but eventually I locate the security gates and bustle my way through, throwing my bag into a plastic tray to be X-rayed, along with my jewellery, belt and shoes. It feels as though it takes forever, but finally I'm through without incident. Nobody questions what I'm doing here or tries to stop me, even though I have no intention of getting on a plane today.

I stumble headlong through the winding and inescapable duty-free shops, past all the tempting offers on perfumes and spirits, and emerge, blinking, into an expansive lounge crowded with people.

It's absolutely heaving, and somewhere amongst them is Sammy with my son. At least I must be close now, although finding them won't be easy. It's like looking for a solitary star in an infinite universe. They could be anywhere. And even if I do find them, how am I going to stop them? Jacob's had his mind poisoned against me and I can't physically stop them getting onto that plane if they won't listen to reason.

Have I bitten off more than I can manage on my own? Should I have called the police as soon as Polly handed me those emails? I thought threatening Sammy with them would be enough to bring him to his senses and force him into handing Jacob back, but all it's done is pressure him to flee. I should have seen it coming. Now my fate's in the lap of the gods, while the clock continues to tick.

I scour a digital screen listing all the flights due to depart within the next two hours, searching for Sammy's flight to Tehran. It's still showing a thirty-minute delay but I'm grateful to see the plane's not yet boarding. That means I still have a chance to intercept them. The problem is, they could be anywhere. And I'll need to keep an eye on the departure boards, because if I can't find them before their flight's called, I'll have to try to head them off at the gate. It's beginning to feel like an impossible mission.

I probably have no more than thirty minutes before the gate opens. Thirty minutes to scour the departures lounge in the hope of spotting them. But with thousands of people circulating around the terminal, it's not going to be easy.

I begin by scanning a vast swathe of seats and recliners, looking up and down the rows, my eyes flitting from one face to the next. Men. Women. Children. Some of them nursing cardboard cups of coffee. Others sleeping, reading books or chatting. All of them with a familiar look of boredom you always see on the faces of passengers in airports around the world. People killing time, wearied by travel.

I'm confident Sammy and Jacob aren't among them, but there are a hundred other places they could be. There are countless shops, restaurants and cafes. It's entirely possible I could chase around after them in here for hour after hour and never spot them. I need a stroke of luck.

I walk in a large circle around the outside of the lounge, peering into the business premises around the perimeter. So many people. So many faces. And I'm only looking for two. It feels like a hopeless task, but I can't give up. It's too important and after ten years, I can't face my son disappearing once more.

I've come almost full circle when I pass a coffee shop. It's one of those big chains, famous throughout the world. There's a long, winding queue at the counter, and behind it, a dozen members of staff in matching shirts are frantic, trying to keep up with the orders. It looks like hell. I'd kill for a decent coffee right now, but I don't have the time. I need to keep pressing on.

Within the confines of the cafe, there are around twenty tables, all of them occupied with people eating, drinking or simply idling away their time.

By now, I'm becoming adept at quickly scanning faces, waiting for that click of recognition as my eyes move rapidly from passenger to passenger. I'm confident that when I see either Jacob or Sammy, I'll know it in an instant, even though one face is beginning to look like every other. Is that what they mean by face blindness? Or is that something else?

*Come on, Karina. Focus!*

There are half a dozen tables obscured from view behind an arch which has created a cosy snug. A quieter area next to the busy kitchen. I can't quite see everyone inside, unless I crane my neck and stand on tiptoes. At least I don't look out of place here. As far as anyone knows, I'm just looking for an empty table or a husband I've become separated from.

I count at least another fifteen faces. Two or three families. A group of students, all of them on their phones, and a mother breastfeeding a baby. None of them is Jacob or Sammy.

I'm about to walk on and head up to the upper levels when I catch sight of the back of a head. Blonde hair. Shaved at the back. Jacob?

I snatch a breath and freeze, uncertain. Until the head bobs backwards, revealing a man sitting at the table with him. It's Sammy, so preoccupied with his phone he doesn't see me. Head down, thumbs dabbing at the screen. Jacob's mirroring him, doing exactly the same. They might as well be strangers.

My stomach bubbles with nerves and excitement. I've actually found them. It's a miracle in itself, but now I need to find a way of stopping them from getting on that plane.

# Chapter 42

Sammy's blank expression quickly gives way to surprise, shock and then horror when he looks up and sees me approaching their table.

'Karina? What are you doing here?'

'I could ask you the same.'

Jacob lifts his head at the sound of my name. His eyes grow wide and dark as he studies me.

'I'm on a business trip,' Sammy says, smoothing down his silver-coloured tie over his stomach.

'With Jacob?'

'It was a chance to see his family now the schools have broken up.'

'Is that right?' I say. 'And how long has this trip been planned, exactly?'

Sammy looks over my shoulder, his eyes darting left and right. It reminds me of how India reacted when I confronted her in her kitchen. Like a cornered rat, looking for a hole to dive into.

'I don't have to answer to you,' Sammy says, standing. 'Come on, Jacob. Let's go.'

'You picked up my messages, then?' I ask.

Sammy stoops for his briefcase, picks it up and puts it on the table, eyeing me warily.

'Look, Karina. I have nothing to say to you.'

'Really? Maybe I should show Jacob the emails. I'm sure he'd be interested in knowing the truth about what his father's really like.'

'What emails?' Jacob asks, lowering his phone.

'Do you want to tell him or shall I?'

'Karina,' Sammy growls in warning.

'Did your father ever properly explain why I've not been around for the last ten years?'

Jacob looks at Sammy and answers nervously. 'He said you weren't well and that you couldn't cope with being a parent.'

'I'm sure he did.' I fix Sammy with a dagger-like stare. 'It wasn't that I couldn't cope, Jacob. Your father abducted you when you were small. He took you away from me and he made me think I'd had a mental breakdown. But it was a lie.'

'Dad said you'd say something like that.'

'He's been lying to you. For all these years, he's never told you the truth.'

'If you don't leave us alone, I'll have to call security,' Sammy says, but for the first time, I see the worry in his eyes. 'You need help, Karina. Are you still taking your medication?'

'I don't need medication. There's nothing wrong with me.'

Sammy rolls his eyes at Jacob as if to say, 'I told you so.' Fury burns in my chest.

'Do you remember the holiday?' I ask, focusing my attention on Jacob. Sammy can say what he likes, but it's my son I need to convince to stay. 'We went to Turkey with your stepdad, Ronan, when you were four. There was a pool and you were so excited you dived right in without your floats. You almost drowned. Ronan had to dive in to save you.'

Jacob looks down at his hands and blinks. 'Yeah,' he says. 'I do remember that. Was that my stepdad?'

'Ronan, yes. You sunk to the bottom like a stone and I nearly had a heart attack.' I laugh, but I don't know why. It wasn't funny at the time and it's certainly not funny now. 'It was your first time on a plane and you were so excited. We'd been talking about the holiday for weeks and all the things we were going to do. Do you remember?'

'Sort of.'

'Except it wasn't a holiday. It had all been planned by your father and Ronan. They put sedatives in my wine and while I was sleeping, Ronan took you from your bed and handed you over to your father.'

'What utter nonsense.' Sammy slams his briefcase on the table noisily, causing several people sitting close by to turn and stare. 'Can you hear yourself, Karina? How ridiculous you sound? You're not well.'

'As far as I know, he took you to Iran and was planning to keep you there, where he knew I couldn't find you,' I say.

Jacob shakes his head. 'I vaguely remember something.'

'You weren't very old.'

'That's not what happened and you know it. You had a breakdown. You couldn't even re-member having a son, so it was decided Jacob

was best off with me,' Sammy says with authority. It almost sounds true. Except it isn't.

'Ronan and your father were in it together
and tried to convince me you didn't exist. What
was I supposed to think? You'd vanished. Ronan
denied any knowledge of you. And they even
went as far as destroying any photos I had of
you,' I say, ignoring Sammy while keeping my
gaze firmly fixed on Jacob's face. Imploring him
to believe me.

'Dad? Is it true?'

'Of course it's not. I'm afraid your mother's
not been right in the head for some years. She's
a fantasist. She makes things up. Come on, ignore her. We have a plane to catch.'

Right on cue, an automated voice crack-
les through invisible speakers announcing that
passengers for the Tehran flight should make
their way to the departure gates and that the
plane is due to board imminently.

Sammy pushes past me, swinging his briefcase. When Jacob doesn't immediately follow,
he turns back with a dark scowl. 'Jacob! I said
let's go.'

Jacob looks uncertain. 'Is it true?' he asks
again. 'Is any of it true?'

Sammy sighs. 'You see, she's getting in your
head. This is what she does.'

'Is it true?' Jacob repeats.

'Why would I need to abduct my own son?
You see, it doesn't even make sense. We really
don't have time for this.' He tries to grab Jacob's
arm, but Jacob pulls away.

'He's right. He's my dad. Why would he go to
all that trouble to take me from you?'

I run my fingers through my hair. I'd rather not be having this conversation in the middle of a heaving coffee shop in one of the world's busiest airports, but I can't avoid it. 'Because he hated that I had custody of you.'

'I don't understand.'

'I'm afraid your father didn't want much to do with you when you were small. When we split up, I tried to make sure he could see you whenever he wanted, but he wasn't interested. I didn't think it was good for you, so I told him I was taking full custody and that if he tried to fight me for access, I'd go to court. But you know what your father's like. He doesn't like to lose at anything.'

Jacob stares at me like I've grown two heads.

'I know it sounds insane. And it was. But I've never stopped loving you. There hasn't been a day when I haven't thought about you, even when they were all trying to convince me you were just a figment of my imagination.'

'Jacob! We need to leave,' Sammy hisses.

'Just a minute.'

'I'm so, so sorry I haven't been around for the last ten years, but it's not my fault. I love you so much. Since I discovered you were living in London, I've been finding out all sorts of things about you. And I'm so proud of the young man you've become. You're kind and thoughtful. Popular at school and obviously doing really well with your studies. I even saw you at sports day when you won your race,' I tell him.

'Really?' His face lights up momentarily.

'Yes! It was amazing. All I wanted to do was to run up to you and tell you how brilliant you were.'

'Maybe I could see you when we get back?' he offers.

I shake my head. He wants to do the right thing and not upset Sammy, but he still doesn't understand the seriousness of the situation. How could he?

'Jacob, if you get on that plane to visit your family in Iran, you won't be coming back.'

A darkness falls over his face. 'We're only going for a few days.'

'Your father knows he can't fight me over this. I have evidence of what he did, and if I take it to the police, he'll be arrested and I'll be granted custody of you,' I say softly. It's so much for such a young mind to take in. 'That's why he's planned this trip at such short notice. My guess is that he only mentioned it to you last night?'

'I'm warning you, Jacob,' Sammy snaps. 'We need to go this instant or the flight's going to leave without us.'

Jacob reaches under the table for a rucksack which he throws over his shoulder. 'I'm sorry,' he whispers.

'You know if you go, your father will never let you come back. You'll never see your friends again. And he'll send you to an Iranian school.'

'What?' Jacob throws a puzzled look at Sammy.

'I've told you, don't listen to her. She's crazy. She'll say anything to get her own way.'

'I could show you the emails your father sent to Ronan when they were planning to kidnap you,' I say, struggling to keep my tone even. I don't want to give Jacob any reason to think I'm not of sound mind. 'Although, it'll be hard reading.'

'Show me,' he says.

Reluctantly, I find my phone and pull up the email chain. Jacob scans the messages, his mouth hanging open and his Adam's apple bobbing up and down.

I really didn't want to have to show him, but Sammy's left me with no choice. It's going to be a heart-wrenching read, but he needs to know the truth.

'Is she right?' he asks at last, looking up at Sammy. 'Were you planning on stopping me from coming home?'

'No, of course not. Why would I do that?' Sammy says.

'Because of these.' He holds up my phone.

'Look, it's not what it looks like. She's doctored them to twist your mind against me.'

'How would she have doctored them?'

The speakers in the ceiling announce the final call for Sammy's flight.

'I'm not asking you, I'm telling you. Come on, we're leaving.'

'I'm not going,' Jacob says defiantly, dropping his rucksack on the table.

'Don't be ridiculous. We can talk about it on the flight.'

'I said I'm not going.'

My heart flutters and I take a deep breath.

'Don't argue with me. Get your bag and hurry up!' Sammy shouts.

'Jacob,' I say softly, putting my hand on his arm. 'You don't need to do anything you don't want to.'

Sammy looks anxiously at his watch. 'Maybe I should tell him about the abortion. How do you think he'd feel about that?'

My heart races like startled wild horses. That's something Jacob should never know about.

'I think it's time we involved the police, don't you, Sammy?' I say, allowing a sly grin to cross my lips.

He glares at me like he'd happily rip out my throat.

'Bitch!' he snarls. 'You know she isn't even your real mother. Why don't you ask her about that?'

'Sammy, don't you dare.'

'Why not? I thought you were all about the truth. You're not his mother any more than I'm his father. How's that for a plot twist?'

'What's he talking about?' Jacob gasps, staring at me, bewildered. 'What does he mean you're not my mother?'

'Don't listen to him. He'll say anything to get his own way. It's more lies.'

'Believe what you want. I don't care what you do,' Sammy growls at Jacob. 'You know what? You two deserve each other.' Then he turns and runs, out of the cafe and disappears among the crowds.

A stunned Jacob stares after his father. Sammy didn't even glance back.

'Why was he talking about abortion?'

I reach for Jacob's arm and give it a reassuring squeeze. 'It's nothing. He was trying to upset you, that's all.'

Sammy's vanished. Maybe if he , he'll make his flight. I really hope so.

'You can go with him if you like,' I offer. I don't want Jacob blaming me for his decision later. It has to be his choice. 'Or you can stay with me. It's entirely up to you.'

Jacob turns his head slowly, looks at me, and my heart almost bursts as I see the little boy I used to know in his eyes.

'What happens now?' he croaks.

'Whatever you want.' I take my phone out of his hand. 'You've read the emails. You know what your father did, or at least some of it. It's up to you what happens next. If I call the police, he'll be arrested the moment he returns to the country. If I don't, he'll be back and I don't know what he'll do, but if I know your father, he won't let this go without a fight.'

It's a horrible decision to thrust on anyone, let alone a fourteen-year-old boy, but he has to choose. It's not about me or what I want anymore.

Jacob pulls out a chair and slumps at the table with his head in his hands.

'I don't know,' he mumbles.

'I can call the police right now. I can make a statement and show them the emails.'

I pull up a chair on the other side of the table and we sit in silence for a few minutes.

And then Jacob looks up, wipes his nose with his sleeve and sniffs.

'Do it,' he says. 'Make the call and tell the police everything.'

# Chapter 43

'I always knew something wasn't right,' Jacob says as I return with a latte for me and a salted caramel frappe for him.

He toys with his drink with a straw, poking it around in the cream and syrup, unable to look me in the eye. Ten years is a long time. I guess it's going to take a while to rebuild our relationship. I never thought he'd throw himself into my arms when we were finally reunited, he's an awkward teenage boy after all, but I wasn't prepared for how much of a stranger my own son has become.

'What do you mean?'

'I don't know. I guess I've never been that close to Dad and it was weird to think you'd abandoned me when I was so young.'

'I told you, I didn't abandon you.'

'Yeah, I know that now, but it's what he'd always told me. He said you were crazy and that you probably ought to be locked up.'

'He said that?'

Jacob nods, his eyes sad. 'I'm sorry I believed him.'

I reach across the table and rest my hand on top of his. He stiffens and I withdraw my arm.

It's going to take time. I can't expect miracles. 'It's not your fault. You didn't know.'

'Why did he say you weren't my parents?'

'I guess he was angry. He was lashing out,' I say.

'Right.' I can see my answer doesn't satisfy him. I agree, it's a weird and cruel thing to say to your own son.

'Look, I can prove it's another lie. I downloaded your birth certificate.' I pass him my phone and show him the digital certificate I found with Freida's help.

He glances at it. Reads the names. Nods. 'Okay,' he says.

'I never thought I'd see this day.'

'I feel terrible for what he did to you.' Jacob taps his fingers nervously on the table.

I shrug. 'I can't lie, Jacob. It was awful. You have no idea what it's like to think you're losing your mind. For ten whole years I genuinely thought that all my memories of you were imagined. Do you remember our house in Norfolk? It was right by the beach.'

'Vaguely.'

'You and I decorated your room together. You helped me paint it and we chose astronaut curtains and a matching duvet cover.'

'Yeah, I think I do remember.' The hint of a smile appears on his face.

'When I came back from Turkey, it was all gone. Ronan had arranged for it to be redecorated while we were away and all your things, your toys and books and games, removed. It was as if you'd never been there. It was terrifying.'

'Really?' he says. 'And did you really have no idea what was going on?'

'None. Ronan made me take strong sedatives that stopped me thinking straight. And then he arranged for me to see a psychiatrist. Of course, I believed I was going mad at that point and the psychiatrist confirmed what I feared.'

'I still don't understand how you could suddenly think you'd only ever imagined me.'

'I know, but I was confused and Ronan was a master at manipulation and control. He convinced me I'd lost a baby while I was pregnant, and that was what caused me to imagine you.'

'What happened to him?'

'We divorced a few months later.' I leave it at that. He doesn't need to know that Ronan's currently in hospital or that he nearly died because of me. If he hadn't arranged to meet me to beg me not to involve the police, none of that would have happened. 'I've not seen him since,' I lie.

'Oh,' he says. 'I remember he was nice.'

'He was a charmer, but he conned us both. You still want me to call the police?'

'I think so.'

'You have to be sure, Jacob, because once it's done, there's no going back.'

He stabs at his drink with his straw and licks a lump of cream off the end of it. 'You have to,' he says. 'You can't let him get away with what he's done.'

'Okay. I think that's the right decision.'

I make the call there and then. I'm transferred between various different people until I'm finally put through to a female detective who listens attentively. When I'm done, she doesn't laugh or call me a liar. She asks me to come into the station to make a statement.

'What happens now?' Jacob asks when I hang up.

'What do you mean?'

'Will I have to come and live with you?'

'If you want.' I'd hoped he'd jump at the chance of moving into my pokey little flat in Muswell Hill, but I'm not naive. It's a massive upheaval for him and we need to take it slowly. 'But not if you don't want to.'

'What about Mu... I mean, India? I like her. She's really nice. She's been my mum while you were...'

'I don't know. We'll sort something out.'

'It's just that it's my home. It's where all my things are and all my friends are near. Will I have to move school?'

I laugh. He has so many questions I don't have the answers to. I've not even thought about it. My mind has been entirely focused on getting my son back. I'll probably have to move to somewhere bigger. There's not much room for both of us in the flat, but I can't afford the prices in Richmond. He might have to change schools.

'Don't worry, we're not going to do anything rash. Shall we get you home?'

I finish my latte and smile across the table at my beautiful boy. After ten years, I can't believe we're going to be together again.

'Where's that?'

The poor child. He looks so confused.

'Wherever you want it to be.'

# Chapter 44

FOUR WEEKS LATER

The police officer I saw was far more understanding and sympathetic than I'd expected. We met at a red-brick station in Wood Green where she brought me a weak coffee and listened patiently to my story. She didn't raise an eyebrow or suck in a breath of disbelief. She just took notes and asked lots of questions. I showed her the email correspondence between my two ex-husbands and explained how Sammy had fled the country to Iran when I'd confronted him at the airport. She said it was one of the worst cases of gaslighting she'd ever heard of.

'I'll have to discuss the case with my colleagues, but I imagine we'll be issuing a warrant for his arrest, based on what you've told me,' she assured me. I could have hugged her. I never expected anyone to believe me, but having a detective taking my word so seriously opened the floodgates on my emotions. 'Unfortunately, it's difficult while he's in Iran with the current extradition process, but the moment he lands back in the country, we'll pick him up.'

Sammy's not an idiot. He's not coming back. At least not for a long, long time.

'What about Ronan?'

'We'll want to talk to him as well, but first we'll need to assess his mental capacity after what you've told us about his accident.'

I've kept in touch with Polly and she was grateful to hear about everything that's happened since she sent me that first email. When I told her Jacob and I had been reunited and that Sammy had run off back to Iran, she sighed and told me how happy she was for me.

She's decided against leaving Ronan. She thinks it's her duty to help him with his rehabilitation.

'He's still in a bad way,' she told me over the phone. 'They think he hit his head hard against the front of the van and it's caused some significant cognitive damage.'

What she meant was that he was struggling with his memory, he couldn't concentrate and he'd developed terrible mood swings and irritability. That was in addition to the horrific facial wounds he'd suffered, although I found it hard to show much sympathy after what he'd put me through.

'It's going to be months before he heals,' she told me. 'He's had to have plastic surgery to rebuild the left side of his face and his nose. So much for his looks. He's going to be permanently scarred.'

I don't want to say he deserved what happened, but who knows how many women he's charmed with that twinkle in his eye and his rugged good looks. I don't think he'll be doing much charming in the future. He's lucky to have Polly by his side. Maybe she'll finally mould him into the man she's always wanted him to be. And good luck to her. They deserve each other.

A young man with acne-pocked skin hands me my coffee without so much as a smile. I take it to a table by the window and wipe down the grease with a paper napkin before I sit. I hardly ever venture into these types of fast-food burger restaurants, and now I'm reminded why. But it was where Jacob suggested we meet, and if this is where he's comfortable, who am I to argue?

He ambles in with his head down, staring at his phone.

I spot him instantly. I've been watching the door, waiting for him.

'Hey, Jacob. Over here,' I call out, waving.

He glances up and his cheeks flush.

'Alright?' he says, trudging over.

'Are you hungry? Do you want a burger?' I ask.

He shakes his head as he slides onto a plastic seat on the opposite side of the table. 'Nah, I'm fine.'

I persuade him to at least have a milkshake.

'So, how are things at home?'

'Alright.'

'Okay, that's good. Have you heard from your dad at all?'

'Nope.'

Secretly, I'm delighted. Jacob's fourteen. I can't stop him communicating with Sammy if that's what he wants, but I hope that now he knows who he really is, he'll choose not to.

'And India? How's she coping?'

'She cries a lot,' he says. 'Sometimes I hear her on the phone shouting. I think she's talking to Dad. She says they're getting a divorce.'

'And how do you feel about that?'

He shrugs and slurps through his straw. 'Yeah, whatever.'

It's yet more upheaval in his young life, but it's for the best. We came to an agreement with India that for the time being, Jacob will continue to live with her. He's happy in the house with his brother and sister, and I don't want to tear the family apart. Besides, there's not much room in my flat. I've started looking for somewhere bigger, but prices are so expensive. I've discovered I definitely can't afford anywhere in Richmond and Jacob is adamant he doesn't want to change schools. With his exams not that far in the future, I can accept that a major disruption like that's not going to be good for him.

It's not exactly the perfect outcome, but at least I have Jacob back in my life. And it's not all about what I want, anyway. The main thing is that Jacob is happy. India's obviously a good mother and I realise now she had no idea how Sammy came to have custody of Jacob.

He'd spun her the same lies as he'd told Jacob, that I was an unfit, unstable mother with serious mental health issues, who'd walked out on her son when he was small. She had no reason to disbelieve him.

The arrangement we've tentatively hammered out is that we'll co-parent. Jacob will continue to live with India and her two children, but I'll see him whenever I like. We'll make joint decisions about his future and share any other parental duties, like parents' evenings, attending sports days and helping him with homework and choosing options. It's all a bit unorthodox, but nothing about my story is normal.

'Do you fancy going to the cinema this afternoon?' I ask. 'There's that new Marvel film I thought we could see.'

'Nah, thanks. I've arranged to meet my mates to play football.'

'Oh,' I say, deflated. I thought we were going to spend the day together, but he's not a child anymore. I've missed those years when he'd happily spend his time with his parents. He's a teenager now, spreading his wings, finding his own way in life.

He must sense my disappointment. 'I could tell them I can't make it,' he offers.

'Don't be silly. We can go to the cinema another day. Or do something else you'd like.'

'Okay.'

'Actually, there's something I wanted to ask you.' I finish the last of my coffee. It's possibly the worst coffee I've ever had. Bitter, weak and served scalding hot.

Jacob pushes his milkshake to one side.

'Tell me if you don't want me to go, but there's a job that's come up that I'd really like to take, but it means being away for a few weeks and I wouldn't be able to see you,' I say, watching his face carefully for any kind of reaction, although I've discovered teenagers are virtually impossible to read.

'What kind of job?'

'A photography job. Similar to what I used to do before you came along.'

'Cool.'

'You don't mind? It's not exactly what I did before, but it'll be helping another photographer on a project in Brazil.'

I'd completely forgotten about the job Freida had mentioned until she told me she'd put my name forward anyway and they approached me directly. I must have sounded a complete clown on the phone, blustering and stammering like an idiot. It didn't put them off arranging a formal interview a couple of weeks later, and Caz, the photographer, and I really hit it off. We spent more time chatting than discussing my CV and why there was a gaping great ten-year hole through the middle of it. She offered me the job on the spot, but I've been delaying making a decision.

At first, I thought there was no way I could accept. I'd only just been reunited with Jacob. How could I leave him? It would be unforgivable. Abandoning my only son when I'd just turned his life upside down.

It was Freida who convinced me to give it a shot.

'Jacob's going to be fine,' she said. 'You've put the last ten years of your life on hold, convinced you'd lost your mind. Now everything's falling into place, you need to do something for you. Take the job, Karina. You'll regret it if you don't.'

'I can't leave Jacob.'

'It's only temporary. He's a teenager. He doesn't need you to hold his hand. I know you've only just found him, but now you're going to have to learn to let him go again. And anyway, you can call him everyday. It's not as if you're going to be totally out of touch.'

It was hard to argue with her reasoning, but still a part of me felt bad about sacrificing my time with Jacob to pursue my own dreams. I needed to hear what Jacob had to say about it.

'Nah, I don't mind. You should do it if you really want it,' Jacob says.

'You mean it?'

'Of course,' he shrugs. 'I'll be alright. I've got Mum - I mean, India - and anyway, school's starting again next week.'

'I don't want you to think I'm running out on you again.'

'I won't,' he says. 'And anyway, you didn't run out on me, remember? Dad took me.'

'Yeah,' I say, a smile playing across my lips. 'I remember.'

'Good, so you'll take the job?'

'Yes.'

Jacob picks at his thumbnail, his gaze directed at his hands on the table. 'I'm glad you found me,' he mumbles.

'Me too.'

'It must have been horrible, thinking you were going crazy.'

'It was the worst thing that's ever happened to me. I'm sorry I wasn't around for all those years. I've missed out on so much.'

He smiles. 'You didn't miss much.'

'I'm going to make it up to you. Every birthday, Christmas and Easter I wasn't around.

You'll have more chocolate than you'll know what to do with.'

He laughs. 'You don't have to do that.'

'I know, but I want to. You've missed out on so many things.'

'Not really. I still celebrated my birthday and Christmas, but it's sad to think you weren't there.'

'Let's not think about the past,' I say. 'Let's look to the future and all the things we can do together.'

'I don't even have any photos of you,' Jacob says, chewing his lip. 'Dad deleted them all. Do you think I could get one now?'

'Oh god, of course you can,' I gush. 'Let's have one together we can both keep.'

He leaps out of his seat with his phone and scoots around to my side of the table. Puts his arm around my shoulder and holds up the phone. We stare back at our grinning faces on the screen and hold our smiles as he snaps three pictures.

'You've got your eyes closed in this one,' he laughs as we review them together.

'God, I look awful. Will you share them with me?'

'Sure.' Two of the photos, the ones where I have my eyes open, ping onto my phone. 'I'll tell you what though. Glad I didn't inherit your hair. Imagine how badly I'd have been bullied if I'd been ginger,' Jacob says, laughing.

'Hey, I like my hair,' I giggle, although at school I wish I could have been blonde or mousy brown. Something that didn't mark me out. For years, the other kids used to call me

'Gingerlocks'. Now I love it and wouldn't change it for the world.

'Mind you, you're getting a few greys there,' Jacob says, peering at the top of my head.

'You cheeky bugger!'

'There's at least four.' He plucks a hair from my head.

'Ow!'

'Look,' he says, holding a strand up to show me.

'That's not grey.'

'It's greyish.'

Teenagers. I guess I'm going to have to get used to this.

# Chapter 45

**JACOB**

The letter is waiting on the table in the hall. Thankfully, it's come in a plain white envelope with no distinguishing markings, return address or company logo. Nothing to suggest the truth that awaits inside. I race up the stairs with it hidden under my blazer and almost make it to my room before my stepmother hears me.

'Hey, Jacob, is that you? Did you have a good day?' she shouts from the kitchen.

'Er, yeah, it was okay,' I yell back.

'There's a letter for you—'

'Thanks, I've got it.'

She doesn't ask what it is or who it's from, which is just as well as I don't want to lie to her. She's been tiptoeing on eggshells around me since Karina, my mum, came back into my life and I guess she doesn't want to seem to be sticking her nose into my business.

The last few weeks have all been a bit weird. I've known India as my mum since I was six when she married my dad. That's more than half my life. She's always been more of a parent to me than he ever was. He was never here for a start, always flying off on business. Even when he was around, he never showed much interest in what I was doing. He never came to see me play football. Or helped with my homework. I doubt he could name even one of my friends. I guess that's why I'm closer to Mum, I mean India, these days.

I suppose it's why I wasn't that upset when he chose to leave me at the airport. It's probably for the best, especially when I found out the truth about what he'd done and how he'd tricked Karina into believing she was going crazy. That's some pretty lowlife shit. It's no wonder she didn't come looking for me. But she's not his only victim. He's been lying to me about her for years and I don't think I'll ever be able to forgive him for that.

I toss my bag under my desk and collapse on my bed with the letter. My mouth's suddenly dry, my fingers like sticks of ice. Once I open it, there's no going back. I'll finally know the truth once and for all.

I'd thought for a while that something didn't add up, especially after that biology lesson when we were taught about how genetics influence our appearance.

We learnt about melanin, pheomelanin and eumelanin, the pigments responsible for our eye colour, and how it's determined in all of us by variations in our genes. If one parent has brown eyes, that's a dominant trait that influences the colour of their children's eyes.

My father has eyes so dark, they're almost black, whereas my eyes are the colour of a

Mediterranean sea. It could be that my father's genes carry recessive traits of blue, because apparently that's entirely possible, but neither Henry nor Amelia's eyes are light coloured, even though India's are blue. But that's not the only difference between us. We couldn't look any less alike. While my skin is pale and freckly and burns at the first hint of sunlight, my father is olive skinned, his hair as dark as coal. And he has a prominent hooked nose. My hair is blonde. My nose straight.

I rip open the letter impatiently. Inside are two sheets of thick paper which I unfold in my lap. I scan them hurriedly, looking for a conclusion. An answer to my biggest fears.

The first page is laced with scientific language and intimidating combinations of letters and numbers which mean little to me. What I'm looking for is right at the bottom of the second page. A single sentence in plain English.

I already know the truth about Sammy. I sent away some samples of his hair I collected from his comb and a strip of dental floss I fished out of the bin in the bathroom a few months ago, long before my biological mother reappeared in my life. The analysis concluded his DNA didn't match the markers which would have had to have been present for him to be my father. Sammy wasn't my dad.

I never confronted him about it. What would have been the point? I knew the truth and that was all that mattered, although it left me wondering about my real father. Who he was. What he was doing. How he'd met my mother. And then Karina turned up with the revelation that

Sammy had effectively abducted me. It made no sense. If I wasn't really his son, why go to so much trouble? Unless he didn't know himself.

And then there's Karina. She's beautiful in a bohemian kind of way. She has stunning green eyes and a head of thick red hair that she wears so long it falls over her shoulders and frames her face. I guess I look more like her than my father, in colouring at least, but the differences are still stark.

My suspicions were first raised at the airport when Sammy made that accusation that she wasn't my real mother, any more than he was my father. By then, I knew he wasn't really my dad. She showed me my birth certificate on her phone, but what did that prove? Nothing.

When we sat and talked, I studied her face. The shape of her eyes. Her lips. Her cheekbones. Even her ears. I couldn't see any similarity with the way I looked at all. I'd have loved to have believed she was my birth mother and we'd finally been reunited after the most bizarre of circumstances, but it didn't ring true and I had an unsettling feeling she was lying.

It took a few weeks, but I finally managed to collect a sample of her hair without her realising what I was doing when we met for a drink. Then I sent it off by post for analysis to the same DNA testing firm who'd confirmed Sammy wasn't my father. Because *Veracity DNA* are based somewhere in Europe, they didn't require any of those awkward consent forms and were willing to carry out parental testing with no questions asked. It wasn't even that expensive and I had more than enough money saved up to pay for it.

I clung onto Karina's hairs tightly and hid them in my wallet when she wasn't looking. They were in the post the following day, packaged up safely in a plastic bag inside a cardboard box the company supplied.

It's taken almost six weeks to get the results back, but finally they're here in my trembling hand. I draw in a deep breath. One way or the other, I'm finally about to find out the truth.

# Chapter 46

The jet engines roar, the plane creeps forwards and, as it accelerates sharply, my seat punches me in the back. And then we're off the ground, my head feeling as if it's floating as we soar into the sky through the thick, grey clouds above London.

I never thought I'd be back doing the job I love, flying off to far-flung locations with a camera and a head full of aspirations. But here I am. Next stop, Brazil.

Caz has her eyes closed, her head back, completely oblivious to the landscape disappearing below us like a toy town. It might not be my own shoot, but I'm glad to be part of something so exciting. The chance to return to the Pantanal to capture jaguars in the wild is a dream come true, even if I'll only be assisting. Helping Caz with the equipment, priming her cameras and choosing the right lenses. If I'm lucky, she might even let me take some of my own shots. I'm still a little rusty, but I've been spending the little free time I have playing with my cameras again, refining my technique and my knowledge. To be honest, I'm just glad to be back in the field.

Things are going well with Jacob. Really well. Although if it hadn't been for the arrangement we came to with India, I wouldn't have been able to take this job. I don't have to worry about him. I know he's in safe hands. And sure, it still irks me when he calls her 'Mum', but I guess I have to re-earn that title. He's happy and that's the main thing. He doesn't seem upset in the slightest that India's filing for divorce or that he might never see Sammy again. I guess he's finally seen through him and what he's really like.

I'm not working full time at the studio with Freida anymore. I'm down to two days a week and she's brought in a bright young thing straight out of college to cover the rest. She probably deserves it more than me. I've had my shot and thanks to Freida, I've been given a second chance. Everything is finally going my way. And I couldn't be happier.

Caz's eyes spring open, and she lays a hand on top of mine, smiling.

'Everything okay?' she asks as my ears pop and the plane levels off.

'Absolutely. Couldn't be better.'

'We're going to have fun,' she says. 'It's going to be epic.'

'Yeah, I know.'

I've had such a run of bad luck in the last ten years, I deserve some happiness. It's not exactly how I thought my life was going to map out, but it's turned out okay.

Polly's still in touch. She gives me regular updates on Ronan's progress and recovery which seems to be painfully slow. I couldn't really care any less about him, but I don't mind hearing from Polly. I think she's lonely, especially as caring for Ronan appears to have become a full-time job. I only hope he appreciates it. It's more than he deserves.

I still can't understand why she stood by him when he was married to me. Surely it couldn't have been worth it even for all that money Sammy paid them. I certainly couldn't have stood by and watched my boyfriend seduce another woman, propose to her, marry her and move in with her and her young son.

It's perverse. But I'm not Polly and Polly's not me. Her love for him must run deep and he's lucky to have her. I just hope he treats her right. If he doesn't, he'll have me to answer to.

I've not heard from Sammy at all. He's gone to ground, but I'm not surprised. He'd be an idiot to attempt to return to the country, especially as the police have issued a warrant for his arrest and have taken my complaint that he abducted Jacob far more seriously than I thought they would. Sammy's name might be on Jacob's birth certificate but it gave him no right to take my son to Iran without my consent. It was the lengths he went to to deceive me, the complexity of the plot, that I think shocked the police and swayed them to take action.

I'm not that bothered whether he's prosecuted or not. What's done is done and nothing's going to change that. I'd rather he stayed in Iran with his head down and none of us had to see him again.

The police tried to interview Ronan, but his memory's been so badly affected by the accident, they decided he wouldn't be fit to stand trial. Nor would it be in the public interest to proceed with a prosecution, and after talking to me about what I wanted, we agreed it was best not to proceed. I hate Ronan for what he did, but he's suffered enough and will continue to pay the price for the rest of his life.

'My sister's so jealous,' Caz says, interrupting my thoughts as the seatbelt lights above our heads ping off and people begin moving around the aircraft, grabbing bags from lockers and queuing for the toilets. 'She's always wanted to go to Brazil.'

'I've been a few times. It's a fascinating country. Is she older or younger?'

'Younger, but you know, she's settled down now. Three kids. A husband. A mortgage.' Caz rolls her eyes theatrically.

'What's her name?'

'Michaela.'

A lump hardens in my throat and my pulse beats a little quicker. It's a long time since I've heard that name, but it still has the power to evoke a visceral reaction.

'I knew a Michaela once,' I say.

'Oh, really?'

'But it was a long time ago.'

# Chapter 47

JACOB

The words swim in front of my eyes. The results conclusive. Not even enough wriggle room for there to be a sliver of doubt. It says it in black and white. The probability of the result being incorrect is less than one per cent.

*Karina McHugh does not show the genetic markers which have to be present for the biological mother of child Jacob Templeton.*

I stare at the letter and read the sentence over and over until the letters blur and the tears from my eyes dampen the paper.

Karina *isn't* my mother.

Sammy isn't my father.

So who the hell am I?

# Chapter 48

Michaela wasn't much more than a child herself. Far too young to have fallen pregnant and to be thinking about bringing an infant into the world. She was still at school. She had her exams ahead of her. A life to live. She didn't want to be burdened by the weight of motherhood at her age.

And what hope for her child if she'd gone ahead and tried to bring him up on her own? She'd be living on benefits and lucky if the hapless boyfriend didn't walk out on her at the first chance he had, while her authoritarian father was likely to throw her out of the house as soon as he found out what his precious daughter had been up to behind his back.

I don't know what prompted me to speak to her that day outside the abortion clinic. Maybe because she looked so lost? So lonely? A frail and breakable doll cowering inside an oversized coat, shivering in the cold. And my hormones were all over the place. I'd just taken the second pill that within hours would confirm my own termination, and I was already having regrets.

The words spilled from my mouth with no thought as to what I was saying. 'Is everything okay?'

Her voice was so timid, so weak, when she replied and tried to tell me she was fine, that I wanted to pull her into my arms and hug her.

Instead, I persuaded her to go with me for a coffee. And we talked. She opened up to me about what she was feeling and thinking. She told me about her fears. Her anxieties. Her desperation. I think it helped because I was going through the same, and although I was a thirty-three-year-old married woman with a house of my own and a good job, we were sharing a similar experience. The same doubts. The same guilt. The same uncertainty.

I'd made my choice, but she still had hers looming ahead of her. And she didn't know what to do. The idea of terminating the pregnancy appalled her sensibilities, but keeping the baby wasn't an option for her either.

'It's a big decision,' I warned her. 'Whatever you decide will have an enormous impact on you, possibly for the rest of your life.'

'But I can't keep it,' she whimpered, her fringe falling over her eyes.

'How many weeks are you?'

She shrugged. 'Six. Maybe seven.'

'In which case, you'd be able to take the pills at home.'

She burst into tears again. 'I don't think I could.'

'What about your parents? If you talked to them, maybe they'd be more understanding than you think.'

'No, my dad'll kill me. And then he'll kill Nathan. It's all a big mess.'

'Whatever you decide, you have to be sure. If you decide on a termination, there's no going back. You may regret it forever.'

She looked up at me over the top of her latte. 'You've done it. Do you regret it?'

My hand furled around my imaginary bump, picturing the tiny foetus inside me, already doomed. Why had I done it? Out of selfishness? Because a child wouldn't fit in with my lifestyle or our plans? It's not as if we couldn't afford to have a baby. Or couldn't give it a decent home. Love.

I'd tried hard not think about the baby inside me, but I'd already given him a name. Jacob. Because I instinctively knew he was a boy.

I choked back my emotion, tears rimming my eyes. 'Yes,' I gasped, 'I think I do.'

After we'd chatted for a while, she agreed to go back to the clinic with me at her side where her mother should have been. Someone to support her and guide her. An emotional crutch as much as anything.

And when we walked out together, a wedge of leaflets clutched in her tiny hand, chipped blue polish on her chewed fingernails, I came to a decision. I didn't want her to go through with a termination. It would haunt her for the rest of her life.

'There is another option,' I said as we stood outside on the street corner, neither of us sure what was supposed to happen next. 'There's always adoption.'

'You mean go through with the pregnancy? I don't know if I—'

'Just hear me out,' I said, a wonderful idea forming in my head. 'What if I took on your baby?'

'You?'

'Yes, why not? It would be perfect.'

'But you've just had—'

I didn't want her to say the word. 'I made a mistake. A terrible, terrible mistake. I don't want you to do the same.'

My mind was in a whirl, the possibilities and expectations pinballing around my head in a gush of euphoria. Sammy and I could take on Michaela's baby and raise it as our own.

'But how?'

'We'd need to talk to your parents, obviously, and square it with them, but I'd be by your side every step of the way. We'll help you with whatever you need. You won't want for anything and it means you don't have to go through with the termination or keep the baby. When it's born, you'll hand it over to us and we'll register it as our own.'

She blinked rapidly and I could almost see the cogs in her head turning as she thought it through. I was confident Sammy wouldn't object. He didn't seem to care either way whether we had children. He was more concerned with building the business.

'Is that... legal?'

I shrugged. 'Probably not. But who cares? We'll sort all that out, if your parents agree.'

'I'll still have to tell them?'

'I promise, it won't be that bad. We'll treat you like a surrogate mum. We can even pay you for your trouble. I bet your parents would appreciate that.'

She thought about it for a moment, the trace of a smile appearing on her lips. 'Yes, probably.'

'Is that a yes?'

Michaela shrugged off her hood and brushed her fringe out of her eyes. 'I guess,' she said.

# Chapter 49

JACOB

I dry my eyes with the sleeve of my blazer, telling myself to get a grip. So what if I don't know my real mother and father? There must be plenty of kids in the same situation. It's not as if I'm alone, fending for myself. I have a family and they love me.

I fold the letter back into its envelope, lift my mattress and slide it underneath, on top of the other one.

I have zero regrets about finding out the truth, but now I know it, I'm not sure what to do with it. I could confront Karina but what's the point? There's been enough upheaval in both of our lives lately.

Maybe when I'm eighteen I'll take it further. I'm sure that's the age I can legally find out about my birth parents. There must be a good reason they gave me away. Perhaps they couldn't afford to keep a baby. Or I was a mistake. An unhappy accident. I could have been the victim of a rape or a teenage pregnancy.

The possibilities are endless, and one day I will find out more.

But for now, I have enough on my plate. I've started my GCSEs this year and what with Sammy and India getting a divorce and Karina co-parenting me, it's plenty for me to get my head around.

I don't suppose I'll ever see Sammy again. Even if he returns to the country, India and Karina both said the police will arrest him for child abduction, and there's a chance I'd have to go to court and give evidence. I sure as hell don't want to do that. I'd rather he stayed in Iran and left us all in peace.

Karina's away for at least three weeks. I'm pleased she's gone. Her whole life has been on hold for the last ten years and now she's getting to do something she loves. She's been so excited about the trip. And, actually I do miss her. A bit. I like her. She's funny. And she listens to me. She understands me. I don't think she'd take it too well if I announced I'd sneakily taken DNA samples of her hair to prove my parentage. In fact, it would probably kill her after all she's been through.

So for now, I'm not going to say anything.

I'm going to keep it to myself.

But who knows, one day, when life has settled down and I'm feeling brave, I might dig out those letters again and try to find my real parents, because they're the root of my story. The genesis of my being. And without them, I'm not sure I'll ever feel whole.

One day.

# Chapter 50

A crying baby wakes me with a jolt and for a moment I'm completely disorientated. The rumble of jet engines in my ears. The hiss of cool air blasting from a vent above my head. Flight attendants floating up and down the aisles with fixed smiles and searching eyes.

Of course. I'm on my way to Brazil, Caz by my side, and a world of adventures ahead. I glance over my shoulder to identify the source of the noise. A hassled-looking woman is pacing up and down, jiggling an infant on her shoulder, patting its back rhythmically. Eventually its cries grow weary and become a disgruntled grizzle. The lights are down low and the skies are dark outside the cabin.

I remember when Jacob was a baby. I didn't have a clue what I was doing. Sammy and I paid for Michaela to give birth in a private hospital in a suite all to herself where we thought she'd be most comfortable and there would be fewer questions asked.

It was a relatively easy labour. Uncomplicated. We picked her up by car when her contractions began and drove her and her mother straight to the hospital. Her father was still in denial and wanted nothing to do with the whole thing, although I expect he happily spent the money we paid them for their trouble. Within three hours, Michaela had given birth to a boy. Jacob.

He yelled for the first hour, his face all angry and red and crinkled. But Michaela refused to feed him. Or even hold him. She turned her back on him when the midwife tried to hand him to her and refused to look at him.

Instead, I gave him his first feed from a bottle and he gulped down the whole lot and still seemed hungry.

The next day, we took him away in the brand-new car seat we'd bought, dressed in an oversized white sleepsuit and cotton cap. We drove him back to the house and started our new life as a family together. It was as simple as that. A ready-cooked baby without the morning sickness, swollen ankles and stretch marks.

I never heard from Michaela or her family again. That was the arrangement we all agreed. A simple transaction. A way of solving all our problems.

I often wonder what happened to her and where she is now. Whether she went on to have a family of her own. Lots more children. A caring husband.

'You're awake,' Caz says, rolling her head to face me, her eyes bleary with sleep, a blanket pulled up to her chin.

'I heard a baby crying.'

Caz pulls a face. I have the impression she's not the kind of woman to settle down and have children. She's too much of a free spirit. She reminds me of me in the months before I fell pregnant.

'Who's looking after Jacob while you're away?' she asks.

I hesitate for a beat. 'India, his stepmother.'

Caz lifts her head and raises an eyebrow. 'Stepmother?'

'It's complicated,' I say, pulling my own blanket over my shoulders and closing my eyes. 'You wouldn't believe it if I told you.'

'Try me,' she says.

'Yeah, one day, maybe. One day.'

# Acknowledgements

The Phantom Child was probably one of the hardest plots I've ever tried to pull off but I'm really pleased with how it turned out.

What did you think? Did you see where the story was going? Did you see the twist coming?

If you did enjoy the book, I'd be delighted if you could leave a rating and / or a review. I love to see readers' comments.

The book started with a vague idea. What if a mother woke up to not only find her child missing but that her husband flat denied they had a son?

I thought it was an intriguing hook, but it took some work to flesh it out into a cohesive story.

Because how could you make a child completely disappear, especially in the modern world? It meant having Karina totally cut off by Ronan and Sammy. All pictures of Jacob vanished. His passport removed. Even his belongings at home discarded.

And as much as Karina wanted to believe her son was real, the pressure Ronan put on her and her heavy use of sedatives, finally persuaded her that she must be losing her mind after all.

And that, I thought, was a really frightening prospect.

Can you imagine being in her situation where you were being told that everything you thought you knew was in fact all in your head?

To my mind, it's what defines it as a psychological thriller, rather than a domestic thriller. The fear Karina had that she was going insane.

I couldn't have done it without my wonderful editor, Rebecca Millar, who helped me shape the outline of the story at an early stage, which is the first time she'd been involved at the inception phase – and it definitely benefitted from her wise words and experience.

A big shout out too to my amazing wife, Amanda, who proofread The Phantom Child for me while juggling writing two of her own psychological thrillers, which she publishes under the name AJ McDine.

Her eye for detail and her fastidious attention to grammar is second to none. Oh, and she can write a pretty damned good story too. Do check her out.

Kudos to my designer Nick Castle for the stunning cover and putting up with all my ridiculous suggestions when I've no idea what I'm talking about.

Finally, a big thanks to all my Street Team advanced readers for their continued support and dedication to spreading the word about my work.

Plus, to all the bloggers, advanced readers, secondary proofreaders – thank you. You're too many to mention individually by name, and I wouldn't want to inadvertently miss someone, but I really couldn't do it without you.

Adrian

# Also By AJ Wills

### The House Guest
When Marcella is invited to stay with Carmel and Rufus, she thinks it's a chance to steal their perfect lives. But the couple have other ideas and Marcella soon realises they may not be who they're claiming to be.

### The Lottery Winners
When Callum and Jade win the lottery, they think all their dreams have come true – until they're approached by a stranger begging for help and they discover the cost of their winnings may be more than they're willing to pay.

### The Warning
When Megan discovers a text message on a phone hidden in the loft of her new house with a chilling warning about her husband, she's forced to confront some dark truths about their relationship...

### The Secrets We Keep

When a young girl vanishes on her way home from school, a suspicious media suspects her parents know more than they're letting on.

## Nothing Left To Lose

A letter arrives in a plain white envelope. Inside is a single sheet of paper with a chilling message. Someone knows the secret Abi, and her husband, Henry, are hiding. And now they want them dead.

## His Wife's Sister

Mara was only eleven when she went missing from a tent in her parents' garden nineteen years ago. Now she's been found wandering alone and confused in woodland.

## She Knows

After Sky finds a lost diary on the beach, she becomes caught up in something far bigger than she could ever have imagined - and accused of a murder she has no memory of committing...

## The Intruder

Jez thought he'd finally found happiness when he met Alice. But when Alice goes missing with her young daughter and the police accuse him of their murders, his life is shattered.

Printed in Great Britain
by Amazon